"ATTENTION ALL PERSONNEL. CODE BLUE. RECOVERY ROOM."

Adele paled, Cynthia lost her smile. Adrenaline propelled the two of them into the hall, where all the phones at the nurses' station came alive at once. Before Gayle could get the words "Adele, go!" out of her mouth, Adele took off running in the direction of the double doors.

Fueled by panic, Adele sprinted the length of the west wing to the stairwell in three seconds flat. . . . She flew down fourteen flights of stairs, feet barely touching the steps, driven by the words going through her head like a continuous LED sign: *Don't let it be Chloe. Don't let it be Chloe. Please don't let it be Chloe. . . .*

By Echo Heron
Published by The Ballantine Publishing Group:

INTENSIVE CARE
MERCY
CONDITION CRITICAL
PULSE
TENDING LIVES: Nurses on the Medical Front*
PANIC*

*forthcoming

This one is for Adella E. Cramer.
It's all in the genes, Ma.

ACKNOWLEDGMENTS

I AM DEEPLY GRATEFUL FOR THE GENEROUS help and support I received from the following people:

Ken Holmes, Assistant Coroner, who at every turn kindly shared his wealth of information on law enforcement, forensics, and just about anything else I wanted to know;

Simon D. Heron, who came through with invaluable details in matters of the mortuary sciences; and

Nurses everywhere who have continued to influence and encourage me.

And, once again, I wish to thank Tom M. Meadoff, M.D., and James Scheller, M.D., for supplying and clarifying the medical facts; Margie Dingfelder, MFCC, for input on various psychological profiles—even when it proved unnerving; Jean Touroff, who did yet another great job of copyediting and finding the loopholes; J. Patrick Heron, Esq., for sharing his expertise in legal matters; Eleanor Boylan for the commiseration on the woes of mystery writing; Laura Gasparis Vonfrolio, R.N., for the ongoing support of my writing and my nurse soul; Linda Stone, R.N., Catherine Murray Barnes, R.N., and Debbie and Dave Hannaford, for supplying bits and pieces of

facts and information; my editor, Leona Nevler, and her
assistant, Louis A. Mendez; and Dominick Abel, my
agent—for the chance to run it up the flagpole. Public
libraries everywhere—for sharing your treasures, you
have so often been my salvation.

And lastly thank you so much to my friends and
family. It all boils down to love.

PROLOGUE

October 12, 5:31 A.M., Bellevue Hospital

DR. JOHN GANET NOTED THE TIME—5:31 A.M.—
and began scrubbing in, attacking his fingers with the
soft brush as if they were the enemy. As a surgeon, albeit
a junior partner, he resented the fact that his twenty-four-
hour-call days weren't entirely over. He also resented
twelve-year-old Derek Wickstrom's appendix for waiting
until 4:00 A.M. to kick up a fuss.

Dr. Ganet sighed. Well, the bright side was that he
could sign off to Dr. Wortz at 7:30, then stop by Sonya's
new apartment on the way home. She'd just be getting
off graveyard shift at Ellis and would be eager to release
some tension with his help.

At 5:36 A.M., whistling softly, he finished the scrub of
his left elbow and began on his right fingers. He knew he
shouldn't complain about taking OR call three times a
week for Milton and Wortz, the senior blades. After all,
it gave him all the legitimate excuses he needed to get out
of the house. Plus, there was no way Colleen could find
him, especially since Nettie, Bellevue's night switchboard operator, thought he walked on water. His gratis,

1

after-hours tummy tuck was one of the best deals he'd ever made in his life: whenever Colleen called to check up on him, Nettie gave an automatic "Sorry, Mrs. Ganet. Dr. Ganet is in the middle of an emergency case and can't be disturbed right now."

Nettie didn't seem to mind; in truth, it sounded like she got some kind of vicarious thrill out of playing accomplice, judging by the excited, breathy quality of her voice when she called Sonya's to give him Colleen's messages.

A rush of pleasure at the thought of Sonya straddling him caused him to stop whistling. He wanted her as much now as when he met her five years ago during his community service stint. For any woman to hold his interest that long was a record. But then Sonya wasn't any woman.

The exotic, petite brunette remained cool and in charge during any crises, medical or personal. He would never have admitted it aloud, but she was more competent than most of the physicians he knew. He'd once observed her single-handedly run a code on night shift, intubating the patient within thirty seconds, defibrillating, choosing and pushing the appropriate drugs, and doing effective CPR until the patient stabilized.

Then there was the period of time that Colleen suspected he was fooling around and tightened the reins so that he couldn't even go to the bathroom without her watching. Sonya hadn't complained or gotten clingy the way most women did—she simply went on about her life, as full of that solid self-assurance as always. No commitments. No strings. See ya around, pal. Give me a call when you're in town.

As it turned out, he was the one who'd almost lost his mind. Sonya's brand of sex had been hard to live without. She was always ready, always a hot tumble in the sack— or wherever he chose. The back of a taxi, or an alleyway. The best was the time in the men's room at La Lanterna, while Colleen waited for him at their table less than twenty feet away.

Sonya wasn't exactly averse to games either. She was the only woman he'd ever known who really loved everything about sex. Like the times he'd brought the young blonde in. Sonya went glassy-eyed crazy, moaning like an animal, doing things to the two of them at the same time that would forever be etched in his memory.

John looked at the tent which had formed in the front of his scrub pants. Glad for the oversize surgical scrubs, he checked the clock and pressed the faucet foot control to rinse. Hands up, tip of fingers to elbow.

He turned to call for the nurse to dry him off, accidentally bumping into the figure standing directly behind him. John Ganet jumped slightly.

Clad in surgical scrubs, head cover, mask, and safety glasses, the person held up a hand and took a quick step back, as if to apologize for startling him. John let out his breath and started to say, "Jesus, you scared the shit out of me," when the figure stepped close again and rapidly reached toward his left ear.

The young physician's reaction to having his throat slit was one of complete and utter surprise. There was enough time, however, for that surprise to turn into rage as his last realization was that his hands—a surgeon's most valuable instruments—were being amputated.

October 12, 7:30 A.M., Ellis Hospital

Nurse Abby McGowan swore under her breath as the key finally turned and released the lock. It irritated her that numerous previous work orders had yet to get an engineer up to replace the lock barrel. The heavy metal door to the Ward 8 supply room was a bitch to get open on a good day, but today it was harder than usual . . . and more time-consuming. The struggle to turn the key had taken over three minutes, which was three minutes she couldn't spare.

The nurse shoved open the door with her hip. She'd make sure the lock was fixed before she left work, even if that meant doing it herself. Searching the wall to her left, she located the light switch and flipped it up.

The switch was already up. Up was on. Down was off. She flipped down, thinking that maybe what she knew to be a certainty wasn't. The two industrial bulbs located somewhere toward the middle of the ceiling remained unlit and the condition of total darkness prevailed before her.

Abby weighed her next move. She could go back to the nurses' station, fill out a stat work order, call the engineer, wait for him to finish his coffee, find the bulbs and a stepladder, then sashay upstairs to change the damned things, or she could get her clean bed linens in the dark.

An impatient, compulsive type A, Abby was driven by the need to have her patients bathed and in fresh, immaculate linen before the onslaught of physicians hit the ward at 8:15.

Keeping a foot in the door, she stretched herself around

the corner and swore. Not a living soul, let alone a nurse who could bring her a flashlight, was in sight. It was one of the drawbacks of being first out of report on day shift.

Her eye fell on the crash cart, which stood well within her reach. A red plastic flashlight sat right on top.

It was against the law to remove so much as an alcohol wipe from any Ellis crash cart for any purpose other than resuscitation of a coding patient. Except it'd only be two seconds; nobody was going to code in two seconds. Feeling the same way she did when she parked in a handicapped zone, she grabbed the flashlight and slipped inside the supply room.

Before the door clicked shut behind her, Abby pressed the flashlight button, waited a second for her eyes to adjust, and bustled past the aisles of supplies toward the linen racks at the back of the room.

The shadows made by the tall metal racks and their contents brought to mind black-and-white images of horror movies and haunted houses. Yet Nurse McGowan was only vaguely aware that she felt uneasy, troubled by a host of disturbing difficulties and subdifficulties.

The flashlight battery was low, and the dim light flickered. *Crash cart wasn't checked properly—night shift would have changed the battery. What if the flashlight goes out? Hate the dark. What if the door sticks? Can't get out. Trapped. Can't breathe. Scream? Hate embarrassing myself.*

There was a strange noise that wasn't supposed to be there. A muted crinkling noise like someone opening a candy bar under a winter coat. *Noise means movement. Movement means alive. Rats. Ugh. Hate rats.*

There was a smell that wasn't supposed to be there. Familiar, but not to the supply room. It was a smell that belonged to the operating and emergency rooms. *Earthy. Human. Trauma. Blood. Running out of time. Eight patients. Eight baths. Eight bed linen changes. Efficiency. Get done early. Be on time. Brownie points with Gayle the Bitch. Promotion.*

The floor was slippery. *Spilled coffee? A leaky roof? It looks dark. Heavier than water. Betadine soap? Careful— fall and break a hip. Can't afford time off. Disability pay terrible. Gotta pay rent.*

Abby turned left at the last rack, directed the beam of light to the tier that held the bed linens, and several things happened simultaneously. She saw the sheets were soaked with blood, something dripped down the neck of her scrub dress and onto her right calf and ankle, the crinkling noise happened again very close by, she sucked in a breath but did not let it out, the flashlight fell from her hand, and she was again pitched into darkness.

Fear caused her temples to burn and her body to crouch and back against the wall. Totally blind, she struck out at the darkness around her while her mind ran an unwanted replay of the pitch-black cellar scene in *The Silence of the Lambs*.

The scream, barely restrained by the massive gate of social embarrassment, died completely when her hand grazed flesh and panic overload shifted into survival mode.

Getting down on her hands and knees, the nurse groped through the slimy puddles on the floor searching for the flashlight. Her hands found the object, fumbled with the on/off button, hitting it against the palm of her hand until she got a dim yellow shaft of light. She swung it upward and saw a leg sticking out from under a short stack of thermal blankets.

Catapulted into shock, she stood and stared dumbly at the limb. A woman's leg, bent at the knee, with the shoe still on the foot, dangled at the level of her waist. Abby pulled off the bloody mat of blankets covering the rest of the body and let them fall in a heap at her feet.

Sonya Martin, senior staff R.N., lay upon the blanket cart. Her eyes, thinly clouded by a milky film, were open and staring at the ceiling. A wide garish smile of a gash began under one ear and ended at the other. The blood had soaked and congealed on the top of her uniform, creating a maroon satin bib.

Abby stared back into the dead nurse's eyes, her breath coming in short, hoarse gasps. "Sonya?"

She desperately wanted her coworker to sit up, wipe off the fake blood, and laugh. Ha ha, only joking. Happy Halloween.

Sonya didn't answer, but the crinkling noise did.

It was so close her eyes went right to it. That was when she noticed that Sonya was spread-eagled and naked from the waist down, save for her nursing shoes. The end of a small white plastic shopping bag—the kind with a drawstring handle—protruded from her vagina.

The crinkling came again, and with it, the end of the bag moved ever so slightly.

In a this-is-a-bad-dream-and-I'll-wake-up-soon daze, Nurse McGowan hooked the drawstring with her pinky and pulled the bag from its tight quarters. The end of the bag relaxed and opened.

The flashlight flickered, and the edges of the bag moved, ready to release its prisoner. Transfixed, though not quite wanting to see what was going to come out, Abby took one step back. The weak beam of light jiggled, strayed left, right, then went back to the opening of the bag.

There was a rapid, smooth movement.

The flashlight went out for a last time, but not before Abby saw the snake slither over the toes of her nursing shoes.

ONE

"SEE? YOU CAN BARELY TELL."

Adele Monsarrat, R.N., held up the top of her uniform, away from her flat abdomen, and pointed to the faded scar to the right of her navel.

Chloe Sedrick, R.N., squinted through a Vistaril haze and leaned forward until her forehead rested against Adele's rib cage. The young nurse was so drugged from the preop medication she not only didn't see the scar, she couldn't have named what part of her coworker's anatomy she was viewing.

"S'nice," Chloe slurred, smiling lopsidedly. "Damn 'pendix. Hurts like a mothersmucker. I hate that."

Amused, Adele sat down on the bed, and without thinking, automatically felt for Chloe's radial pulse. Chloe, the innocent lamb of Ellis Hospital's Ward 8 nursing crew, would be mortified at herself when she came out from under the drugs. Adele guessed the twenty-five-year-old had never so much as passed wind without blushing, let alone lapsed into construction worker language. This was the nurse who, during report, rapidly mumbled over such clinical terms as "penis," "flatulence," and "stool."

The young woman's pulse was high, though not unusual considering the preop circumstances. "Now, Chlo, settle down." Adele laughed. "You don't want to jeopardize your sterling reputation over a cheap shot of Vistaril."

The pretty young woman giggled and waved over Adele's shoulder. "Hey you! Bring your shweet bod on over here, you segzy ol' fart!"

Dr. Aaron Milton entered the room, gave his patient a kiss on the top of her weaving head, and patted Adele lightly on the back. Dressed in surgical greens, the silver-haired surgeon was strikingly handsome in a scrubbed, bohemian kind of way.

"No more preop meds for this one." He chuckled. "You ready to part with your appendix, Chlo?"

Chloe nodded, then let out with a piercing scream, which caused both Adele and Aaron Milton to cover their ears. "Oh, I love you both so mush," she said, her eyes filling with tears. "I never told you how mush I loved you, did I?" Chloe put her arms around Adele, while sloppily kissing Dr. Milton's hand. "Soooo mush."

The surgeon and Adele exchanged amused glances over the top of Chloe's head.

"Why, Chloe, you surprise me," Aaron said. "You've never been so verbal. Back in our clinic days together you couldn't even hand me an instrument without blushing. Heck, we could barely get you to speak above a whisper, let alone make declarations of love."

Tears instantly dried, Chloe shrugged and waved the man's words away. "Sanks. S'nothing."

The ancient Seth Thomas wall clock clicked, and the minute hand jumped ahead. The sound caused Adele a split-second memory of grade school cloakrooms, institutional-green linoleum, and real wooden desks with the permanent ink stains and the initials carved in. Sixteen years spent in educational prisons, Adele thought, only to graduate and spend another seventeen in a public institution with the same depressing linoleum and the same old clocks.

She checked her own watch and was disappointed to find it in synch with the Seth Thomas. There were twenty-five minutes in which to say goodbye and make her way up to Ellis's most notorious ward before nursing report began.

"Okay, sweetie, I've got to get upstairs to find out what torture night shift has doled out to us poor day workers. Can't wait to see who they've called in to cover your shift today."

"Prob'ly Helen," Chloe said, making a face at the thought of the nurse who always smelled faintly of untrained puppies. Helen made her nervous with her talk about making her the princess of some utopian world that was supposed to surface after the bombs from hell destroyed everyone else. From what she could make of her ramblings, Helen was going to find her a worthy mate and together they would populate the new world. That, and all the unsolicited cleansing of her chakras and auras— whatever they were—made her apprehensive whenever Helen was near.

"More than likely," Adele said, watching Chloe space out. "Maybe she'll come down to the operating room and give your lower chakra triad a good spring cleaning while Dr. Milton has you open."

"She came already," Chloe said, absently trying to

grab her tongue, which felt like a strip of flypaper. "Five-thirty in zah damn morming, talkin' 'bout savin' me from hell. Creepy. She'd prob'ly take my 'pendix an' make a voodoo doll outta it."

"Or feed it to those dogs of hers," Adele added.

Aaron Milton, only half listening to the women's chatter, shuffled toward the door. He had to have a cup of joe. His first case of the morning, a total hysterectomy, had taken longer than he'd anticipated; now he was already bone tired, and he still had six more cases to go before lunch. At least Chloe would be easy; an appy on a healthy young girl wouldn't cost him more than thirty minutes, skin to skin. He might even be able to fit in an hour's nap. God knew he needed it after his escapade last night. He smiled at himself—sixty-four and still able to satisfy a woman half his age.

"See you later." He waved from the door. "After you get back to your room. Any orders you want me to write? Special drugs you might like to try? Back rubs?"

Chloe sobered. "Please," she said in a funereal tone, "don't let me die."

The request startled him, not only because the girl even thought it a possibility, but because of the absolute earnestness of her plea. He pulled his graying ponytail out from the collar of his scrub top and clucked his tongue—the sound of dismissal. "Now Chlo, you know I wouldn't allow so much as a hair on that precious head of yours to be split. I'll be quick and gentle."

"Sounds like my last boyfriend," Adele said dryly, washing her hands at the sink. Of course she was only joking; she hadn't had a boyfriend since her husband pulled his disappearing act two years before.

"Del?"

"Umm?" Adele dried her hands and gathered her over-size purse—an Adele Monsarrat trademark.

"If anything happens to me"—Chloe worked an exquisite cameo ring off her finger and slipped it onto Adele's naked one—"give thish to my sister Lesa. Lives in Pacifica off two-eighty? It was my greatgramma's. It's my most favoritest possesshion in the whooooole, wide world."

Adele sighed in mock exasperation as she admired the ring. "Oh brother, I've got to get out of here. Even Helen isn't half as morbid as you."

"Come on now, Chlo," Aaron said, sneaking a glance at Adele's long, shapely legs as she passed. "Next thing you'll be dictating your own living will."

Tall and lithe, Adele had the body of an athlete. The physician recalled reading in the *Pacific Intelligencer* that she'd recently won the San Francisco Bay to Bridge race and had done notably well in the previous year's Boston Marathon. Aroused, he purposely shifted his gaze to her shoulder-length black hair and was dismayed to find it as stimulating as her body. Under the thick straight bangs, her eyes—huge and almond-shaped—drew all of his attention. They were an extraordinary shade of light brown . . . more gold than brown. He felt mesmerized, unable to take his eyes off her.

"I got a doom feeling," Chloe continued.

"Oh yeah, yeah." Adele waved the hand now sporting Chloe's ring. "Every time I get on an airplane I get the same feeling. As I strap myself into my seat, I envision 'Midair Disaster' headlines and the *Newsweek* photos of one of my ripped-off legs hanging by a tendon from someone's chimney."

"Oh, euew," giggled Chloe. "Zhat's 'sgusting."

"Do you really?" Aaron asked, suddenly fascinated by the woman. Recently widowed, he'd found himself bewitched by women everywhere—nurses he'd known for years, neighbors' wives, even the meter maid had gotten him going this morning.

Adele nodded matter-of-factly. "Oh yes. When it comes to flying . . ." She gave the doctor a closer glance, noticed the lust look and shook her head. ". . . or men—my rationality is always challenged.

"I'll hold the ring for you until you get back from recovery." Adele shifted the nineteen-pound canvas purse from one shoulder to the other and squeezed Chloe's toe through the bedsheet. "I'll try to have you assigned as my patient, although I'm sure we're going to end up in a fight over who gets to take care of you. Gayle will probably make us draw straws."

"Anybody 'cept Helen or Meg," Chloe said, her eyes rolling back in her head.

"Oh Chloe, Helen and Meg both love you. They probably think you're the only one worth saving out of the lot of us." Adele hesitated at the door and waved a final time. "Personally, I don't think they're far off the mark."

The county sitting on the north side of the Golden Gate Bridge, known to San Franciscans as "Somewhere Over the Rainbow" or, more popularly, "the Land o' Plenty" (plenty of snobby yuppies, conservative Republicans, BMWs, and million-dollar condos), sported a wealth of two hospitals, thirty-seven privately run drug rehabilitation centers, eleven shopping centers, forty-seven parks, nine recycling plants, thirteen golf courses, and nine yacht clubs.

For an in-depth look at the nature of the place, the Marin phone book pretty much told the whole story: it listed forty-two plastic surgeons; well over two hundred psychiatrists, psychologists, and counselors; thirty-five various psychic healing centers; seventy acupuncturists; twelve dating services; and eighteen yellow pages' worth of listings for attorneys. The county was reported to have the third-highest per capita income in the United States, and the highest incidence of breast cancer in the entire world.

As a lifelong resident, Adele Monsarrat had served a tumultuous seventeen-year sentence as registered nurse at Ellis Hospital, a 374-bed institution set in the middle of the county. Ellis was the one and only competitor of the 250-bed Bellevue Hospital some five miles north in the town of San Andreas—a lovely little place situated directly over the fault of the same name.

One day, not so many years before, when the air was just a bit smoggier than usual, and the traffic congestion (with the accompanying road rage) had grown to monumental proportions, Adele had simply handed in her Sisters of Masochism membership card to the Director of Nurses and taken a year sabbatical. Uprooting her life, she traveled the dustier, less civilized corners of the world looking for answers, the questions of which were somewhat fuzzy. She returned to Ellis Hospital a slightly disillusioned, though wiser soul—except this time around, Adele's soul did not belong to the company.

Kissing off her benefits and retirement packages, she contracted as an independent on-call per diem—in other words, a free agent who could pick and choose her own show. Still afflicted with traces of codependency and masochism, the circus she chose was Ward 8, four day shifts per week.

Adele stepped into the sixteen-room, forty-bed ward and found it bustling with the sounds and smells of people in need. Immediately she scanned the assignment board. Working with her, shouldering the responsibility of thirty-four patients, were Helen Marval, Ward 8's own mentally deranged Annie Wilkes; Meg Barnes, a quiet rookie who'd been hired to replace the nationally famous but still dead Sonya Martin; and Cynthia O'Neil, the ward's own mortician-turned-nurse semisuccess story.

Also with them was Gayle Mueller, head nurse and major termagant. Typically management, Gayle was not expected to get her hair mussed, let alone ever lay her hands upon a patient. She was consistently negative, old-school, pro-administration, humorless—a control freak with an iron hand and an alcoholic/workaholic personality to whom nothing meant more than being a Professional Nurse with lots of alphabet soup after the R.N.

Yet, despite these things, there were aspects of Gayle that Adele admired. Like the get-down-to-business no-nonsense part. Too, there was no guessing as to where you stood with Gayle—she either hated you and made your life a living hell, or she had no opinion about you one way or the other and let you go about your business unhampered.

Adele fell into the unhampered category along with Meg, Linda, Abby, all the doctors, and most of the aux-

iliary staff. Falling into the hated slot were the patients as
a whole, Helen, and Skip, the ward's only male R.N.
Cynthia held a spot all her own in Gayle's eyes, which
seemed to be one of extreme wariness. Of course, Chloe
was the darling upon whom the sun rose and set in
everyone's eyes, especially Gayle's. But the person that
Gayle loved, or more appropriately, worshipped—the one
no one could figure out—was Ellis and Bellevue hospitals' chaplain, the Reverend Roger Wynn.

Gayle was crazy for Reverend Wynn. The rest of the
hospital staff, especially the nurses, abhorred the man. It
was a joke among hospital personnel that the austere
chaplain, with his white-streaked goatee and spiked eyebrows, closely resembled a storybook picture of Satan.
What wasn't funny, however, was that Roger Wynn
was a condescending, the-woman-belongs-in-the-kitchen
right-to-lifer who, not so deep down, disliked women—
including Gayle.

The chaplain had been transferred to Marin due to
some trouble he'd gotten into up in Oregon. According to
one of the *Unsolved Mysteries* research crew (the Sonya
Martin/John Ganet murders made an exciting—though
still unsolved—eleven-minute segment), Roger Wynn had
been charged with sexually molesting a twelve-year-old
parishioner and her ten-year-old brother in Coos Bay. The
charges were eventually dropped, and he'd been shipped
to another parish Somewhere Else—the clergy's usual
way of dealing with their sex offenders.

Cynthia's theory was that Gayle wanted to sleep with
the chaplain, which was as close as she could get to
fucking the Devil—or Jeffrey Dahmer. Adele disagreed;
she figured Gayle was just one of those unfortunate

women who couldn't be happy with a man unless they were being abused.

"Were you planning on attending report this morning, Monsarrat, or did you want us to wait until you came out of suspended animation?" Gayle's ice-laced voice came from behind her.

Adele turned. The woman's eyes, of that electric-blue color that she so admired, were carrying some serious baggage underneath. Adele smiled; she'd learned long ago that the best way to deal with Gayle was with a grain of salt and a total absence of attitude. "I saw Chloe off to surgery," she said, falling into step with the charge nurse as they moved down the hall toward the report room.

"Oh yeah?" Gayle smiled in spite of herself. The expression, foreign to her face, took ten years off her age. "And how was our Sunshine Girl?"

"Loaded and slurring her words on one shot of Vistaril."

Gayle's peal of laughter gave Adele the courage to ask favors. "When she comes back from recovery, I'd like to have her as my patient."

The laughter stopped at once. "Nope." Gayle shook her head in a way that said there was no room for negotiation. "Your assignment is too heavy—you're already getting four of the patients you had yesterday plus both acute patients in eight-oh-three and then two more in eight-eleven. Everybody else's assignment is as heavy or heavier than yours. We can handle one more admission. If we get another patient before Chloe's ready to come up, she'll have to go down to Ward six."

Adele opened her mouth to protest, then snapped it shut. This was Gayle's way of letting her know that she and she alone was the one who had control over any and all decisions.

"Oh, well . . . maybe that's best." Adele sighed deeply. "At least Helen won't be able to bother her anymore."

Gayle stopped. "Excuse me?"

Bingo. "Helen was down in preop at five-thirty this morning doing her usual bedside psycho number on Chloe. It freaked the poor kid right out."

Rage sprang into Gayle's eyes on cue.

"She went into surgery thinking she was going to die on the table. She asked me and Aaron to make sure nothing bad happened to her and that Helen be kept away from—"

Gayle abruptly turned and walked back toward the front desk. Her graying blond Dutchboy bounced with each angry step. "Tell them to start report without me." The words barely made it past the woman's clenched teeth. "I'm going to let admitting know Chloe has reservations on Ward Eight."

Report proved not to be a smooth transition between Ward 8's going off and Ward 8's coming on. It was, in fact, a comedy of errors. Gayle was not there to rule the proceedings with an iron fist and hostile glares, Meg showed up twenty minutes late, Cynthia spilled hot coffee on the copy machine, Helen made a big commotion about being given her report first, and the night shift charge nurse kept forgetting what she was saying and dozing off midsentence.

The only odd thing about the procedure, however, was Helen insisting on taking report first. Helen usually thrived on hearing everybody else's business. She often showed up for work two hours before her shift began so she could read all the patient histories. And when she ran out of charts, she would sit in the computer corner and watch the night staff work, taking notes or sometimes chanting.

Helen also had a tendency to prolong her reports by asking numerous inane questions no one could—or would—answer. "How long has her aura been that awful red color?" "What do you think is going on with his fifth chakra?" "Whose spirit is that hanging out at her bedside?" "Does he take qi-toning herbs for his prostate?" "Did you try to look at the patient with your third eye?"

This morning, however, when Helen made a beeline for the door at 7:25 after a conspicuously questionless report, Adele felt a tug of concern somewhere in the vicinity of her temples.

"Spread your knees *apart*, Mrs. Vinter." Adele jammed an elbow into the inner aspect of Mrs. Jeraldine Vinter's left knee and pushed. Mrs. Vinter pushed back with an incredible amount of might for an eighty-three-year-old in congestive heart failure.

Cynthia shut off the flashlight and put down the silicone urinary catheter she was aiming at Mrs. Vinter's ancient and very swollen meatus.

"Jesus, Mrs. Vinter, stop with the reluctant-virgin routine. Make believe I'm . . ." Cynthia glanced at the wrinkled face. ". . . ah, Rudolph Valentino trying to—"

Mrs. Vinter's tissue-thin eyelids flew open and her head began to tremble. "How dare you say those dirty things to me."

Adele decided to take another tack. She held up a hand.

"Okay, okay. Let me explain this again. You need this catheter. It'll make you feel better by keeping your bladder empty, and that will make the nurses feel better because then they won't have to keep coming in here to change your bed." Adele smiled broadly. "So. You have to stop fighting us and relax so we can put it in, okay?"

The nurse searched among the wrinkles of the old woman's face for signs that she'd understood the simple logic.

"No, you can't do it." Mrs. Vinter's mouth was set in a thin, stubborn line.

Cynthia sighed. "Why not?"

"Because you say dirty things."

"But if you let us put in the catheter," bargained Cynthia, "we wouldn't have to say dirty things."

"I can't."

"Why?"

"Because you say dirty things."

Cynthia and Adele gave each other the nurse's look of resignation. They'd both had this conversation—or one very much like it—on a hundred different occasions with their elderly, slightly confused patients who did not want their bodies violated by medical warriors.

Adele leaned close to Mrs. Vinter's "good" ear—the one without the hearing aid. "Tell you what, Mrs. Vinter. We're going to leave you alone for now and you can think this over. Cynthia and I will come back in about a half hour and we'll try again. Okay?"

"Dirty things," Mrs. Vinter repeated, the vacant look of the insulted elderly clouding her rheumy eyes.

Simultaneously, Adele and Cynthia checked their watches. Adele's watch said 9:02; Cynthia's said 9:32. The reason for the discrepancy was that Cynthia, a watch-driven individual, was also a habitually tardy person. No matter how early she got started, she would inevitably happen upon odd and unavoidable occurrences which would make her late. This slight defect had caused more than a few problems in her life.

The problems escalated eight years before on the day she showed up thirty minutes late at San Francisco Civic Center, where the apprentice mortician had been scheduled, at 11:30 A.M. sharp, to be married in a civil ceremony to the love of her life, multimillionaire John J. Woolsey, Jr. By the time she arrived, the judge had left for lunch, forcing the couple to reschedule for one week hence. As things went, a Hyde Street cable car slipped its cables the following day, leaving John J. Woolsey, Jr., quite dead, and Cynthia brokenhearted, unmarried, and having to work for a living for the rest of her life instead of idly hobnobbing with San Francisco's elite.

The ill-fated incident left Cynthia a faithful commitment-phobe living one half hour ahead of the rest of the world.

Adele removed her latex gloves and covered the confused Mrs. Vinter with a blanket, more for modesty's sake than warmth. "Why don't we try this debacle again after Mrs. Vinter's ten A.M.—ten-thirty your time—magic Haldol pill."

"Sure." Cynthia flipped back the loose braid which had slipped over her shoulder. The light brown hair with its mix of autumnal colors glinted like new copper in the morning sun. "That'll give me time to get Mr. Coomb's bowels whistling."

Adele regarded the younger woman; the characteristically Irish face set with intense green eyes was both beautiful and impish at the same time. She always felt inadequate next to Cynthia. Where Cynthia was of a normal, manageable height and voluptuous, she was tall and thin, almost reedy. Where Cynthia radiated rounded, erotic feminine sensuality, she fell into the angular, athletically gawky category. Her aging, wrinkled elbows didn't help either.

"What does that mean, exactly, Cyn? The whistling part?"

"You know, the whistling clean three-H enema?"

"Three-H?"

"High, hot, and a hell of a lot? Don't you remember that from your second-year clinicals?"

"Whistling, though? I mean, couldn't you use another word?"

"But it's true!" Cynthia protested. "After the enema—especially if it works—haven't you ever heard that high-pitched whistling noi—"

Gayle Mueller, looking as though she'd died but forgotten to fall down, appeared in the doorway, pointed at Adele, and opened her mouth. At that moment, the general PA system activated with a blast of static.

"ATTENTION ALL PERSONNEL. CODE BLUE. RECOVERY ROOM."

Adele paled; Cynthia lost her smile. Adrenaline propelled the two of them into the hall, where all the phones at the nurses' station came alive at once. Before Gayle could get the words "Adele, go!" out of her mouth, Adele took off running in the direction of the double doors.

* * *

Fueled by panic, Adele sprinted the length of the west wing to the stairwell in three seconds flat. Usually she was in total command when responding to a code. Level-headed, organized, and quick to identify problems and solutions—these were qualities that made her one of Ellis's best code-blue team leaders. For resuscitating patients who were checking out of Motel Life and headed down the legendary Dead Man's Tunnel toward the famous white light, few were more adept.

She flew down fourteen flights of stairs, feet barely touching the steps, driven by the words going through her head like a continuous LED sign: *Don't let it be Chloe. Don't let it be Chloe. Please don't let it be Chloe. . . .*

The stairs brought her to a set of metal doors outside the surgical suites. Adele pushed the automatic wall plate, and the doors sporting the warning "!RECOVERY ROOM—NO ADMITTANCE!" in glossy stop-sign red swung inward with a loud whoosh. Somewhere in the blur behind her, an obese woman with a bad case of impetigo shouted that she couldn't go in.

Mindful of nothing except the face of the coding patient, Adele raced into the large open unit and toward the throng of uniforms surrounding a gurney.

As she got close, she saw a small white hand hanging off the side of the bed, the fingers jiggling rhythmically as Dr. Milton squeezed Chloe's heart, trying to get it to move. Unconsciously, she took the cool wet hand in hers and, for the second time in a few hours, felt for a radial pulse. This time, Chloe was pulseless.

Adele avoided looking at the red gash that was Chloe's

chest, and stared into her friend's fixed and dilated pupils. The delicate mouth was streaked with blood and mucus. An endotracheal tube protruded obscenely from between her teeth. Her once pink and healthy skin was now gray and mottled.

"Time down?" Aaron Milton asked in a voice that was flat yet husky with emotion. His scrub top was stained with dark streaks of perspiration, and even darker splatters of blood.

A code team nurse looked up from her task of suctioning blood from under the steel retractors holding open Chloe's chest and checked the wall clock. "Forty-one minutes."

"Have the results come back from Bellevue lab? What's her calcium now?"

An older woman Adele recognized as the senior surgical nurse waved a Bellevue Hospital lab slip. "Same as our lab. Panic value—off the scale."

For a brief moment, Aaron and Adele locked eyes. She read his plea to stop the nightmare and turn the hands of the clock back. Shaking off the shock, she slipped smoothly into the role of professional.

"Is the Isuprel wide open?" She checked the three IV lines running into Chloe and frowned. The left antecubital IV had been Z-taped—an old military method of securing the IV needle which, to her knowledge, no one but Helen ever used anymore.

"Yes," Aaron answered.

"Atropine? Intracardiac epi?"

"It's all been given," Aaron said quietly. "Her heart won't respond."

Adele put on sterile gown and gloves and stepped

close to Aaron. "Let me do that," she said. "You rest for a minute."

As soon as the physician let her move into his place, she inserted her hand into Chloe's chest. At the first touch of the heart, Adele was stunned—it was as tight as a marble egg. She shot a questioning glance at Aaron as she worked to squeeze the constricted muscle. "Christ on a bike, Aaron, what the hell is this?"

The physician simply stared back without answering. The shadow in his eyes said what they all knew—that Chloe was dead and nothing they did was going to get her back again; the brain had been too long without oxygenation.

The heavy, familiar silence that always preceded the ending of an unsuccessful code was broken when Nan Farley, the ER physician, asked for an update of how long Chloe had been down.

Fifty minutes.

Adele ignored the answer, working the frozen muscle.

Dr. Farley looked at Aaron, then at Adele, and announced in no uncertain terms the code was ended and would someone please call the coroner?

Adele found Aaron in the hospital chapel, sitting in the dark of the last pew, staring straight ahead. Several strands of silver hair had pulled loose from the rubber band holding his ponytail. A surgical mask hung limp around his neck.

Not entirely purged of her childhood religion-from-hell nightmare, Adele awkwardly crossed herself, but resisted the impulse to genuflect, and slid in next to him. She silently stared at the front of the nondescript, multidenominational chapel along with him, steadily running a finger over Chloe's ring as though it were a rosary bead.

"I don't know what happened," Aaron said finally. His voice was so low she had to lean close to hear him. "I've operated on thousands of people . . . most of them strangers." He held out his hands as if asking for absolution. "I've had people die on the table, but there were concrete reasons—their hearts were shot to hell, or they had such extensive injuries nothing would have saved them.

"Chloe was a baby—a perfectly healthy kid with a mildly inflamed appendix. Shit, we could've treated her with antibiotics and . . . I mean, there was no reason for this."

The surgeon closed his eyes. "She called it, didn't she? That bit about doom. I should have paid attention to that." He opened his eyes and turned to her. "There was a time when I would have listened—talked to her for as long as it took to make her feel confident. All I could think about was how quick I could finish her up and have a break."

Adele edited out the overt anger from her voice and asked, "Why wasn't the code announced earlier? Chloe was already dead by the time it came over the PA. Didn't anybody think that just maybe there might have been other personnel in the house who could have done something more . . . something different?" She stopped as the physician's face twisted and his eyes welled up.

"What else was there to do? She was young. I thought it was a delayed vagal response . . . you know, a squirt of atropine and we'd get her right back. Happens all the time." He wiped away a tear that had rolled halfway down his cheek. "But she wouldn't come out of asystole no matter what the hell we did. The minute I cracked her chest, I knew . . ." He trailed off.

Adele pulled herself to the edge of the pew so she was facing him. "How the hell did her calcium level get that high?"

The physician again shook his head. "Don't know. When the first electrolytes came back, it was so high we figured it was a mistake and redrew. But the calcium kept climbing. We thought maybe the lab's machine was screwed up. I had them run the blood at Bellevue's lab. It came back even higher."

"How . . . ?" Adele let the question die on her lips.

The physician shrugged. "A medication error? A defective IV of pure calcium chloride? The bag she had hanging when she coded was lactated Ringer's. Hell, before we got the lab work back, we ran it in wide open. She got the whole liter." He sighed. "I don't know. Doug Collier said he'd let me know after the preliminary autopsy this afternoon."

At the mention of the county's coroner, Adele cringed. That Chloe's body would undergo the horrors of an autopsy made her sick. It was, without question, a violation of enormous proportions against the human body.

She studied the physician's face a moment longer, wrote her home phone number on the back of a lab slip belonging to an anemic patient, and handed it to him. "Call me if you need to talk."

He tucked the yellow slip into the breast pocket of his scrub top. "Thanks," he said, searching her face earnestly, as if he would find the answers to his troubles there. "I might take you up on that."

"I hope so," Adele told him, hurriedly moving into the aisle. Sudden anxiety that she had given him the wrong impression caused her to forget herself long enough to make the sign of the cross and genuflect.

<u>TWO</u>

HELEN SAT ROCKING, ONE HAND CLASPING the crucifix hanging between her breasts as if it were a lifeline. The other hand worked over a crystal. Tina, the ward clerk, fidgeted with the disconnected end of her phone headset. Meg sobbed quietly into a Kleenex, at the same time leaning against the wall for support.

Cynthia stared at Adele in slack-jawed disbelief. "How did this happen?" she whispered.

"We don't know yet," Adele answered, in a voice that seemed to float out of her. Even though the initial shock was gone, she felt as if she were outside her body looking in on the scene.

"They're doing an autopsy," Gayle said in the same monotone she had used to tell them that Chloe Sedrick was dead. She looked like she hadn't slept for days. "I'll let you all know the results as soon as I'm told." Abruptly, Gayle opened the door to her office—her usual sign of dismissal. The din of several call bells going off at once added to the atmosphere of confusion. "Please show up in the conference room as soon as report is over this afternoon. I've asked Reverend Wynn to come by. I'm sure we can all benefit from his spiritual . . ."

Cynthia and Adele automatically rolled their eyes. The very mention of the man set most of the nurses' teeth on edge.

". . . guidance in this time of need. Until then, pull yourselves together and go about your business as usual." Gayle held up a warning finger. "Not one word of this is to be discussed on the ward, and I don't want any displays of hysterics.

"Helen and Adele, I want to speak to you."

"C'mon, let's get back to the war," said Cynthia, pushing Meg and Tina ahead of her. "Before *all* the call bells go on and blow the fuse again."

"What the hell were you doing down in the recovery room this morning, Helen?" Gayle fought to keep control of her voice and her fists; she hadn't wanted to punch someone so much since her last bad bout of PMS. "The surgical clerk told Tina you were thrown out of the unit because you were upsetting Chloe."

Out of the corner of her eye, Adele saw Helen stop rocking, frown, and then furtively search her uniform pocket.

"I was cleaning Chloe's space of negative energies." Helen's voice trembled. "There were some evil . . ."

Gayle groaned and sat down heavily. She lowered her head into her hands.

". . . spiritual entities hanging over her, more than I've ever seen except that one time last autumn when It first found us." Helen rose from her seat as if she remembered something important that had to be tended to right away. "It was that same bad guide hovering over her that I saw last year when—"

"Damn it!" Gayle yelled, and pounded her fist on the side of the filing cabinet. The noise made both of them jump. "Did you touch her in any way? Chloe coded less than two minutes after they threw you out. Did you do *anything* to her? Did you give her one of those god-damned Chinese herbs of yours that would have caused her to choke or have a reaction? What the hell did you do to her?"

The fleshy folds of Helen's neck flushed scarlet, her eyes turning to slits of contempt. "All I did was clean her aura and give her a healing crystal to hold." She paused. "And I retaped her IV properly."

Helen lowered her voice. "It was the usual Milton sixteen-gauge gouge job—too big and too far above the antecubital." Her chin tilted defiantly. "The real reason they kicked me out was because most humans can't be exposed to that much positive energy. I didn't do anything to Chloe except to clear her aura of the evil influences."

After a second, Helen changed again, nervously twisting and pinching her fingers. "But maybe I overdid that part . . . made her too pure, you know? Every once in a while, if the spiritual plane is too much in order, the soul is misled into believing it's free to leave the physical body. It really depends on—"

"Shut the hell up!" Gayle's neck veins were bulging. "Do you hear what you're saying, or do you actually believe this New Age horseshit?"

"I . . . How can you . . ."

"Because if you *do* believe it, you're certifiable, and if I ever catch you practicing that bent shit around this ward, I'll fire you in two seconds and you can go find work on the other side of the Golden Gate with the rest of the freaks. All I want to know is whether you did anything that might have caused Chloe—"

"I said no!" Helen answered in a high, cracked voice. The smell of her nervous perspiration permeated the room. She had stopped torturing her fingers and was furiously playing with the object in her pocket. Adele guessed it had to be one of the twenty crystals she reportedly carried on her person at all times.

"I wouldn't do anything to harm Chloe. We were friends. She was a princess. She was scared, she *wanted* me to—"

"She wanted you to stay the hell away from her." Gayle turned and looked pointedly at Adele. "Adele, tell Helen what Chloe told you this morning."

Adele hesitated, twisting Chloe's ring on her finger. She looked first at the angry, hurting Gayle, then at a tortured and somewhat vacant Helen. "Sorry, count me out," she said, firmly decided. "I'm not going to play in this game. This is between you two." She opened the door and stepped into the now quiet corridor.

It was noon by the time Adele got her patients settled and medicated. She and Cynthia had been each other's comforting shadow. Whenever their eyes met, there was between them a glance of understanding, or, in passing, the brief touch of a shoulder.

All of them on the ward were silent—not so much because of Gayle's warning; this was the silence of grieving. Tina, usually loud and brash, was subdued. She answered the phones not with the customary harsh "Yeah,

Ward Eight!"—which usually translated as "How dare you call here, you imbecile!"—but in an almost timid tone.

Meg sniffled constantly into a handkerchief. Adele couldn't help but notice how badly the girl's hands shook when she sorted through her patients' lab work. That Meg would be among those who took Chloe's death the hardest wasn't surprising; Chloe had been Meg's mentor when she first came to Ellis. Since that time, Chloe was the only nurse to whom Meg ever spoke voluntarily.

When pressed, Chloe once confided that she felt sorry for the thirty-two-year-old who led an isolationist's existence in a dump of an apartment over the Granary, a bar and grill situated on the outskirts of downtown San Rafael.

Cynthia believed that Meg had a schoolgirl's crush on Chloe. Adele had to agree; the way the girl gushed and blushed in Chloe's presence was beyond a doubt infatuation.

Adele sat down to chart, though her mind wandered elsewhere.

In the past 24 hours, pt. Salucci's scrotum has swollen to approximately the size of a medium cantaloupe . . .

The day Sonya was murdered had been different.

. . . the sac is inflamed and excoriated, with a quarter-sized bleeding area on the posterior portion of . . .

That day everyone was hysterical too, only not with grief, but with fear. Sonya was not well liked . . . that is, unless one was male and had high levels of testosterone, or female and swung in that direction.

. . . left larger than right. When squeezed, pt. reacts violently and screams in Italian . . .

First there had been the encounter with Helen in the locker room before Sonya's body was even found.

... greenish tan exudate oozes from surgical puncture at base of ...

And the snake. People were jumping and screaming at the slightest movement and shadow flicker. Then there was the bizarre scene wherein Helen played the role of a snake diviner and went straight for room 819's radiator—under which the snake had taken refuge. When Helen got the thing to come out and slither onto her arm just by talking to it, the hair on the back of Adele's neck stood straight up.

... the texture of tiny pebbles just under the surface. The penile shaft from base to approximately one half of its length is covered with ...

Worse than the snake were the sheriff's deputies—as in Keystone Cops. Useless macho morons strutting around barking warnings at anyone who came within ten feet of them, their nightsticks drawn and ready for use like so many wooden phalluses. At their helm was Harold Marval, a bumbling, overweight fool ... much like Dr. Watson in the Basil Rathbone Sherlock Holmes series. But then again, whoever married Helen would have to be a little ...

... discussed personal hygiene with Mr. Salucci. Pt.'s English is poor; but keeps repeating something about the Pope's corn bread and mortal sin ...

The only leads that came out of that fracas had been the sensationalized details of Sonya Martin's full, and amazingly varied, sex life. From the way the story was presented in the *Pacific Intelligencer*, the suspect could have been any number of betrayed wives and girlfriends, or, for that matter, boyfriends or husbands.

Dr. Ganet's murder was so overshadowed by Sonya's it got almost no press at all ... except, of course, for the severed, missing hands and the two newly fatherless children. Adele thought the front-page photographs, side by side, of the toddlers and a close-up of their daddy's bloodied stumps nauseatingly gauche. In a letter to the editor, she'd criticized the way the police had handled the case, but of course, it was never ...

... *sac and member* ... Adele smiled briefly—Boys Only Club member. ... *covered with Silvadene and suspended on penis hammock to keep pressure off* ... She paused to search for the right words. ... *the already stressed appendages.*

Because of the long-standing affair between John and Sonya, Cynthia thought the prime suspect should have been Colleen Ganet, but Adele hadn't agreed. If made angry enough, a normal jealous woman might slit a throat or two, she might even amputate a couple of hands (this was a nation of potential Mrs. Bobbitts, after all), but she wouldn't have been touching snakes, let alone inserting them into another woman's ...

Foley catheter patent and draining cloudy, foul-smelling tan urine. Dr. Greenwald notified.

One week after the murders, a twenty-six-year-old Ellis orderly, Henry Williams, was arrested and held on suspicion of murder when it was disclosed that he and Nurse Martin had had "stormy relations" (Cynthia insisted it was poorly disguised S&M). Despite the high school dropout's fat Troubled Youth file, Henry was released sixteen hours after his arrest as the number of Ellis and

Bellevue hospital employees who'd had "relations" (also mostly stormy) with Ms. Martin grew to upward of thirty men and seven women.

. . . hands restrained, as he keeps pulling on his . . .

By the new year, it seemed like the whole lurid case was forgotten. The *Pacific Intelligencer* rarely mentioned it except to say that the Sheriff's Department and the San Andreas Police Department were working together with the DA's office to track down leads as they came up— which was never. All other information was classified.

Classified information. What the hell did *that* mean? It meant, Adele thought, slapping Mr. Amerigo Salucci's chart closed, that they were dropping the case. After all, who cared that most Marin County nurses and doctors were still having anxiety/panic attacks anytime they found themselves alone?

"I'm going to lunch," Adele announced to those sitting at the nurses' station.

Meg and Helen didn't look up from their charts, though Helen did mumble "Okay" without much interest.

"My patients are of alive and breathing status. Mr. Salucci needs to be checked every so often to make sure his hammock is still in place, and Mrs. Vinter is in soft wrist restraints so she doesn't pull out her catheter, but she's still pretty agitated."

"Sure," Helen said, and turned to the graphics page in her chart. Meg gingerly spread open her flow sheet, wiped away some tears, and began to chart vital signs.

"Mrs. Lee's piggyback IV will need to be hung at . . ."

"Okay." Helen tugged on a strand of badly damaged red hair as she drew a line from the 37.0 Celsius dot to the 39.5 Celsius dot on the body temperature chart. Meg, in ambidextrous indecision, suddenly switched her pen to her left hand and continued writing.

Adele stared at the two of them. "I've set a bomb to go off in four minutes. It will kill everyone in the building."

"Will do," Helen said, scratching a painted-on auburn eyebrow. Meg sniffled and nodded in blind agreement, continuing to write.

Ward 8 doors weren't yet closed behind her before she set off in an easy jog toward the recovery room. Something didn't feel right. Adele's intuition, that overactive gland which sat in the middle of her gut, was competing with her grief for attention.

For the second time that day, she pushed the metal plate on the wall outside the recovery unit, this time without interference from the obese clerk, who was busy chowing down on a powdery jelly doughnut behind a bodice ripper entitled *Ruby's Red Love*.

Inside the large open unit, the smell of benzoin and fresh laundry hung in the air. Two nurses were sitting at the desk situated in the center of the room, while a third took the blood pressure of the only patient to be seen. When she entered, all three turned to stare at the intruder, their expressions belligerent.

Adele shrank, not for the first time amazed at how some nurses could be so unfriendly; it seemed incongruous with the very nature of their profession. She smiled at the darkest of the three, a Hispanic woman whose name tag read "Rosa." She decided to direct her attention to the Latina, who she figured would have the most *simpatía*.

"Hi. I'm Adele. I worked with Chloe Sedrick on Ward

Eight, and . . . I'm . . . I was her friend and . . ." The hostility of the stares made her falter. "I'd like . . . Can you tell me what happened right before she coded?"

The Latina shook her head. "Uh-uhn. The coroner, he come and took her away. He tell us, don't say nothing to nobody."

"Well, can you tell me if anyone was here when—"

Rosa shrugged. "Can't say nothing."

"If you want to know what really happened," interrupted the anorexicly thin nurse sitting next to her, "you should talk to that nutcase who works with you up there. She was here, doing all this hocus-pocus . . ."

Rosa snickered.

". . . hand-jive witchcraft to your friend."

The thin woman, whose name tag read "Mary R.N.," spoke in a whiny Cockney accent. Her long, narrow face reminded Adele of a whippet. "A very ballsy lady, that one was," she continued indignantly. "Took it upon herself to be hanging IVs on your friend, *and* messing about with the equipment, mind you. I chucked her out on her ear. Wasn't a minute later your friend coded." The blonde turned back to the chart lying on the counter. "She'll be the first the coppers hear about from me, I can tell you."

"What kind of IVs did she—"

Hands on abundant hips, Rosa piped up, "She was crazy. She hang a new bag on your friend and she no check with me first, like she the boss. Then she turn off the pump, and leave the IV to run in wide open."

"*And* turned off the monitor alarms so that we almost didn't catch the asystole," said the blonde.

"And turn off the wall suction too!" added Rosa, getting excited.

"You mean she . . ."

The third nurse, obviously the one in charge, joined the group, looking at Adele as though she were something that had crawled out of a suction canister full of unspeakable things. The woman's stare sent chills through Adele, who instantly felt pity for all the people who woke up from anesthesia to that cold, unfeeling face.

"Why is she here?" she asked, jerking a thumb at Adele.

"She's asking about the one who coded this morning," answered the blonde.

"Christ on a bike!" Adele interrupted. "The woman had a name. It was Chloe Sedrick. She was a nurse in this hospital. She was a friend and a coworker. We're all nurses here—why the attitude?"

"You're not supposed to be here," said the charge nurse in a high, breathless voice. "Get out now or I'll call the supervisor."

The Seth Thomas clicked behind Adele. Without thinking, she glanced over her shoulder and saw her lunch break had been over for five minutes. And yet, she didn't want to give the contentious nurse the satisfaction of seeing her leave.

"How long have you worked here?" Adele asked.

"Three years. How long have you been here—one month?" The woman tittered. Behind her, Rosa laughed and said, "Oh-oh. Now we gonna get down to business. Gonna be fireworks now, baby."

It was like a scene out of *West Side Story*, thought Adele. "I've worked here for seventeen years."

The nurse's face fell, but Rosa's laughter went up an octave. She snapped her fingers the way the homeboys did and said, "Oooh baby! Doncha go messin' with this girl. She's hot!"

Adele walked to the doors, and turned back. She wanted to tell them about Chloe, about what a delightful soul she'd been and that she deserved more than their indifference.

All three waited with cold stares.

"What happened to your compassion?" Adele asked. "Don't you realize that a young girl—a nurse—died here today? She was one of us. Don't you . . ." The pressure in her throat strangled off her words.

She kept the anguish down until she hit the fourth-floor landing. There, she held herself at the middle and let it out in a long, tormented moan.

Reverend Wynn's appearance on the ward did not, as Gayle predicted, give spiritual guidance. His idea of grief counseling was to stand over them preaching about how they needed to take a good look at their own faulty, selfish lives. "You girls need to clean up your acts and look to the Lord for forgiveness," was how he put it.

Lapsing into fourth-grade-clown standard, Cynthia sniffed her armpits, then clasped her hands and rolled her eyes beseechingly toward the ceiling. Tina snorted and whinnied out her famous chicken laugh.

Reverend Wynn's eyes bugged out of his head, making him look even more like Satan. "You think this is *funny*?" he screamed at them. His face and neck had turned an alarming shade of purple.

Helen put her hands over her ears.

"Is nothing sacred to you? Get down on your knees in the sight of the Lord and pray for forgiveness. Pray that your young departed friend asked for forgiveness before she left this earth. Pray that she was pure."

Temper snapped, Adele stepped to his side, as if she were about to whisper a secret. In close proximity, she noticed his eyes were bloodshot and there was a faint smell of bourbon on his breath. It didn't surprise her; she had always suspected he might be a closet alcoholic. He seemed lonely enough.

"How dare you preach to us. You don't know anything about Chloe. She didn't need to ask for anybody's forgiveness, Mr. Wynn."

"It's Reverend Wynn. Please address me as Reverend, Ms.—"

"Mister," she shot back, "as far as I'm concerned, you are about as far from being a man of God as . . ." She had to stop and think. ". . . Beavis and Butt-head. Hypocrites always claim to have God on their side, Mr. Wynn. Christ on a bike, I thought we locked up our religious fanatics in this state!"

"Adele, get out!" Gayle was out of her seat and headed for the door. She held it open. "You're out of line. Reverend Wynn has taken time out of his busy schedule to speak with—"

"Oh please," Adele said, bristling. "He came here to pump himself up. It's the nature of his job to bullshit people. He doesn't know anything about Chloe, let alone spirituality."

"On the contrary, Ms. Monsarrat," Roger Wynn said sadly, lowering his eyes, "I knew Miss Sedrick better than . . . you think."

Adele hoisted her purse onto her shoulder with some effort. "Oh, gag me with a cement mixer," she snorted.

"What a crock of verbal flatus. You think you knew Chloe better than any of us here? Man, where do you get *off*?"

As the door closed behind her, Adele heard Roger Wynn announce solemnly to his audience, "There goes a deeply troubled girl who needs some serious help. Let us pray for her soul."

Adele's scowl was at once transformed into a smile when the clergyman's request was followed by a short burst of women's laughter.

In the nurses' locker room, Adele buttoned her black wool skirt, staring at the Nike advertisement taped to the inside of her locker door—a photograph of a trim, athletic woman walking out of a locker room. She derived a sense of *assuredness* from the photograph—a quality which she'd failed to assimilate during her upbringing.

After years of availing herself of the abundance of counselors and self-help books and workshops, she'd managed to build within herself a secure foundation of self-confidence. Small reminders, such as the realization that life was, in fact, relatively short, or even the Nike advertisement, all worked to bring about an instantaneous hit of inner strength. The Nike slogan "Just Do It!" was a phrase she often employed.

The door opened and the atmosphere of the room changed to one of restraint. *Helen.*

Adele glanced at the advertisement again, mouthed, "Just do it, Adele," and closed the locker door. In the middle of the room Helen stood studying the palm of her hand.

"Helen?" Adele spoke in the soft, obsequious tone she

used when she and Helen were alone. It was reminiscent of the way Melanie spoke to Scarlett in *Gone With the Wind*. Helen looked at her as one hypnotized. The veil of madness fallen, Adele shifted into their Twilight Zone mode.

"Helen, what happened this morning with Chloe?"

"It was there again, Adele, like before."

"What was there?"

"The Devil," she explained. "I call it It. If I say Its name, It's drawn from the dark world—like an incantation.

"It's strong now . . . stronger than when It killed Sonya. Put the evil eye to me again and said not to tell."

"Tell what?"

"What It told me to do."

"Did It tell you to hurt Chloe?"

"No, but It was whispering bad things about her. I told It to stop. Chloe was scared." Helen frowned, picked at the small pink crystal in her hand, and began rocking on her feet. "The Devil tricked us—It took our princess anyway." She hesitated; then she said in an offhanded manner, "It likes killing."

Reluctantly, Adele looked into Helen's eyes and drew a shuddery breath. The vacant eyes were not at all unlike those of a Stepford Wife. It was almost impossible to tell if the woman was telling the truth or relating some insane hallucination.

Helen broke the blank stare with a frown of concern. "You should be scared, Adele. I'm afraid It will kill my dogs. Look what It did to poor Chloe."

"What did It do, Helen?"

"I said I can't tell!" Helen whispered crossly, pulling an imaginary zipper across her lips, in the manner of a child. "It'd know I told. It knows everything. Let's talk about nice things."

Adele sat on the bench and needlessly retied her shoe-laces, giving the woman time to calm down. She'd pushed Helen once before and had no desire to repeat *that* mistake. The rage which hid behind those vacuous eyes was truly scary. "Listen, do you think it would be okay if I brought Nelson over to see you? I know you breed Labs and I thought you might like to meet him . . . maybe even clear his chakras. He's been acting out lately, and I'm not sure what to do."

Distracted from the dark side, Helen smiled. "That'd be nice. I love dogs, you know. I can read their minds. They're so . . ." She paused. ". . . accepting." She opened her locker.

Painted on the inside of the door were pentagrams and other symbols associated with astrology and the tarot. In the center of it all was a color portrait of the Virgin Mary holding a golden-haired baby Jesus. She touched Adele's arm briefly. "You are very nice to me, Adele."

Adele nodded. "Well, you and I need to pull together to bring balance and peace to the ward now that Chloe isn't with us, don't we?"

Helen opened a shoe box lined with jeweler's cotton and felt around inside her pocket. Directing a line of baby talk to her empty palm, she set some invisible thing on the pad of cotton, reseated the lid, and turned her full attention to Adele. "I'll ask the spirits to protect you from being the next one."

Rotating her purse and empty lunch sack, Adele stopped at the door. "The next one?"

"It told me," Helen said, "the killing isn't over."

* * *

Roger Wynn's leg joints throbbed with pain. He pressed his bare knees harder into the hardwood floor. It wasn't much of a punishment considering the crime—certainly not all that he deserved. Ezra Wynn would have found a harsher punishment for his son, but then again, the grim-faced fundamentalist had been more creative with his disciplines.

Being on his knees was familiar; Roger had spent his life on his knees, first paying homage to his father's righteous wrath, then later the rage of his God. It was all one and the same, since judgments were delivered with Ezra's open hand and sharp tongue.

Ezra's mission was well executed; beating—whipping—his fourteen children and his wife into pious servility. It was, the elder Wynn avowed, the will of God. He claimed to anyone who dared to question his strict ways that he received his instructions personally from God during the most holy of fundamentalist rituals.

An instant flash of his father dancing around a fire, poison snakes in each hand, seared through his mind. His father was a Chosen One—nothing could harm Ezra Wynn.

The closeness of the dark closet choked him. Perspiration soaked his shirt. Clasping his hands as tightly as he shut his eyes, he gasped for air. "Unworthy soul, I throw myself at thy holy feet. I beseech thee, O Lord . . . forgive me, forgive me, forgive me. . . ."

His mother crept into his vision, and his testicles retracted, causing a wave of nausea. Emily, who used her continuous pregnancies as insurance against Ezra's cruelty; each confinement meaning an automatic nine-month reprieve from punishment. It was also the only time Ezra treated her with something akin to affection.

Ezra Wynn being kind or thoughtful was a wonder to behold, for he was as niggardly with his affections as he was generous with God's many punishments. But the unborn child was supremely holy. Often Ezra would wonder over the miracle of it: his seed, taken by God himself and planted in the soil of the sacred womb and then delivered through the body of Emily—his chosen vessel.

The infant was a personal gift to Ezra Wynn from God. Fresh from the Maker . . . the scent of his hands still new upon the flesh.

As far as Roger could guess, the child stayed holy and without sin until just after its third birthday. Then, he guessed, the scent of the supremely chaste began to go rancid in his father's nose.

Emily, the look of suffering pasted on her pharisaical face, always stood to the side, hands clasped as his were now, watching them all be viciously beaten. "Bear up under the hand of God, child," she'd said over and over, until it became a prayer.

Later, she would sometimes sneak in to them, soothing their wounds with Bag Balm and their hearts with a kiss or a gentle touch of her swollen fingers over a fevered forehead.

Roger began to cry. His tears mixed with his sweat and ran down his arms and face. "O dear God," he prayed, gasping for air, "forgive me. Through my cowardice, I have killed my beloved. I have . . ."

Bear up under the hand of God, child. Bear up under the hand of . . .

". . . another innocent soul upon my conscience."

Roger fell forward, striking his head on the floor of the closet. He picked himself up and struck his head once again, and then again, and again . . .

Bear up under the hand of God, child. Bear up . . .

THREE

ADELE EXITED ONTO HIGHWAY 101 WITH TEETH clenched—the usual condition of her jaw whenever she drove the Beast. Driving the 1978 Pontiac station wagon was a health hazard; every time she got behind the wheel, something went wrong that caused her blood pressure to soar.

The problem was twofold. If she took her eyes off the road for a second, the shandrydan automatically swerved in the opposite direction she was looking, or ran into things or persons.

The other problem lay with the car itself. It was a clever thing; hell-bent first on draining her bank account for gas and repair bills, and then on killing her. She often told people the Beast was Christine's brother.

The mechanical demon especially hated to be driven on the freeway—a hard thing to avoid in Northern California. It would behave itself until it hit a major multi-lane highway during rush hour traffic. Then it began to act up—rather like a werewolf on a full moon—with sudden, high-pitched noises, or the front tire would fly off, or a brake line would rupture, or the tailpipe would drop.

But what the vehicle did best was what Adele called its going-to-sleep trick. For this prank, the car had to be doing over sixty on a busy highway, or it required that torrential rains and heavy fog prevailed or that it was speeding down a steep hill with a crosswalk full of schoolchildren at the bottom, or a cop needed to be directly behind her as she approached a red light at a busy intersection, or she needed to be entering a sharp curve with an extra-wide-load semi in the opposite lane. As soon as any one, or a combo, of these conditions was present, the Beast would, without warning, go to sleep. This meant no brakes, no steering, no control—just two tons of undisciplined steel moving in whatever direction it had previously been headed. Each time the Beast played the trick, she swore she would never get behind its wheel again ... until the next time she drove the damned thing.

Out of the very corner of her eye, Adele could see the sun sinking behind the hills. She imagined it was a beautiful sunset, but didn't dare take her eyes off the road to be sure. She didn't have time to be playing around with another accident.

Gripping the wheel very tight, she lowered her eyes for a tenth of a second to her watch. She veered slightly into the right lane. The driver in that lane swerved and lay on the horn.

It had taken her only an hour to get to the overpriced pet store for a bag of the hard-to-find vegetarian doggie health-food kibbles that cost a fortune. She figured if it stopped the neurotic behavior patterns Nelson had developed over the last two months, the price would be worth it.

She still had fifteen minutes to get back to Ellis for her meeting with Dr. Douglas Collier, Marin County coroner. Relaxing her shoulders and arms, she shook out the cramps which had settled into her muscles.

That Dr. Collier had agreed quickly and cordially to meet with her after business hours was amazing; she expected more of the county-civil-servant gestapo attitude. But then again, she'd never met the man, even though they worked in the same building—he in the basement, she on the top floor.

Envisioning what a coroner might look like, she came up with the image of someone hobbled and sickly as a result of years of exposure to formaldehyde. There would certainly be graying ear whiskers and age spots.

It would be just as well if he was old, she thought. She was often not herself with men her age or younger. If there was even a distant attraction, she'd be nervous, and when she got nervous, she either became rude or turned into a fumbling idiot. Besides, she'd been divorced only a year. Not enough time had elapsed to get into that business again, especially since Gavin, her ex-husband, was still missing.

Adele turned onto Sir Francis Drake Boulevard without a complaint from the Beast and let out her breath. The car was behaving. She'd have to remember to give it an extra quart of some hearty-weight oil as a treat.

Gavin had been one of her patients. He'd come in with a severe concussion after the drainpipe that he was climbing came loose from the apartment building it was attached to and fell, taking him from two stories to ground level in two seconds. He didn't remember why he'd been climbing the drainpipe at midnight, but then again, Gavin couldn't remember a lot of things.

His mother admitted she thought Gavin had begun to unravel a few years after his stint as a Green Beret in Vietnam. After his fall, it was her opinion that he'd gone quite off his cracker.

He had been sane enough to participate in a moderately boring marriage with Adele for three years—at least until one hot August morning two years before. She'd been on the phone with Cynthia, writing down a no-fat, no-sugar, no-nothing recipe for the oatmeal cookie from diet hell, when Gavin entered the bedroom talking to himself.

He smiled, blew her a kiss, threw off his clothes, then showered. Emerging from the shower—still giving voice to an endless monologue—he'd done a bit of toenail maintenance and pulled a storage box from the top shelf of the closet.

It was hard to follow both him and Cynthia simultaneously, but Adele recalled later for Detective Chernin of the Marin County sheriff's office that his monologue was peppered with words like "night maneuvers," "forty-four B," "gooks," "half-slips," "tree ambush," and "lovely shoes." Not wanting Cynthia to think Gavin was more of a fruitcake than she already thought he was, Adele didn't mention a word about the David Lynch movie—starring her husband—going on right in her own bedroom at that very moment.

Cynthia had just gotten to the spices part of the recipe as Gavin opened the box and began to dress. The black wool socks went on first, then the green tights followed by a wet-suit top with an army fatigue jacket over that.

After the army boots, like the star upon a Christmas tree, came his green beret.

She'd stopped writing in the middle of the word "nutmeg" and stared at him while he finished strapping a gun belt around his middle and a hunting knife to his leg. As Cynthia said "three hundred and fifty degrees for forty-five minutes or until golden brown," Gavin saluted, turned on his heel, and goose-stepped out of the house.

No one had seen or heard from him since.

Police investigations turned up nothing except an opinion that he had gone to another state, perhaps another country, changed his identity, and started over.

Careful not to swerve into other lanes, Adele sniffed the underarms of her sweater. She was glad she'd decided to change out of her scrubs. When she took off her uniform, she went from the Nurse mentality of blood, death, and pus to a Normal Person mentality of flower arrangements, laughter, and regular sleeping hours.

She wanted to meet with the coroner as a civilian and ask him the questions she felt driven to ask. In the back of her mind, she hoped the man was someone she could trust. There were things that she had shared only with Cynthia that she now felt needed to be told to someone who would make use of the information.

Adele smoothed her hair back from her face and turned Chloe's cameo ring around her finger. Chloe was dead. Nothing she could do would change that. She would miss her and her childlike innocence tremendously, but she would not think about Chloe saying how "mush" she loved her that morning, or the way her eyes widened and lit up when she laughed.

A red light somewhere on the Beast's dash (she thought

of it as the car's chest) flickered on and off. Adele tensed, swept the dash with her eyes for an instant, but could not tell what warning light it had been.

The 1994 Metro Storm cruising in the left lane slammed on his brakes to let her swerve in.

The room, a wonder of clutter, smelled like straw-berries, formaldehyde, and dusty books. Fascinated by the plethora of items decorating the salmon-colored walls and shelves, Adele was glad for the phone call that came before they'd finished introductions—it gave her the chance to explore the bizarre museum that was Dr. Doug-las Collier's office.

Sitting in the overstuffed pre–World War II chair oppo-site him, she let her eyes wander. One of the walls was lined floor to ceiling with books and magazines, most piled on their sides, some with papers sticking out, some opened and stacked binder to binder.

In the corner behind his desk stood an old-fashioned metal filing cabinet on top of which were two large jars. Floating in the one labeled "Testimony Evidence—1992" was a human heart with half a bullet protruding from the smooth grayish pink surface. The other, marked "Strawberry Yields Forever," was filled with red gummie worms.

Behind his desk hung myriad diplomas, framed car-toons, and an assortment of photographs. Overcome by curiosity and progressive myopia, she went closer for a better look at his collection of wall art. Surrounding the medical and forensic pathologist degrees were several law enforcement certificates, a Homicide Investigators Association certificate, and a membership certificate from

Mensa. The cartoons were, predictably, by Gary Larson and Charles Addams. The sign directly behind his head read, "I am the person your mother warned you about."

Adele bent down to take a closer look at a photo of the coroner with a group of schoolchildren and bumped the coatrack. Turning quickly to rescue the pole, she got tangled in the wardrobe of sixty or so neckties. A picture frame, wedged between the filing cabinet and the wall, slid onto the floor at her feet. The photo was of Dr. Collier and a dark-haired woman, both astride camels. In the background, barely discernible through the haze of air pollution and glaring sun, the pyramids rose up behind their backs like so many secondary camel humps.

Adele studied the picture closely. It was such a familiar face she felt certain she knew the woman, yet could not place her.

She shoved the frame back in its hiding place and moved to the main shelves, which held an assortment of crudely made weapons. A toothbrush with a razor blade melted into the handle and marked "San Quentin—1971—Davis homicide" lay next to a white knife labeled "Alcatraz—1939—steak bone/Johnson and White murders." The prettiest one, a beautiful hand-serrated glass shard made from an old Coke bottle, was tagged "North Beach—Wong rape/mutilation—1956." The lower shelf held an old-fashioned pharmacist's jar filled to the brim with a thousand different types of pills, a variety of handmade syringes, and other street drug paraphernalia. On the shelf closest to the floor were a variety of poisons, guns, scarves, and ropes, labeled with date and crime, in the same fashion as the other weapons.

She debated whether to go on to his book collection,

decided that it might be pushing curiosity beyond the
limits of propriety, and returned to the wall behind him.
Making a pretense of brushing off her skirt, she glanced
through the curtain of her hair at the two frames on
his desk. The smaller, silver filigree frame was empty,
but inside the black frame was the familiar dark-haired
woman again—unsmiling yet pretty in an uptight CEO/
cheerleader kind of way.

Settling into the chair once again, she let the worn
velvet cushion caress the backs of her legs. She peered at
him over a huge pile of papers, waved, and smiled. The
gesture seemed to confuse him, for he stumbled over
what he was saying about the district attorney and made
an awkward movement with his hand that she supposed
was a wave.

He held up his finger to indicate he'd be off in a
minute, then made the yappity-yap sign and rolled his
eyes. Self-consciously, he pushed back the thin shock of
sandy hair which had fallen over his forehead. He did not
have ear hair.

When he'd first opened the door to his office, she was
still looking for the gray old man, stooped and hobbling
with a cane; she was hardly prepared for the fortyish man
with the receding hairline who smiled kindly and seemed,
in turn, surprised and pleased by her. His immediate
offering of condolences brought the blind urge to fall
upon his shoulder for a good cry. Thank God the phone
had rung before she could act on *that* display of emotional instability.

"I'm sorry to keep you waiting," he said, replacing the
mobile handset on its charger base. "Miss Sedrick's death
has caused a lot of excitement around here."

"I hope so," she said, amazed at how much anger came up the back of her throat.

He looked at her uncertainly. "Why is that, Mrs. Monsarrat?"

"Because if Chloe's death is another nurse murder, there are going to be a lot of very upset people demanding the police find the person doing this."

Adele looked him in the eye. "Chloe *was* murdered, wasn't she?"

"Mrs. Monsarrat, I can't—"

"Adele. And it's Ms. Why can't you tell me?" She heard the PMS bitchy witch creeping into her voice, stopped, sighed, and started again, this time in a softer tone. It was a well-known fact that American men stopped listening when a woman began to vituperate.

"Please, Dr. Collier, I came here because . . ."

Adele panicked. What she had come for suddenly seemed childishly naive, but the momentary embarrassment only served to bring up her anger again. She didn't care what he thought. A valuable human being—someone she cared for—was dead.

"I came here because Chloe Sedrick was a healthy young woman. She ran the San Francisco Marathon last year and was the sixth woman to finish in—"

"I'm sorry, Ms. Monsarrat. I know Miss Sedrick's death was unexpected and untimely, but you must be—"

Adele leaned over his desk. A migraine, the bane of her adult female existence, was beginning behind her right eye. "Dr. Collier, I am a nurse who lives in a county where there have been two, possibly three, murders of medical personnel in one year.

"I'll guarantee you that whoever killed Sonya Martin

and Dr. Ganet also murdered Chloe—appendectomy or not."

"Why do you think you can guarantee me that?" he asked, tapping his pen.

"Because as seasoned medical people, we both know that a healthy twenty-five-year-old doesn't go into asystole and have a panic off-the-scale calcium level for no reason."

She sat down in the overstuffed chair and lowered her voice. "All I want is to ask a few questions and I'll—"

"I can't. Everything about this case is classi—"

"Don't. Please don't give me the standard 'classified information' speech." Adele let her shoulders and her voice drop to more reasonable levels.

"Listen. I know you don't know me, but I swear on my life you can trust me. Whatever you tell me stays with me. I . . ." She hesitated. "I need to do something. I need to help. I'll do anything you ask, and I won't step into anything you don't want me to. I know some things that might help. I—" She bit her lip to stop her tongue. She hated begging, plus she had promised herself not to give away any information before deciding if she could trust him.

He studied her for a long time with an intensity that made her sweat. "Well, you seem to know as much, if not more, than I do. Hypercalcemia seems to be the probable cause of death. I've sent everything to the forensics lab, but I—"

"What's everything? I mean, what did you send them?"

He paused and looked at her strangely. "The usual tissue and body fluids, plus the IV bag, all the syringes and tubing. I won't get those results back for a week or two, so it's a matter of working with what—"

"A week or two?" Adele heard her voice whine and tamed it.

"Yes. It's the normal amount of time." He was indulgent.

"Did anyone take photos before she was moved?"

"Ms. Monsarrat . . . Adele, I've been doing investigations for fifteen years. Even though this death took place in a controlled environment, I've taken it upon myself to treat some aspects of it as though it were a murder case. Everything was covered, believe me."

"Well, would you . . . Could I ask some questions about what happened in the murders last year?" Adele grimaced at the naive tone, readjusted her attitude, and continued. "I know some things about what happened last year, and I think somehow it might be tied into Chloe's death. A lot of the facts don't make sense, but if I could piece some things together, I think I can help.

"I'd like to know I could trust you. Actually, I'd like it better if you'd trust *me*."

He didn't say anything right away, but played with his pen, the advertising strip along the side of which read "Chapel of the Hills Mortuary—A Peaceful Farewell." "Ms. . . . Adele, are you aware that besides being the coroner, I'm also an officer of the law?"

Her heart sank; she was about to hear his rendition of the Bureaucratic Bullshit Oration.

He studied her some more, stretching his lower lip over the top one. "I'd like to know something about you before I break the law."

Her tight, "social" smile grew into a real one. "I'm so clean I squeak." She stood up. "No points on my license,

I don't do drugs or drink, there aren't any hidden psychological traumas, I mean, I love my mother and what I can
remember about my dad, and I'm—"

He smiled patiently. "Great. Would you like to have
dinner with me?"

She let out a breath as though she'd been kicked, and
slumped at the shoulders. A second later she gripped her
purse strap and faced him, her cheeks reddening. "I
didn't come here to solicit a date, Dr. Collier. A good
friend of mine was murdered this morning. I came
because I thought we could help each other." She walked
to the door and yanked it open.

In a flash he reached out and caught the door before it
could slam into the display shelves. "Hold on, please."

Adele stopped and gave him the coldest look she could
muster. In college, she'd spent hours in front of a mirror
perfecting it—the Sharp Icicle Through the Eyeball into
the Brain Stare.

"I didn't mean anything by offering dinner. I'm
starving—I haven't eaten since six this morning. I've
been up to my neck with this case."

She looked at him more closely and saw for the first
time that he did, in fact, look wasted.

"Did you really think you could walk in off the street
and I'd hand over the files?" he continued. "The only
polite way I can talk to you and eat at the same time is to
ask you to accompany me. I should have been more
direct." He pushed back the bit of stubborn hair again.
"Lord, what hath feminism wrought?"

Unwilling to melt so easily, she kept a slight freeze on
the edge of her expression. "Is this a placation?"

Douglas Collier sighed. "My gut feeling is that you

probably have some valid insights and information. After all, you do work on a ward which employed two of the victims. I think I would very much like to talk to you— that is, if you don't mind me talking with my mouth full."

"So, why did you—"

"You seem like someone I can trust," he interjected, putting on his jacket. He switched off the lights. "And God knows I need a trustworthy soul on my side right now."

He ordered the thick-cut prime rib. This amazed her. How, she wanted to know, could someone who dealt with cutting open bodies and slicing up livers and brains like so much meatloaf, eat any kind of flesh?

"I don't relate the two," he said in answer to her question.

"Oh come on." She laughed. "When you're cutting into a piece of meat, you can't tell me you don't think about cutting into a human body. They look identical. You know, as in a liver is a liver is a liver?"

He sliced through the meat. Blood ran onto the plate and mixed with his parsleyed potatoes. "I hate to disappoint you, but my work stays in the morgue—I don't think about it when I eat." He glanced over at her plate of steamed vegetables. "Is that why you're a vegetarian— because of your work?"

"No, but I'm sure that if I did eat meat, I wouldn't be able to pack wounds without thinking about it."

He shrugged as a way of letting the argument go, then pointed to the cameo on her finger. "Nice ring."

"It's Chloe's. She made me promise I'd give it to

her sister." Adele hesitated. "Were you aware that Chloe thought something was going to happen to her in surgery?"

He nodded, chewing ravenously. "Aaron mentioned it this morning."

She cut through a yellow beet and bit into it. "Okay, so ask whatever you'd like to know."

He cut another piece of meat. He would be the type, she thought, who ate all of one item on his plate before beginning on another. Organized or anal-retentive? That was the real question.

"How long have you been an R.N.?" he asked around the steak.

"Seventeen years."

"Always worked at Ellis?"

"Except for two years during college when I worked as a nurse's aide at Bellevue. It was part of the nursing program requirement."

"Have you ever worked in a doctor's office or a clinic?"

"Never. Too slow. Too limited. I like chaos and action, and a hospital is the only place you find that."

"Where did you . . ." He bit into a piece of fat. The sight made her queasy. ". . . go to school?"

"Graduated from Redwood High at sixteen, and went right into nursing school at University of California. At the time I was sort of the Doogie Howser of nursing."

"Where do you live?"

"I rent a one-bedroom cottage off Magnolia in Larkspur. Thirteen Baltimore Avenue."

"Married?"

"Divorced."

"Children?"

"I haven't had time, but someday I'd like to—that is if I find the right person to have them with before the chariots of youth leave tire tracks. I'm already past the automatic amniocentesis age."

"How old *are* you?"

"Old enough not to answer that question," she answered after a pause.

Embarrassed, he ducked his head and blushed. "Oops, sorry. Do you live alone?"

"Well . . ." She lowered her eyes. "I live with myself, but we're having a platonic relationship right now. I also have a roommate. His name is Nelson, and I'm madly in love with him."

The coroner's face fell the minutest bit.

"Yes," Adele continued, "I've been in love with Nels since he was a four-week-old fur ball of a pup."

"Ah." He chuckled. "Breed?"

"Black Lab."

"Religious affiliations?"

"Nelson is Lutheran. I was raised as a Catholic. I'm an agnotheist now—half agnostic, half atheist."

"Have you ever been involved in a police case before?"

She thought while she transferred the bulb of baked garlic to her bread plate. "Sort of. I mean, never formally. But when I was a kid—we lived in Novato then—the man next door murdered his wife and five-year-old daughter, cut them up and buried them in his yard."

His eyebrows rose a fair distance up his smooth forehead, bringing his upper eyelids with them. "You mean the DeBergua murders? Late sixties, early seventies? *You* were 'the neighbor's child' we read about?"

Adele nodded, pleased that he recognized the case. "I swear, it was right out of *Rear Window*, except instead of Jimmy Stewart and Grace Kelly, it was the nosey little girl next door with the binoculars.

"Mr. DeBergua told everybody who asked that his wife had gone to visit her ailing sister in New York and taken the kid with her. No one seemed to think much about it except me.

"Mrs. DeBergua sometimes took care of me when my mother had to stay late at the library, so I knew that the daughter and the mother were scared to death of him. He was a schizoid—one minute he'd be right on the verge of blowing up, the next minute he'd be clowning around, acting silly. But it was always strained—he never got rid of that short-fused edge. I mean, Mrs. DeBergua used to *duck* every time he raised his hand.

"About a month after they'd disappeared, I waited for him to leave the house one morning and took my Mr. Greenjeans junior-gardener shovel to the place in his yard where he'd recently taken to planting lots of fruit trees. I dug a few holes and came up with a human toe."

Adele sipped her wine. "After I hyperventilated for a while, I wrapped the thing in my little embroidered hankie, put it in a shoe box, and bicycled directly to the police station on the next block."

The man was staring at her intensely. "Brave girl." He shook his head and returned to masticating a bit of meat. "You must have made an impression that day."

"Yeah." She laughed. "But mostly it was the impression made on me. My mother was a librarian at the San Rafael branch. As soon as she realized where my interests lay, she started bringing home Nancy Drew books. When I got bored with those, I moved on to true crime and basic criminology. By the time I went to UC, I'd read everything the Civic Center library had to offer about criminology and investigations.

"For years I hung around the detectives at the police station, getting them coffee, filing reports, cleaning up the offices—doing everything I could to be near them. They thought I was a goofy kid, but they liked me. I was like a mascot.

"When I got older, they began inviting me to join in when they'd brainstorm a difficult case.

"A semiretired detective by the name of Kitch Heslin humored me by teaching me things—tricks mostly— about the law and criminal psychology. He actually taught me a lot about routine investigations." Adele smiled warmly at the thought of the detective who had once played the role of mentor, confidant, substitute father, and knight in shining armor.

"It's like a pet hobby," she added.

"So if you were so interested, why didn't you go into law enforcement?"

"I'm a natural-born codependent." Adele sighed. "I wanted to heal people, not shoot them."

He regarded her. After a minute, he raised his eyebrows and cut another piece of meat. "Any addictions?"

She nodded. "I'm powerless against peanut butter, but I've not had so much as a spoonful in almost two years. Popcorn runs a close second, but I keep that down to a bowl a week. Then there are mystery thrillers and whodunits, but I've tapered down from four books a week to one a week, mostly because my friends started dropping hints that I was pathological." Adele bit into a pepperoncini, briefly choked on the vinegary brine, and continued.

"Running is probably my strongest current addiction, but I've cut down to only eight miles a day."

He gave a strangled cry and swallowed. "*Only* eight? What *were* you doing?"

"Twelve."

"Boy, I'd love to see your hips and knees," he said, shaking his head.

"Excuse me?"

"I mean, well, you know, under surgical conditions . . ."

They both laughed. She leaned forward, resting her chin in her hand. She wasn't used to drinking alcohol and the bottom half of her glass of wine was having its way—her lips were going numb. He really was a very nice-looking man.

"Does your wife mind what you do?"

"We're separated." He paused and considered for a minute. "Dana left me over a year ago." His smile faded, and was replaced by an expression Adele could only describe as a strange combination of detachment and pain. The way his eyes went, she sensed the subject was a sore spot.

"Kids?"

His eyes lowered. "No, no children."

"Religion?"

He stabbed the last piece of rib eye—fat and all. "I'm secretary-treasurer of St. Hilary's. It's more a political, community service, good Samaritan–type deal than a religious commitment. My personal jury is still out on the deeper issues of religion."

"You mean Reverend Wynn's St. Hilary's in Tiburon?"

He nodded.

"Addictions?" she asked.

"Strawberry gummie worms, since the first time I put one in my mouth. Traveling, but there's never any time. Computers are the latest fascination. I'm totally absorbed by the graphics, the Net, and all the different software. It's an amazing science." He removed a slice of seeded sourdough from the basket and dipped it into a saucer of olive oil. "And you? Are you computer-literate?"

"I dabble when I have time. Mostly I use my computer for E-mail. Occasionally, I search the Web for information and old news.

"Tell me . . ." she said, hoping to steer him away from computers. Amateur hacks had a way of going on about computers that was guaranteed to turn any evening into long, boring hours of complicated monologues about Web pages, search engines, RAM, and gigabytes. "How do you get just one flavor of gummie worms? Nobody ever gets just one flavor."

"I buy them by the gross and weed out all the strawberry ones."

"What do you do with the rejects?"

"Put them in jars and leave them in the vestibule of St. Hilary's. I don't know who eats them, but they're always gone in a few days. I suspect Roger eats most of them himself, although he denies it."

He studied her. "Why don't you like Roger?"

"How do you know I don't?"

"I watch people's reactions to certain words and

names. You tightened your jaw the minute I mentioned St. Hilary's, then you started jiggling your leg when I said Roger's name."

She shrugged. "He's not a fan of women, he's condescending, and I don't believe he has a kind or tolerant bone in his body—you know, your typical Bible-quoting Christian. His antiabortion views are primitive, and God only knows what that pedophile scandal was about."

"You're pro-choice?"

"Let me put it this way." She sighed. "I'm all for women having control over their own bodies, but I don't much care for the practice of using abortion as a method of birth control."

He was silent while he thought about her answer, nodding and chewing. Then, as if coming to terms with what she'd said, he began on his zucchini, actually turning his plate so the squash was closer to him.

"You're sure you've never had any run-in with the law or given cause to be tagged—demonstrations in college, or some other radical political group?"

"No," she answered slowly. "Nothing like that, unless you want to call the murder investigation last year a run-in. I was questioned like everyone else—which is to say I was treated like a criminal."

"But you withheld information?"

She eyed him, a flicker of discomfort crossing her gut.

He smiled as if to dispel her fears. "It's okay. You're bright . . . and careful. I'd have been surprised if you'd spilled everything to people you didn't respect."

She took a noncommittal sip of water and played with her napkin.

"I've made death my profession," he said after a while.

"It's bad enough when people die naturally. Even with the death of a derelict, there's always some tragedy or sorrow which eventually comes into play. But murder—now that's another story. The taking of another life is a monstrous act. The violence of murder has creeper vines—it kills a part of everybody involved."

Adele started to say something, but hesitated at the sight of his jaw working.

"I don't condone capital punishment," he continued. "A murderer should be made to endure the pains of his guilt every day of his life. *That's* the worst punishment I could imagine." He brought his gaze level with hers. "So, what does your gut say, Ms. Monsarrat? Do you trust me?"

She pushed back her hair and flashed him an awkward smile. "I think so. It depends on what your favorite color is."

"Salmon. And my lucky number is six."

"Okay," she said, laughing. "I trust you."

He didn't move away, but stared directly into her eyes. Adele wondered who would be a wimp and look away first. "Good," he said, "because if we're going to share information of this caliber, we should probably trust each other."

"Are we?" she asked. "I mean, going to share information?"

"You didn't go to this trouble to pass off hearsay. I want to hear what you have to say, as much as you want to know what I can tell you."

"But why have you . . ."

His gaze made her self-conscious to the point of pain. She looked away.

"Intuition and good judgment."

"Okay," she said, aware of the small rivulet of sweat trickling down between her breasts. "So, where do we start?"

For the tenth time in two hours, Aaron Milton studied the number on the crumpled lab slip and reached for the phone. His hand rested on the handset as he glanced at the TV. The title credits for *ER* were flashing on the screen. Maybe it was too late to call. He sighed in disappointment. But she'd seemed sincere when she insisted he call anytime he felt he needed to talk. Hell, Adele was a sensible, modern woman, not one of the pre–sexual revolution, closed-thigh dinosaurs he grew up with, whose every movement was dictated by the current women's magazine and what the neighbors might think.

He picked up the handset. He desperately needed to talk to her before he went nuts. He had to tell her about going to St. Hilary's cemetery after work, and how, as he stood next to his wife's grave, pieces started falling into place in his brain, like a jigsaw puzzle come together.

He had to tell her what he'd seen, who he suspected— no, *knew*—had murdered Chloe and the others. He couldn't believe he hadn't realized it before.

She wouldn't think he was crazy if he explained it carefully. He wouldn't go to the police until he talked to her—he'd decided that right away.

He pressed the first three numbers. He would suggest they meet at a coffee shop; he didn't want to put her off.

Sweet Chloe. Gentle character. Jesus, to be killed by *that* psycho. God only knew who else . . .

Quickly he pressed the last four digits. He didn't want

to think about it until he could talk to her. He'd avoided dark nights of the soul for sixty-four years—she'd get him through this one.

The phone rang twice before an answering machine picked up. So sure was he that she would answer that he listened to the message and had gone several seconds after the tone before he remembered to hang up.

Panic crept into his chest. He couldn't stand to be alone . . . not now. The image of his lover's legs wrapped around his torso imposed itself over his fear and he picked up the phone. It wouldn't exactly be a sympathetic ear and a shoulder to cry on, but it *would* save him from a dark night of the soul.

"Start with last October." He rotated the plate to his potatoes and fell on them with zeal. Adele made note that he saved the best for last.

"Well, one of the day staff was on the ward when Sonya Martin was actually murdered. This nurse—"

"Helen Marval," he said.

"Right." Instant embarrassment. Of *course* he'd know Helen was there. "Whenever she has trouble sleeping—which is most of the time—she comes to the hospital early. Usually she hangs out and watches people, or reads all the charts, but once in a while she hides out in a corner of the supply closet . . . in the dark. She calls it her channeling place."

He abruptly stopped mastication of his potato and gave her an odd, questioning look.

"Helen believes she can commune with the spirits of the universe in there." She bit into her bread and chewed it down before continuing. He was hanging on her every word.

"I am the only one who knows about this little quirk of Mrs. Marval's. That's why, on the morning of the murders, when no one claimed seeing her on the unit, I was sure she'd been hiding out in the supply room.

"I've worked with the woman for twelve years. I know her moods, and I am here to tell you that morning she was really flipped out. Around six forty-five I found her in the nurses' locker room washing her hands as if she were auditioning for Lady Macbeth. I managed to get a good look at the sink before she rinsed away what looked like blood. I watched it go down the drain with my own eyes.

"She told me the Devil, whom she now calls 'It,' had visited the unit and done evil. She said It had seen her and given her the evil eye.

"Today she was with Chloe right before she coded. The nurses in the recovery unit said she was fooling around with Chloe's IV." She sighed. "This afternoon when I asked her what happened, I got another bizarre story about how the Devil had come and told her to do something and not tell anyone."

He resumed eating, though his eyes never left hers. "What's your relationship with Mrs. Marval?"

"It's hard to describe, really," Adele said, twisting her head until her neck cracked. "I guess I treat her more kindly than anyone else. Usually I'll defend her when I think people are ganging up on her unfairly. Once in a while, she'll seek me out to talk, but she'll only go so far with me. If I push her, she goes berserk and then she won't talk to me for weeks." She shook her head. "I suspect I'm one of the only people she trusts. I guess I feel sorry for her, but I'm afraid of her too.

"She's one hell of an efficient nurse, and the patients love her, which is why the administration tolerates her bizarre behavior. The fact she's married to the sheriff doesn't hurt either. I'm sure the administration isn't eager to put any tension on those political strings."

"What does she say about this Devil?"

"Oh, mostly stuff about It stalking us, causing the blood of evil to flow, and that It will kill again. She carries crystals and Chinese herbs around like fetishes."

Adele brought her chair closer to his and lowered her voice. "See, Helen is convinced that the Master of Evil is going to send bombs to destroy the earth, and only a chosen few will be allowed to survive the holocaust by going into these underground caves. She says she's been selected to be the leader of this new civilization, and there'll be chosen breeders who're pure and . . . oh you know, it's all part of the New Age schizophrenic Holy Roller frenzy."

Adele remembered something and snapped her fingers. "Oh yeah, another thing no one else knew except myself was that for kicks Sonya and John Ganet used to call Helen on her days off and put her in hysterics by saying they were going to get her and her dogs and burn them up out at China Camp." She took a bite of grilled red pepper and chewed slowly. "That was before automatic call tracers.

"Sonya constantly goaded Helen at work. It got to be uncomfortable for everybody. Helen hated it, but she'd keep her mouth shut. She got her revenge in other ways, like arranging it so Sonya would have the heaviest assignment, or turning on her car lights so her car wouldn't start at the end of the day. One time Sonya found all the uniforms in her locker shredded with a knife, but I suppose anyone could have done that—she hurt a lot of people in her quest."

"Her quest?"

"You didn't hear about Sonya's famous quest?" She sat back. "Sonya's goal was to have sex with a thousand different people in twenty-four months. It wasn't any secret. It was part of her advertisement . . . an open invitation of sorts."

"Charming," he said dryly, and wiped his mouth. Something in the gesture made her think of a puritanical old lady.

"Do you think allowing Mrs. Marval to confide in you is safe?" He absently wiped the crumbs off his side of the table with long, slim fingers. Adele noticed his fingernails were perfectly manicured. Anal-retentive for sure. No one could *ever* call this man Dougie and mean it.

"I can handle myself. I've been through four different self-defense programs. My ex-husband was a combat training officer for the Green Berets. He used to wake me up in the middle of the night to put me through defense combat drills."

Without comment, Douglas Collier pushed his plate away and called the waitress over. After the tea and frozen yogurt were ordered, he turned to her, wearing such a serious expression she didn't know whether to laugh or be alarmed.

"Have you told anyone else any of this?"

"I told you I hadn't," she said, hoping he wouldn't notice the telltale blush that colored her neck every time she lied. There was no sense trying to explain her relationship with Cynthia and the fact that she would trust the nurse with her life—not to mention everything that went on in her life. Men, she learned a long time ago, simply did not understand the scope of women's best-friendships.

"Good." He sat back. "And we *are* clear on the fact that anything I tell you is highly confidential infor—"

She gave him a look.

He sighed. "Oh well, it isn't much, anyway. Both Ganet and Sonya were killed with a number twelve scalpel—quite an efficient weapon, I must say."

Adele flinched. Every nurse on Ward 8 used the twelve scalpel, a particularly utilitarian blade. She had a supply of them in her sewing and medicine cabinets and routinely gave them to friends for around-the-house use.

"That scalpel is distributed only on Ward Eight at Ellis and Three North, the surgical unit at Bellevue," he went on.

"Both victims showed no signs of struggle or panic, so we assume they both knew their attacker. Because of the angle of Ganet's throat wound, we assume the murderer was shorter than Ganet, who was six foot. Also, the way his hands were amputated—hacked and sawed rather than cut cleanly through with several hard strokes—indicates a lack of strength.

"The murderer knew both hospital floor plans well enough to get in and out of the place without being seen. This would also indicate that the murderer was familiar with the victims' schedules and probably the schedules and work habits of everyone else in the vicinity."

"You know that Helen works at both hospitals?" she asked.

"Yes, and that she trained as a surgical nurse at Bellevue, and that she has a psych history which includes violent rages, hallucinations, psychosis, and amnesia.

"What's frustrating is that the woman is so protected by her husband we can barely ask her for the time of day, let alone what she was doing that morning. Her carefully coached story was that she arrived at the hospital around six-twenty and then sat on the locker room toilet reading the *Farmer's Almanac* until report started at seven A.M. Swears she didn't see anyone or anything. And, until now"—he raised his eyebrows at her—"not one person at either hospital can recall seeing her or her car before report started that morning.

"Without being able to interrogate her fully, it wasn't likely we'd get anything substantial on her. I tried like hell to get to her, but the investigators were all Harold Marval's puppets. I did manage to find a neighbor who said she witnessed Mrs. Marval driving through town about four forty-five that morning, but when I turned in the report, I was warned to back off.

"Hopefully that'll change now. There's a new guy over there, Tim Ritmann, who seems pretty sharp. Apparently he was appointed to ameliorate the tarnished image of the department. Marval hates his guts, but I don't think Ritmann loses any sleep over it."

His attitude turned softer. "I feel for Marval. It's got to be lousy not to have anything to go on except your own wife."

"And that was why Henry Williams was arrested—the police were in need of a suspect?"

He nodded. "They were up against a wall. The DA wanted a body, so they ran Williams up the flagpole as an offering to see if he'd fly. It was stupid, but when you're under pressure, who cares?"

He set down his teacup and yawned, which made her yawn. They simultaneously looked at their watches and were both shocked to see it was after ten.

"That's about it, I'm sorry to say."

Secretly Adele *was* disappointed, but he had given her some things to think about. "Do you think I could get Chloe's sister's phone number from you? And maybe I could take a look at any nonsacred info you have lying around on the murders last year?"

He hesitated. "Okay. I have to go back to the office anyway. I'll check Chloe's personal information sheet, and look around for anything else I might have. If you want, you can stop by now, or wait until tomorrow after five."

"How about now?" She liked pushing that fine line between assertion and aggression.

He helped her into her jacket, leaning slightly into her to smell her hair. She felt a stir of what she called her romance hormones and purposely turned her mind to Chloe and how she might look right at that moment: cold, unmoving, mottled white and gray with that purplish ring around the lips. She shivered.

"Cold?" he asked. The whole side of his body pressed against hers. It provided a certain comfort for her.

"No. Just thinking of Chloe, and wondering who'll be next."

"Oh God, I pray there aren't any more," he said sadly.

She studied his face in the red neon glow of the restaurant sign.

He noticed her gaze. "I'm not as hardened as you think. It gets to me sometimes. There are a few murder victims whom I've done autopsies on who still haunt me."

Before starting the car he suddenly turned to her, speaking with all the urgency of a man making his last confession. "I deal with the end result of all the worst traits of human beings—hate, greed, rage. Once in a while I have a fantasy about owning a roadside bait shop in Florida. The only things I'd worry about would be hurricanes and whether or not I could afford to get the kids braces and bicycles.

"Instead, I go home thinking about at which angle a throat was cut, or exactly what kind of sick mental processes were involved in murdering a young, innocent girl. It's no way to live."

He looked sad and vulnerable, Adele noticed. There was none of the anal-retentive dryness about him now.

"Sorry. I shouldn't have dumped that on you."

"I'm glad you did," she said, barely above a whisper. "It proves you're human like the rest of us."

It was 11:15 when the Beast glided past the Granary. With the exception of a couple of parked cars, the street was deserted and the bar itself was dark, save for the one neon Coors sign blinking like a lighthouse for wayward alcoholics.

Above, Meg's apartment lights were on. She'd be grieving, Adele thought, and on impulse, slowed to pull over. Maybe she'd stop in and try to comfort her, maybe get her to talk about her relationship with Chloe. Perhaps something might come out of it that would give her more of a lead.

The Beast settled itself snugly behind the car parked across the street from the apartment. Adele glanced at the large accordion file on the seat next to her, still amazed at how much material Collier had given her. It was going to take her forever to go through it all.

Maybe she'd wait to talk to Meg. Unlike Helen, who was a straightforward flaming psychotic, Meg was enigmatic and, in a subtle way, more menacing than Helen.

On the fringe of Adele's peripheral vision there was a movement. Two silhouettes, one tall and one short, appeared in one of the windows. The taller figure seemed to be pulling the other toward the back of the apartment— in the direction of where the bedroom would most likely be. There was a brief embrace, and then the shorter figure pulled the taller one in the opposite direction. After a few seconds, the shorter person won the tug-of-war.

Adele blinked uncertainly. She couldn't imagine Meg allowing anyone to get that close to her—except Chloe perhaps. She immediately put the Beast in gear and pulled away from the curb, missing the fender of the car in front of her by a quarter of an inch.

Suddenly the need to get home before Nelson found something new to destroy was pressing. In two months he'd totaled her mattress, the couch, four pairs of shoes, the dining room table, her new cardiac stethoscope, and two sets of shower curtains. She couldn't afford to leave him alone anymore.

The Beast turned onto Lincoln Avenue, headed toward the highway. Adele could tell by the way it suddenly coughed, bucked, and coughed again that the car was going to be bad.

Somewhere off to the right, Adele heard a high-pitched whine. She turned off the radio and listened, following the sound, trying to find its source and perhaps pinpoint the area of the Beast's affliction.

The Beast bucked once more and went to sleep.

Adele checked her rearview mirror while pumping the brakes. The street was completely deserted. Unable to turn the now frozen wheel, she sat helpless as the front right tire ran into the curb, bounced back, and the car came to a complete stop.

"You narcoleptic son of a bitch!" Adele hit the unmoving steering wheel with her palm. "You're gonna kill me someday, you miserable—"

The high-pitched whine came again. Adele stared at the car's dash chest—it remained asleep. Her ears, diligently searching for the source of the noise, brought her attention to the empty parking lot in front of which the Beast had chosen to take a nap.

Spotlighted by a row of security lamps was a circle of some twelve senior citizens, each playing his or her own bagpipe. Each one wore a tartan of one clan or another.

In wonder, she watched the strange assembly for a few minutes before turning the key in the ignition. The Beast turned over, jumped the curb, and lurched forward.

"Chloe," she said, shaking her head. "It's got to be a sign from Chloe."

FOUR

DOUGLAS COLLIER SHIFTED HIS GAZE FROM the picture frames to his hands. They were capable and strong; like this woman now. He rubbed the knot out of his right shoulder and tried to remember the small details of her. Pretty, certainly. Black hair, drawn smoothly back in a French braid. Sculptured forehead and chin. Creamy skin. High cheekbones and straight nose. And gold—yes, they were actually gold—eyes.

She presented as solid, capable, and yet unspoiled, almost naive. It frightened him that he *did* trust her already. He would have to go slow; he couldn't risk being hurt again. Dana's absence had almost killed him. He'd been no match for the loneliness which haunted him.

It was the loneliness too which had forced him to look at the same truth Adele was facing—at forty-one, he was watching the biological clock and feeling the pressure. He wanted a child—a son—to carry on. He wanted to be in his prime while his son was growing up; there was so much that needed to be passed on. He couldn't afford to wait until he was a doddering old man who couldn't even throw a ball to his boy.

Too, he longed to be loved again, to be the center of

someone's life. It felt like decades since Dana left. He needed a woman to touch, someone to share his world.

His watch alarmed. Without looking, he pushed the off button. It was 10:47—time to stop thinking and move. Today *was* chaos. He'd had to think too hard and much too long. He wondered if other people had thoughts like the ones which tortured him. What did they do about them? How did they live with it?

He removed his tie and hung it with the others, then gathered several files and his black gym bag. He was tired, but wasn't that part of the dues?

Nelson removed the chunk of wood which had only moments before been the corner of the front door. Appearing contemplative, the black Lab chewed the painted piece of pressed pine, letting the splinters and larger pieces fall from his mouth. He'd been working on the door since early morning, stopping only briefly to eat his soy protein Veggie-Kibbles and chopped turnips, drink purified water, and listen to the voices that came from the answering machine.

Dr. Nutt, the doggie psychiatrist, told Adele that Nelson was anxious. Chewing was a way to lessen his anxiety, much like a human who smoked cigarettes when he was nervous. Although the canine shrink didn't offer counsel regarding the root of Nelson's anxiety, he did offer doggie Prozac, which Adele refused—she didn't want a dog who would lick the hand of every homicidal maniac who came to the door.

At the sound of Her key in the lock, Nelson abruptly dropped the corner of the door and wagged his tail. Weighed down by the twenty-five-pound bag of Veggie-

Kibbles, an obese purse, and the pile of files, Adele collapsed onto the couch and did not move.

It was a game they played from time to time. She would remain still until Nelson couldn't stand it—he would whine, lick, and paw until she couldn't stand it. From there, the ritual progressed to petting, kisses, hugs, and ended with the distribution of doggie biscuits—one for each of them. After that came a mutually satisfying, though completely one-sided, conversation about what Adele's day had been like.

Tonight Adele bypassed the game, having only enough energy to raise an arm and blindly search for the playback button on her answering machine.

Gayle Mueller at 8:05: So disappointed in her and couldn't she be a better example for the resh of . . .

She smiled and hit the rewind—better example for the *resh* of the staff? Gayle was in her cups partly due to Chloe's death, mostly due to the fact that Gayle was a closet alcoholic. It was probably the only thing she and Roger Wynn had in common.

A hang-up at 8:12 with soft breathing. Another hang-up at 9:30 with street noises in the background. A hang-up at 10:05 with TV on in the background playing the theme song for *ER*. At 10:47 a long pause, the shuffling of something . . . arms across a table perhaps, a soft sigh, and then the slow drawl of a man's voice saying, "Hey Charlie," followed by a disconnection.

Adele flew off the couch, knocking the bag of kibbles and her purse on top of Nelson. Sensing panic, Nelson barked and ran to the bedroom closet—his version of a fallout shelter—to wait for the storm to pass.

She played the message over six more times, listening

carefully to the background and the voice. There was no mistaking Gavin's voice. And no one else in the world called her Charlie.

Hard, logical thought, her lifelong protection whenever panic and/or fear became uncomfortable, instantly took over.

Gavin Wozniac was alive. That wasn't her problem; she'd done everything to find him, waited a year until he was legally declared a missing person, then filed for divorce. There was no sense in contacting the police, but she would have to tell his mother and hope the woman wouldn't get hysterical.

Adele removed the tape from the machine and put it in a drawer with the other "saved" tapes. Among them was a fifteen-minute monologue of her mother's about the moral dilemma of sick relatives coming to visit and the universal problem of paper towel dispensers in rest rooms consistently being placed above shoulder level so that as one reached up, the water would drip down your arm, ending up on your elbows or in your armpit, depending. Then there was a series of four tapes from Cynthia's cross-country drive—each message left in succeeding accents from the obliterated r's of Maine to classic Valley Girl of California.

By midnight they were snuggled in, Adele with the hot-water bottle at her feet, Nelson curled around his best friend—a dilapidated Mickey Mouse rug—half under the bed, half out.

Propped on her elbow, she zealously went through the wealth of information contained in the accordion file Douglas had marked "Martin-Ganet Murders." There were autopsy reports, police reports, scene reports, and several of the confidential supplemental reports.

She tried not to get caught up in the scene photos.

The interview summaries proved interesting, if only by virtue of the fact that no one interviewed could—or would—give one solid lead. She had a hard time believing that Henry Williams had nothing to say, and that Nettie, the night switchboard operator at Bellevue, reported nothing unusual about the calls she took for John Ganet. As a woman, she knew better; John Ganet was a notorious womanizer and would most certainly receive his "personal" calls at work.

In order of appearance, her overall visceral reactions to the material had been: frustration, outrage, enthusiasm, sorrow, panic, and finally, absolute resolve.

Adele lay back on the pillow. Before she could concentrate on willing herself to dream of who the murderer was, she was snoring loud enough to cause Nelson to drag his Mickey Mouse rug to the far end of the living room, where the noise diminished to sounding like the distant rumble of a faraway train.

FIVE

HELEN MARVAL, R.N., SPED THROUGH TWO STOP signs without even slowing down. It was not postmenopausal zest causing her to break traffic laws; it was simply an easy thing to do when you know for a fact that the only two cops on duty are three miles away at the Qwik Stop fueling up on coffee, sex gossip, and maple bars. It is especially easy when you're married to the sheriff and thus exempt from the laws which govern the unwashed masses.

She was preoccupied with the dream she'd been having before Harold woke her up with his cigar breath and that goddamned groping, poking stuff. Normally she stroked her meditation crystal and let him, but he'd interrupted her REM sleep. Infuriated, she'd kneed him hard enough to send him hobbling to the freezer for ice. She'd have to remember to tone down his second chakra when she got home.

In the interrupted dream, Anthony Robbins stood in front of a drawing of one of the creature-messengers. He'd finished pointing out the details of its physical appearance (pointed ears, spiked tail, snout, and fangs) and was saying, "The origin of these fine creatures who've been sent to you is . . ." when Harold started with his "Oh Mommy, Mommy, c'mon 'n' open up for Daddy."

Helen jerked the dark blue Ford Fiesta into fifth gear, causing her jowls to wobble like Jell-O. The crucifix hanging from her rearview mirror swung forward and hit the windshield with a click.

The creatures had first made their appearance the day Nurse McGowan found Sonya Martin in Ellis's Ward 8 supply closet with her throat cut. The ward was in a total state of upheaval, with deputies, detectives, and coroner's people in everybody's way, keeping them from doing their jobs with their stupid questions and not letting anyone near the supplies. Then wimpette McGowan had become hysterical and had to be sent home. That left them short a nurse because no one was willing to replace her, due to some harmless backyard snake that had gotten loose and couldn't be found.

Helen rolled her eyes. She'd been trying to tone down everyone's aura and channel some peace into the place, plus take care of her patients as well as two of Nurse McGowan's, when the OR called to ask if she wouldn't mind starting a difficult IV on a come-and-go D&C patient. It seemed that Dr. Ganet had had *his* throat cut over at Bellevue, and the surgical schedule was backed up for hours, and the anesthesiologists and the surgeons were all very jumpy and in bad moods and didn't want to be bothered with such menial tasks as starting tedious IVs.

She hadn't minded starting the IV; it was the area of nursing in which she excelled. During her thirty-three years of nursing service—the first five of which had been with the United States Women's Army Corps—she'd never failed to access a vein on anyone, in any situation. Even the doctors called on her to get in on the ones they couldn't.

There was only the one time, when Dr. Milton had made a mockery of her God-given talent. She would never forget the humiliation. The way Milton had pleaded with her to hurry down and start this IV that only *she* could start, she should have known. When she got to the postsurgical suite, the patient was completely covered except for one arm. Milton told her the cold limb was the only available avenue due to the extensive burns which supposedly covered the rest of the body.

It had taken her over twenty minutes, but when she finally got the IV running, Milton and his disciples had laughed, then stuffed a twenty-dollar bill in her uniform pocket, like she was some kind of cheap sideshow hussy. Milton told her it was a bonus for being the only nurse in Marin and San Francisco counties—possibly the entire state of California—who could get an IV going on a corpse. The humiliation he'd caused her would cost him entrance to the New World.

That the OR had called her on the day of the Ward 8 circus didn't surprise her. Nor did it surprise her that the D&C patient was one of those anorexicly thin, desperate, mid-forties divorcées; women like that always had something wrong *down there* (it was the High Spirit's method of punishing them for their loose ways). What had puzzled her was that the woman was such a difficult IV. Despite the heavy layers of makeup covering the plastic-surgery scars (the ones behind the ears never quite faded), the woman was still relatively young—young enough to have good veins. They'd certainly looked good—like ropes. They didn't roll and they weren't tough. They were easy—the needle slipped right in. But when she pulled back the syringe plunger, there was no blood return, only resistance.

The third time she stuck the woman (a disgraceful number of tries—even the corpse she'd had to stick only twice), she'd given the resistance a good fight, similar to a tug-of-war, persistently pulling on the plunger until the blood trickled into the barrel.

She was about to thread the catheter into the vein, when a dark *some*thing slid into the syringe. Tilting her head, she engaged her bifocals while her heart went off like a jackhammer in her chest.

Staring back at her through the side of the clear plastic barrel was a miniature gargoyle with wings. Even as she flung the tube away from her, it boldly pressed its snout against the inside of the syringe, striking the plastic barrel with its minute claws. Before it died, one of its corkscrew fangs had actually punctured the plastic.

It wasn't long before there was another. That one— drawn out of an old woman with lung cancer—she named Adam. Adam lived in its own nest in her locker. He had been the bearer of the first message: that the end of the corrupt world as people knew it was near and the New World would finally have its chance.

All the messengers who came after Adam told her different things. The last one had been over a week ago. The message was: Prepare your servants for Doomsday. Determine those who shall be Named.

That was all well and good, but it was just that she wasn't sure exactly who or where the messages were coming from. Helen sighed and switched the majority of her 163 pounds from right to left buttock, straightening her uniform under her. Even though the white dress was a polyester blend and wouldn't wrinkle if a nuclear bomb fell on it, she didn't want to take the chance of looking anything but perfectly pressed. When one was five feet and pleasantly plump, that was hard to pull off. If anything about her appearance was out of place, her patients might think she was lax, and besides, she didn't want to give Goddamned Gayle anything to confront her about. Head nurses, especially the skinny ones, hated her because she was so much more efficient than they could ever hope to be.

Helen's gas-pedal foot grew heavy as she indulged in a fantasy about stabbing Goddamned Gayle to death. This was unfortunate for the unneutered tom named Puddin who, ignoring the hand of fate, took that moment in time to run in front of the Ford.

At one year of age, Puddin had lived long enough to pick up road smarts. It was simply a matter of being at the mercy of those cruel hormones driving him on to the female Russian blue living on the other side of the two-lane highway. So close, and yet so far.

For approximately two seconds after impact with the Fiesta's front tire, Puddin was still going for the Russian blue.

Helen did not swerve or touch the brakes. Actually, she was glad for the feline roadkill. She hated cats because cats hated dogs and Helen loved dogs more than anything in the world except for children under the age of six. After the age of six, all humans, with a rare exception, were simply not to be trusted. It made her task of choosing the survivors who would populate the New World most difficult.

When the extremely short, high-pitched yowl and the *thumpk-thumpk* noises were over, Helen pulled off to the side of the road and scanned the rearview mirror.

The orange oblong lump lay still next to a reflector post.

Driven as much by curiosity as the cat had been by the call of the wild, she shifted into reverse, her rear wheels coming to a stop a few feet from the lifeless feline. She removed a hard leather case from her purse, got out of the car, and gave her overpermed red hair a pat. It crinkled ever so softly.

The silence that was part of the mist comforted her. She liked the very early hours; it was the only time when the present world did not threaten her and she had complete command of her life as well as everyone else's.

Giving Puddin a none too gentle tap with the toe of her white nursing shoe, she removed a number twelve scalpel from the case and knelt down. Distasteful though the touch of the animal was, she pulled back its head, deftly sliced through its throat ear to ear, and dropped it at once.

She rocked back on her broad haunches. "Come on out now," she coaxed, in a voice that was low and sincere. "I know you're in there."

Two of them, one with wings, one without, slid out the external jugular and onto the reddening fur.

Helen cooed. All her life she had been drawn to wee, helpless creatures (except cats), and these were certainly creatures that needed someone who could see past the horrible outer shell.

The lilliputian monster sans wings tripped on its own reptilian tail and tumbled down the cat's body. At once it stood on hind legs and regarded her through minuscule slitted eyes, cocking its head in friendly curiosity, much like one of her puppies. Helen giggled in spite of herself.

She put out a finger until the tip was less than an eighth of an inch from the ill-shaped thing. "Welcome," she whispered. "Come to the Imperial Empress of the New World. What message do you bring?"

It extended its snout to sniff her, and before she could coax again, scurried onto her waiting digit, straddling it like a pony. Bringing the creature close to her ear, she listened carefully to the small voice inside her head.

Ken Goldstein, producer for KPRC television, hated the cold early-morning fog which daily swept off the bay and over Sausalito. He'd debated leaving the morning paper lodged neatly in the hedges separating his driveway from the Miltons' driveway, but the prospect of a media CEO being caught outside the know of world news was worse than giving one's flesh over to goose bumps for five minutes.

From the pocket of his Giorgio Armani coat, he brought out a red cashmere scarf which he wrapped snugly around his neck and the lower portion of his face. Sure that no one would be up at 4:00 A.M. to witness him traipsing across the yard, he hurried outside, the hem of his flannel nightshirt trailing below his coat, not quite covering his thin, white ankles.

Ken Goldstein mumbled a few negatives about the goddamned, anti-Semitic moron of a paper-delivery person and reached over the top of the hedge, blindly groping for the paper. His breath clouded the air as he paused in his endeavor to violently break off a small twig poking him in the eye. Forty-eight years of deep-seated frustration over being short, overweight, and myopic surfaced in a momentary childish outburst of first punching and then ripping away major parts of the hedge. It was only with the savage removal of one branch that he noticed that the Miltons' outside lights were blazing.

Curiosity replaced the tantrum. He could explain away the lights, but the Mercedes left parked in the driveway was another story.

The producer squinted around his myopia and parted the branches. Despite the post–hippie era ponytail Aaron Milton had been sporting since the old lady died, the doctor was type A about his Mercedes—Milton would never leave his toys out in the driveway. And there was *some*thing . . .

The man searched his overcoat pocket for his glasses and hastily put them on. The something transformed into the shape of someone sprawled across the front seat with his head thrown back.

Later, Mr. Goldstein would report that it was neighborly concern which propelled him heedlessly to the side of the vehicle, though his friends suspected it was more a case of prurient curiosity, impure and simple. Since Mrs. Milton died, the good doctor had been sowing a few wild oats—on more than one occasion, the producer had seen an attractive young blonde leaving the Milton residence via the back door at four o'clock in the morning.

Crouched low, he peered cautiously through the passenger-side rear window. It took almost a full two seconds for the anticipated image of Aaron Milton receiving a blow job to disappear and be replaced with reality. A thick blood smear across the lower third of the driver's-side window and the sight of the blood-spattered beige leather dashboard caused him to promptly open the passenger door.

Ken Goldstein swore once, rapidly stepped backward, and slipped on the brick edging of the driveway. Running back to his house on a broken ankle, he would swear he never felt the pain or the cold.

At 5:00 A.M. Adele crawled out from under the bed holding yesterday's running socks. She crumpled one, testing it for stiffness, and put them on. That the pair did not walk away by themselves or salute meant she could get one more wearing out of them. Feeling a lot like a horse being shod, she slowly worked her feet into running shoes which were already occupied by orthotics, sole cushioning, Odor-Eaters, corn pads, and bunion protectors. While she waited for her left foot to properly seat itself amidst the hardware, she dialed Aaron Milton's home number and waded through the long and humorless message.

She clucked her tongue in disappointment. Recorded answering-machine greetings were an indication of one's core personality, the same way a salad was often the ultimate indicator of a restaurant's worth. In the immortal words of her mother—"If you get iceberg, expect ptomaine."

Call-waiting interrupted her call and she hung up, letting the answering machine take the call. She listened guiltlessly while the Ellis Hospital nursing office came as close to begging as management ever got to begging— there were six admits waiting in ER and they needed her to report to work stat. Call back in five minutes to confirm she was on her way.

Instead of calling Ellis, Adele hit redial, composing the message she would leave Aaron. She was working on her tone of nonchalance when a man answered.

"Hey Doc. Sorry for calling so early, but I thought I'd try to catch you before you left for the hospital. I want—"

"Adele?"

She realized the voice on the other end of the line was not Aaron Milton's. The pronunciation of her name, with the stress on drawing out the *l* sound, was recently familiar.

"Yes?"

"Adele? It's Douglas Collier."

She nodded. Apprehension and dread instantly came alive in the pit of her stomach, overshadowing her surprise. "Why are you at Aaron's . . ."

"I'm . . . I got a call from Detective Ritmann. Dr. Milton has been murdered."

Adele took in a sharp breath and clapped a hand to her mouth. At her feet, Nelson whined anxiously.

"Found him in his driveway. Been mutilated. I just got here a minute ago. Why were you calling him?"

"I . . . I had a question about Chloe's code yesterday, and I wanted to . . ." She went silent, feeling numb.

"Adele? Be careful." There was a pause, then: "Do you have a gun?"

"Yes." Gavin had given her a .32 caliber Colt along with a year's worth of firing drills as his first Christmas gift. She was the only woman she knew who could go from load to accurate fire in under two seconds.

"It might be a good idea if you keep it nearby."

She thanked him and hung up. An acute need to talk to Cynthia shot through her, except Cynthia would want to sleep until the last minute before work.

She sighed. There was always her brain theater— the group of inanimate objects and imaginary characters she sometimes talked to. Or she supposed she could talk to herself—a rapt audience and fascinating speaker guaranteed.

The Labrador placed a paw on her foot and made a noise like a banana would if it could make one.

Then again, there was always Nelson.

"What the hell's going on around here?" Cynthia asked before Adele was all the way through the locker room door. "Damn cops are *every*where, like lice on a transient. Gayle's half loaded, swigging down Listerine in the locker room, and now she's locked herself in her office and hasn't said one word to anybody. Cops are dragging chairs and a desk into the supply closet and acting like—"

"Aaron Milton was found murdered this morning. He was mutilated." Disheartened, she sighed. "Same deal as Ganet, I would imagine."

The young nurse sat down hard on the bench, her mood sobered. "The same person who killed Sonya?"

"I'd say that's a pretty good guess." Adele hung up her jacket. "Is Meg here yet?"

"Why? Do you think she . . ."

"I'll explain everything at the gym tonight. What about Helen?"

Cynthia pulled a face and nodded. "Annie Wilkes is

present and accounted for. Night shift said she came in before five and went into her trance routine in the computer corner."

"Do me a favor today—keep an extra eye on her."

"Sure." Cynthia shrugged. She'd known Adele long enough to know there was a good reason for the request. "I'll try, but shit, Adele, she's so frigging *squirrelly*."

"Hey. Don't talk about my next-best friend like that."

"Your *what*?"

"Damn!" Adele snapped her fingers. "I knew you'd be jealous."

Gayle weaved slightly while she spoke through an almost visible cloud of Listerine vapors. The medicinal miasma was making Adele's eyes water.

"You are no doubt wondering about the presence of the police," she began.

No one out of the two shifts' worth of Ward 8 employees said a word. Adele studied each face, noticing the range of expressions—Cynthia's grim sadness, Tina's snarled lip, Helen's nervous twitch and incessant rocking, Meg's obvious I-could-care-less contempt, Skip's mournful and swollen eyes behind the thick glasses, the night shift LPN's glorious, insipid smile.

"They are here for your safety and . . ." Gayle made a wide gesture with her hand, knocking over Cynthia's coffee cup. A small amount of the mostly cream and sugar mixture spilled over the report sheets which had yet to be distributed among the day shift. ". . . to ask a few of you . . ." Gayle glared at Helen, who immediately stopped rocking. ". . . some questions about the terrible tragedy which took place yesterday."

Silence.

"Also, there will be two mandatory meetings held today down in the Rose Room by the Sheriff's Department—one at noon, and one at six this evening. Tina will call every staff member not present to make sure the turnout from Ward Eight is a hundred percent. You will *all* attend . . ."

The silence was peppered with a few isolated groans, which Gayle seemed not to hear.

"The police will be giving special instruction on how to protect yourselves in case you . . ."

Gayle began to cry, and the ambiance of the room went into hyperfreak. The snarl faded from Tina's lip, and Helen started to hyperventilate, pulling at her Bozo hair, which was more disheveled than usual. Skip put his hands to his face and sobbed freely, as though he'd been given permission to suddenly break down. Three nurses from night shift stared at each other, eyes wide with disbelief. Even Meg looked alarmed.

Adele was willing to bet no living human had witnessed Gayle Mueller cry since infancy.

"This morning, one of our finest surgeons, Dr. Aaron Milton, was murdered. His throat was cut and his . . . his hands were amputated."

The initial silence was profound. Then Meg screamed. Adele hurriedly got to her feet, as if to be ready for the oncoming confusion. Jaws unhinged, people gasped.

"You need to stay calm." Gayle was speaking again, although no one was paying attention. Adele was studying Meg, who had turned a whiter shade of pale. From across the room, she could see the rapid bounding of the nurse's carotid pulse.

With a jerky movement, the blonde suddenly stood, weaved, moaned, and, as one in shock, stumbled to the door and went out.

Adele had started after her, when she noticed Helen again doing her Lady Macbeth number without benefit of soap and water.

". . . you need to stay together at all times," Gayle droned on, oblivious of her audience. "Don't allow your-selves to be caught alone anywhere or . . ."

Helen, like someone in a trance, rose from her chair holding out the crucifix hanging from her neck. Headed for the door, she tripped over one of Skip's size 13 feet, fell to her knees, and crawled the rest of the way without so much as a blink.

Adele pulled Helen to her feet. "Take a deep breath!" she commanded.

The woman opened her mouth and, chest heaving, cried out: "The Devil walks among you. We're no match for this Master of Evil. It will cut us down one at a time. We must prepare for—"

"Oh shut up, Helen!" Gayle yelled.

Helen stopped as though she'd been slapped. With the speed of light, she turned and pointed at Gayle. "It, the Master of Hell, stands at *your* shoulder, Miss Gayle Garbagemouth, Miss Head Bully, Miss—"

"Okay," said Adele, pushing Helen to the door. "That's enough. I think we should all just get report and go on about our—"

"You've been marked, Miss Mighty Nurse!" Helen shouted, letting herself be led out the door. In the hall, Helen yelled loud enough for Mr. Salucci to turn his head

toward the noise: "Screw the whore! I hope It cuts her
g.d. balls off."

Mr. Salucci regarded her with pleading brown eyes, in
much the same manner Nelson had recently taken to
looking at her.

"You really did it this time, didn't you?" Adele asked,
searching under the heap of bloody bed linen for the
truant IV line.

Mr. Salucci said something in Italian that sounded like
"undue noz brutie mare dozie," and laughed uproariously.

In the hour between 6:45 and 7:45, Amerigo Salucci
had freed himself from his hand restraints, pulled out his
IV and his urinary catheter, ripped off his dressings, urinated on his bedside cabinet, bitten through one of the
plastic IV bags, defecated on the floor, elevated his bed to
the "high" position, then hidden the control. The only thing
that remained of his breakfast was the tray. Adele didn't
even want to guess where she would find the rest of it.

For the sake of saving time, Adele called the paging
operator, requesting an orderly to help with Mr. Salucci.
While she waited, she mopped up the floor and bedside
cabinet, restarted his IV, completed and charted his assessment, and gave him his 7:00 A.M. medications late,
and his 8:00 A.M. medications early.

They held a conversation of sorts, she speaking in
English, he in Italian. Neither understood a word of what
the other was saying, but it didn't really matter—the
messages (his insulting, hers professional) got through to
the other.

She had picked up the bedside phone to page the

orderly again, when the mahogany version of a golden Adonis walked through the door.

Dr. Collier turned off the electric saw and moved the splatter guard to the top of his head. With steel tweezers he picked up the four-inch section of wrist that he'd separated from the now very short remainder of Dr. Milton's forearm, placing it carefully under the exam lamp.

Through the magnifier, he examined the tissues surrounding the ulna and the radius, and finally the bones themselves. He nodded solemnly—as in Ganet's case, there were signs of irregular hacking motions rather than a clean, swift amputation. Dictating what he observed, he wrapped, labeled, and placed the wrist segment in the freezer. Once again he studied the handless, disemboweled corpse.

"If dead men could speak, what a tale they'd tell."

The diener—the morgue assistant who helped with autopsies—looked up from her workstation. "Sorry?"

Douglas shook his head. "Nothing. Just wondering what Dr. Milton would say if he could rejoin us for a moment."

The young diener returned her attention to the loose flap of tissue covering Aaron Milton's deeply lacerated neck. "I think," she said, "he'd be reeeeeally pissed."

Sonya Martin had once blatantly described the tall, muscular Henry Williams as her own personal supply of fresh dark meat.

The fresh and dark Ellis orderly stood on the other side of Mr. Salucci's bed, earphones planted firmly over his ears. Adele reached over and pulled an earphone away from one ear. A faraway tinny noise that Adele recognized as rapper Snoop Doggy Dogg spilled out of the foam disks.

Some of the nurses thought the young black man cold and insolent, but Adele knew better. On one particularly hellish day three years before, following the last of two attempts by Alva Williams to give up the ghost, Henry had sought Adele out for comfort. As he wept like a child in her arms, she stroked his head, and reassured him his mother would stabilize and eventually leave the hospital.

Of course she didn't have a clue as to whether it was true or not, but when tending to the walking wounded, she usually went for the power of positive thinking. When Alva left the hospital two weeks later, Henry declared she was a miracle worker. Since that time they had not shared more than conversational pleasantries, but there remained a bond that showed itself in the warmth of their smiles and the tones of their voices.

"Hey man." Henry knelt down to Mr. Salucci's eye level. "Looks like you gone wild on us. You need some help changing this bed, Adele?"

Adele smiled at the way he always pronounced her name—"AhDele," as if it were two words instead of one.

"How about if you put his catheter in first. We'll attack the bed later."

Adele opened the catheter insertion tray and set up the sterile field while Henry washed his hands. The orderly gloved and swabbed the head of Mr. Salucci's penis with antibacterial solution.

She waited until he lubed the tip of the catheter with sterile lubricant before she spoke. "Could I ask you a really personal question, Hen?"

With deft precision, he threaded the silicone catheter into the opening of the man's penis. "You can get personal with me anytime, girl." He laughed, then winced when Mr. Salucci cried out in pain. "Hold on, brother. Take a deep breath."

Henry made the final twist-push which would get the catheter clear of the urethral neck. With the first trickle of thick urine through the drainage tube, he inflated the anchoring balloon at the end of the catheter now situated inside the man's bladder.

"Last year, when you were held and questioned"—Adele lowered her voice—"did you tell the police everything?"

Henry grimaced and moved his head in a gesture that African-American men commonly employed to signal frustration. "Aw Adele, I don't want to be going into any of that bullshit again."

Her face fell in an expression of deep disappointment.

Henry removed his gloves and gave her a brief hug. "Hey girl, why you want to know that shit? You gotta let nasty business stay dead."

"I can't. Now that it's started again, I—"

Henry pulled back. "What? You and them cops going on 'bout that nurse dying yesterday? She got the wrong drug is all. It wasn't—"

"Don't you know?" Adele looked at the blank face and then the earphones and guessed he didn't. "Aaron Milton got his throat cut this morning. And Chloe didn't get the wrong drug by mistake, Hen—she was murdered."

Henry's eyes widened and he made a noise like air leaking out of a tire. "Ah shit, man! They got Uncle Milty?" He shook his head, clearing away the insertion tray. "The man was real good to my mama when she was sick," he said in a softer voice than she'd ever heard him use before. "I don't know why, but he took an interest in me. He's the one who talked sense into this stubborn head about getting my GED and getting my sorry ass to college. When I signed on for my night classes at SF State, he gave me money for books and everything. I didn't want to take the money, but he said it was a loan. He told me I could pay him back by getting a degree."

He lowered his head and turned away from her. For a time, neither of them said anything.

"Hey, there wasn't anything I didn't say," he said finally.

Imitating the African-American manly-man head gesture, she hoped he'd recognize it for what it was and not think she suffered from some kind of tic. "Come on, Henry, I didn't tell the cops everything either, and I'm not going to tell them everything. I'm trying to figure it out for myself, you know?

"You were hanging with Sonya all the time. There has to be something you didn't spill."

They each tied one of Mr. Salucci's hands to the side rails in silence while they prepared to bathe him. Henry refused to meet her eyes.

"Look at it this way, Henry," she said when they were almost finished. "If more good people get killed, there ain't gonna be nobody left to save your poor old mama's ass next time she comes in sick."

Henry crossed his arms and leaned against the sink, shaking his head. To her, the gesture translated into the fact that he was sticking to his silence. Adele glared, then shrugged. In a way she didn't blame him; the whole subject had caused him nothing but grief and humiliation.

"Them," he said suddenly. "Ganet and Sony? They were heavy into the kinky shit, you know?" He reached out and gently pulled her into the patient bathroom, closing the door behind them.

"Yeah, so tell me something half the world doesn't know."

The man frowned at her. "Hush up and listen, girl." Closing the lid of the toilet, he sat down. "A couple times they got into a three-way with a girl that Ganet picked up. 'Cept things got all turned around and the girl got real hooked into Sony, but Sony didn't want any part of her without Ganet.

"The girl went crazy, calling Sony on the phone all hours in the night, crying and carrying on, begging Sony to see her. One night when I was there, she called and Sony got real cold with her and said she was gonna report her to the cops if she didn't quit her.

"Couldn'ta been an hour when the bitch comes barging in the middle of me and Sony getting down to business in the bed, you know? She pulls out a street blade and flang it so hard it got itself stuck in the mattress up to the handle."

Henry snickered in spite of his seriousness. "Didn't almost miss Sony's ass by nothin'."

"Did you know who she was?"

"Sure. I knew who it was from the get-go. She got to working with you right after Sony got killed."

Adele raised her eyebrows in question, because her lips wouldn't work to form the word.

"The blond girl. That Meg."

Adele took a second, breathing deeply. "Why didn't you tell the police?"

Henry stood and rolled his eyes at her apparent stupidity. "Shit, you think the heat gonna listen to a nigger putting the finger on a little white girl nurse in *this* county? Man, they would've strung me up by the balls for sure."

Henry opened the bathroom door and positioned his earphones. "You be careful, girl. Don't be getting yourself into any of this shit. I need you around to take care of my mama."

Adele reached up and pulled one earphone away from his ear. Now it was Jimi Hendrix playing "Castles Made of Sand."

"I'll be around, Hen. You just make sure to let me know if you think of anything else."

Detective Enrico Cini had turned the storage room in which Sonya was murdered into a temporary office. A table and two chairs had been dragged in and set up at the back of the room, not more than five feet from where Sonya was discovered.

Skip had been interrogated first and was spit out in forty minutes, his black-rimmed glasses resting on the middle of his nose. Gayle entered and Cini emerged three minutes later, seeking coffee. Fifty-five minutes later, Gayle gave up the hot seat to Tina, who was out in twenty minutes.

Cynthia had been inside for an hour and a half. Ignoring the handwritten sign that said "Knock before entering," Adele went inside long enough to hear Cynthia say in her best Valley Girl accent, "I mean, it was the ice cream that would *not* die, ya know?"

Adele stole a glance at Enrico Cini. The fireplug of a man had hair which resembled a moth-eaten fur coat—she guessed he cut it himself, using one of the vacuum cleaner systems advertised only on late-night TV. He sat with his head resting in one hand and was looking at Cynthia as though she were from another planet. He seemed dazed, amazed, bored, impatient, and unhappy all at once.

Cynthia spied her and yelled out, "Hey! Adele baby!" while she waved.

Adele gritted her teeth and waved back. She would have to remember to drop a weight on Cynthia's foot at the gym.

Detective Cini shaded his eyes from the glare of the bare bulb hanging over his moth-eaten head. "Are you Adele Monsarrat?"

"Yes?"

The man looked at his watch. "You're next. In about ten minutes?"

"If I'm not busy, that'll be fine."

"Make sure you're not busy."

Oh sure, buddy—you and the vacuum you blew in on.

"Rise and shine, sweetie." Adele laughed as she pulled the sheet down from over the head of Susan O'Day—her adolescent anemia patient. "I need to do your assessment and meds before your doctor gets—" Adele gasped.

The pretty sixteen-year-old's skin was chalk-white and clammy. "I'm gonna have diarrhea quick!" the teen exclaimed, her eyes wide with fear.

Adele grabbed the bedpan from the side cabinet, slipped it under the girl, then quickly took her blood pressure.

"Something's wrong. I tried to get up, but I almost fainted, and I'm so thirsty."

The blood pressure came up 70 over 30. Her pulse was 120 and thready. Within the space of ten seconds, Adele lowered the head of the bed below the foot, opened the IV to a steady stream, and calmly inserted an oxygen cannula into Susan's nose.

The girl licked her blanched lips. "I have to have some water," she whispered.

"Not yet," Adele said. "Let's see what's going on first."

When the girl was done, Adele pulled out the pan and quietly panicked at the sight of more than a quart of congealed blood, otherwise known to nurses as "gut jelly." By the time she had measured and emptied the contents, the teen urgently needed to use it again.

"What's happening to me?" She clung to Adele's arm.

Adele opened her mouth to lie and said instead, "I think you've got a bleed going on inside your abdomen. Try to relax and take some deep breaths until I get Dr. Wortz on the phone."

Not wanting to waste time, Adele called Tina from the bedside phone and ordered lab and a stat call to the physician. She was about to take another blood pressure when Detective Cini appeared in the door and crooked his finger at her—as though she had been a naughty child.

Adele turned her back on him just as Susan's eyes rolled back in her head and her body stiffened, heralding the oncoming seizure. She felt for the young girl's pulse, at the same time listening for a breath. The obnoxious pest at the door ceased to exist when she found neither one.

With the exception of an uncomfortable fall in blood sugar, lunch break for Ward 8 nursing staff came and went unheeded. Ward 8 nurses were used to eating bits and pieces on the run.

Resuscitated and stabilized, Susan of perforated ulcer fame had been whisked off to surgery. Longing for one moment to herself, Adele ducked into the nurses' lounge and slipped into the bathroom stall, locking it securely behind her. She sat, closed her eyes, and bit into the Granny Smith she'd put in her pocket.

It took the average person approximately two minutes to pee, she figured, start to finish. She set her stopwatch.

Chewing rapidly, she picked up the phone conveniently placed opposite the toilet and dialed the number she'd written on the palm of her hand. On the third ring, the phone was picked up and a small voice said, "Mommy can't talk."

The voice was barely audible. Adele was sure the child was speaking into the earpiece.

"Hello?"

"She's . . . My . . . my mommy's crying!"

Adele clenched her fists and made a growling noise deep in her throat. Of all the things on her Bad Things in Life list, this was the all-time worst: adults who, under the false belief it was "cute," allowed young children to command the phone.

"I'm sorry," Adele said firmly. "Tell a grown-up to come to the phone." She was careful not to yell or use obscenities.

There came squeegee noises as the child did God knew what with the receiver. After a long time of listening to the child breathe, she yelled, "Get your mommy right now! Tell her it's about Chloe."

The child whispered something indiscernible and dropped the receiver into what sounded like a metal barrel. Next she heard the sound of small feet running and the child's excited screams of "Mommy! Mommy! Auntie Chlome's on the phone!"

She cringed, hoping the woman wouldn't think someone was playing a cruel joke. Eventually a woman who sounded like Chloe answered with a soft and weepy hello.

"Hello, Mrs. Andreason? Lesa? This is Adele Monsarrat. I worked with—"

"Yes. Chloe told me about you."

Adele hesitated, wondering what Chloe would have possibly found interesting enough to tell her sister. She prayed it didn't have anything to do with that unfortunate day she'd gone to work so exhausted that she hadn't noticed the hole Nelson had chewed out of the back of her scrub dress. Worse yet was the fact that she'd neglected to wear a slip, and she hadn't worn underwear since her thirteenth birthday.

"I'm so sorry about Chloe, Lesa. Everyone here is devastated." Adele let a moment pass. "I was one of the last people to speak with Chloe, and she had a feeling that . . . well, she gave me your grandmother's ring to give to you. I'd like to bring it down personally."

"Oh, not today," the woman said, alarmed. "I . . . I can't see anyone today. I've got to make all the arrangements, plus take care of the children. The newspapers and police have been camped out on my doorstep and the neighbors have been calling all day. It's too much. My husband is in Spain on business and I can't get a message to him and . . ." She started to cry. "Oh dear God. The police said something went wrong, and that maybe somebody intentionally . . ."

Adele felt her throat tighten. "Please, isn't there something I can do? I cared so much about Chloe. I'd like to help."

Chloe's sister blew her nose and cleared her throat. "Thank you, but I'll be okay."

Stubborn—just like her sister.

"Please, Lesa."

There was a pause, and then: "Chloe's being cremated in San Anselmo. It would be a huge help if you could pick up her ashes and bring them down. I'll call Chapel of the Hills and tell them to release her to you. Is day after tomorrow okay? Her memorial service will be at noon."

"That's my day off, so it's fine. Can you think of anything else? Can I pick up anything from her apartment?"

The woman sighed. "I don't think so. The police told me I won't be allowed into her flat until next week, so I don't think you could get in there."

"Wait. The police sealed off Chloe's flat?"

"Yes. Yesterday afternoon when they called for information."

"The police called you *yesterday* to ask questions?" Adele was shocked the Sheriff's Department had moved so quickly.

"I've told them I couldn't talk until after the memorial service. They weren't very nice about it." Lesa paused in her grief and grew indignant. "Can you imagine? My sister is dead and they were callously rude. It made me so mad I . . ." She broke into another round of sobs.

Adele, tired of holding back, began to weep in earnest.

It was the toilet scene right out of *Alice Doesn't Live Here Anymore*. Cynthia rocked a weeping Adele while Gayle pounded on the stall door bellowing, "Adele? What the hell's going on in there? How long are you going to be?"

The women inside the stall ignored her.

"It's okay, Del," Cynthia whispered, stroking Adele's hair.

"No it isn't, Cyn, and you know it. Everybody's scared. I'm scared. It's senseless killing. I hate this!"

The locker room door opened with a single musical note. Gayle stopped pounding on the stall door.

"Adele?" It was Tina.

"What is it, Tina?" Cynthia answered, wiping away the streaked mascara from her friend's face with a ragged piece of toilet paper.

"Mr. Cini wants to know how long you're going to be, Meg went home sick, so Skip says you need to take over her patients, the toilet in Mr. Salucci's room overflowed and the engineer wants to know who tried to flush the box of puffed rice and the banana, and Dr. Wortz wants you to report to ICU stat so he can ask you something about the girl you transferred."

"What should I tell everybody?"

In the warmth of Cynthia's loving empathy, Adele gathered her strength. "Tell everybody," she said eventually, "to back off or I'll sue for damages."

* * *

In a hectic thirty minutes, Adele picked up Meg's end-stage renal patient, admonished Mr. Salucci for the disastrous disposal of his breakfast, helped Skip do a complicated dressing change, avoided the stalking Mr. Cini, and ran to ICU.

She found the now partnerless Dr. Wortz sitting at the nurses' station looking withered and lonely. Seeing her, he asked for a few details about Susan O'Day's case.

As he wrote down the last of the information she provided, she realized that he had lost not only a partner in Aaron Milton but a good friend as well. He was, she guessed, probably terrified as to whether the run on surgeons would continue.

Before she left, she dared to hug the normally austere surgeon and whisper that she was sorry.

The older man's eyes filled with tears. "I don't understand," he said, squeezing her hand. "Why is this happening?"

The stairs that led to the basement were coming up on her left. The hallway Seth Thomas said there were forty minutes before she had to report off, finish her charting, settle her patients, and make sure their rooms, their bodies, and the medical equipment used on them were in order.

There was, she decided, enough time to stop in for a quick hello to Dr. Collier.

His door was ajar. Through the crack, she saw him sitting alone at his desk, talking to himself in an animated fashion. This didn't faze her in the least. As a matter of fact, she found it comforting; though she unashamedly used Nelson as an excuse, she talked to herself or her imaginary friends all the time—even when others were present.

Adele backed up a few feet, and then walked noisily to the door and knocked. "You busy?" she asked, sticking her head into his office.

For an awkward moment, he did not respond. Finally: "Not busy—reeling."

She nodded. "I know the feeling. It's nuts on the ward too. People are pretty freaked. Do you know anything yet?"

"Carbon copy case to the Ganet-Martin murders." He sighed. "The lab is going over the car, the house has been searched. Looks like everything took place in the car.

"He was murdered around one A.M. . . ."

The intercom crackled and a voice came through with information that a reporter was waiting to speak to him on line two.

"The press," he said, with a hiss of disgust. "God, I hate those people. They're like piranhas. *Pacific Intelligencer* is the worst—broke security twice at the crime scene this morning.

"Every man, woman, and child in Marin is going to be assaulted with all this sensationalistic crap the moment they open their afternoon papers. It's amoral.

"Plus they're already digging for dirt on Milton."

"Damn it!" She was instantly furious. "I suppose they've got their claws out for Chloe too?"

"Of course. Uncovering dirt is what they thrive on, and unfortunately there's always some sick soul out there willing to spill their guts about anything. People have to get their fifteen minutes of fame whatever way they can get it."

The intercom voice reminded him about the call on line two and added that Detective Ritmann was now on line one.

He raised his eyebrows apologetically and reached for the phone. She looked at the Seth Thomas and went to the door and waved.

He covered the mouthpiece and whispered, "By the way, they traced a call from Milton's residence to your phone last night, so don't be surprised if you get raked over the coals. They'll want to make something out of it."

Adele remembered the hang-ups and was instantly grateful she'd saved the tape—not that it was going to prove anything.

Between the fourth and fifth floors, the hair on her arms prickled and sat up before she even perceived the presence behind her. Without her permission, her feet faltered and stopped. She strained each of her senses— someone also stopped and was still.

"Hello?"

A faint breath? A slight contact of fabric with fabric?

Alarmed, Adele forced herself to move, humming "Greensleeves" and measuring the distance between herself and the nearest exit door. The presence moved closer. If she looked behind her, she would see who was there.

Concurrent images of the *Intelligencer* photo of her blood-spattered body lying on the stairs, her mother fainting into some policeman's arms, Cynthia kneeling in front of Nelson saying, "I'm your new mom," at first caused her to step faster, then abruptly to howl with laughter.

The presence stopped, and Adele thought she felt—or heard—some confusion or a small breath of surprise.

Taking advantage of the infinitesimal pause, she bounded up the stairs and through the first exit, which took her, befittingly, into the psychiatric unit.

SIX

WITHIN VIEW OF AN AMAZING VARIETY OF sweaty pecs and abs, Adele concentrated on the keypad of the health club's phone. From memory she pressed in the numeric code for her remote room monitor, then listened to the rhythmic scraping sound going on in her living room at that moment.

Nelson was chewing something—hopefully not the piece of plyboard she'd nailed to the front door to cover his latest destruction.

"Damn it, Nelson, no chewing!" she barked into the mouthpiece.

Two older women dressed in matching pink leotards and flesh-tone tights, looked over their health shakes, their mouths hitched up in uncertain smiles.

"Take a walk, hump the ottoman, eat some beets, but stop chewing right NOW!"

One of the ladies frowned. *Hump the ottoman?*

Nelson paused in his chewing of the plywood patch and listened to his mistress's voice. Taking the Mickey Mouse rug in his teeth, he trotted over to the answering machine and whined.

"Oh sweetie, you *do* need more attention from Mommy, don't you?"

Nelson howled in injured commiseration.

"Okay, baby. I'll be home in a little while. Maybe we'll go visit weird old Auntie Helen so she can ream out your chakras and make you normal again. Would you like that, baby?"

Nelson whined, then barked twice.

"Rawhide chews?" Adele interpreted. "Sure, baby boy. I'll pick up a couple on my way home." She paused. "What is it, Nelson?"

The dog whimpered.

"Yeah, I know, but things will get better, I promise."

Over the span of their workout, she gave Cynthia all the details. Starting on the bun buster with the description of her preop visit to Chloe and ending on the deltoid destroyer with the stairwell phantom, most of Cynthia's reactions were predictable—except for the stony silence whenever Douglas Collier was mentioned.

"Collier was one of my instructors at the mortuary college," Cynthia explained from her perch on the Stairmaster. "Uptight one day, Mr. Wonderful the next, depending on whether Dana was being nice to him or not. It made our lives miserable."

"Dana?"

"A girl in my class that he was dating. She was a Snob Hill debutante—the type who has every pubic hair electrolytically removed because it's socially correct. Collier married her right after graduation."

Adele recalled the photos of the vaguely familiar dark-haired woman she'd seen in his office. "Describe her."

"Well, the weird part is that you two could pass for twins—with the exception of the pubic hair, of course. I guess those black-haired exotic types get to him."

"Oh, don't make me laugh." Adele laughed, fixing her gaze on the man in front of her doing 150-pound bench presses. It took her mind off her burning thighs. "The guy just wants to pump me for information. Everybody's desperate to get a lead."

"I think, Del," puffed Cynthia, "he's probably desperate to pump *you*."

"Naw. He's too anal."

"That's exactly what you said about Gavin."

Adele noticed her friend had switched the Stairmaster up to the level before the most difficult one, without so much as a groan or a lapse in pace. "Gavin's problem was he wasn't anal *enough*. He was so loose you could hear his brain flapping on a windy day."

"What are you going to do if he shows up?"

"Nothing to do," Adele said. "Give him a copy of the final divorce papers and send him to his mother's."

"You *really* believe it's going to be that easy? With Gavin?"

Adele shrugged, and in direct opposition to her body's intense desire, advanced her Stairmaster to the next level. "He doesn't have a lot of choice, does he? As far as I'm concerned, that cake was baked and out of the oven a long time ago."

"Speaking of baked cakes . . ." Cynthia pushed the Stairmaster to the maximum workout. Adele was momentarily satisfied to see her beginning to show signs of strain. "What's the plan for Helen?"

"If she lets me behind that brick wall of craziness, I think I'll get some amazing information."

"About what?"

"Helen knows something, Cyn. Either she's witnessed Sonya and Chloe being murdered, or she's actually done the killing herself. She's played some kind of a part in it—don't know whether it was willing or unwilling, though." Adele shrugged. "Who knows? She says she's scared of this It thing, but sometimes I wonder if It is some part of her."

"An alter ego?"

"One of the many. Dr. Jekyll and Mrs. Marval and a cast of thousands—depending on the day."

Unfolding the newspaper she'd pilfered from the gym, Adele propped it against the steering wheel. Sometimes, if the Beast was behaving, and she was on stretches of road without much traffic, she liked to read and drive at the same time. She wasn't half bad at it either. Most of the time she managed to catch up on her mandatory reading without incident. Today, however, she went off the road twice before she could get through one paragraph.

It was as Douglas predicted: The *Pacific Intelligencer* was filled with sensationalistic details and an overabundance of photos showing a blood-soaked Aaron stretched out across the front seat of his Mercedes, one handless arm obscenely displayed. Every page flaunted one or more close-ups of blood spills which had trickled down the driveway, shots of the house and car, a ten-year-old studio photo of a short-haired Aaron Milton next to a more recent long-haired one taken at some charity ball.

It wasn't until she came to the paragraph in the right corner of the back page that she finally pulled off the road.

Dr. Alan Wortz, a senior partner of San Andreas Medical Group, stated that Dr. Milton appeared to be in good spirits throughout the day, despite an earlier incident in which a patient died unexpectedly after a minor surgery performed by Milton.

The patient, Chloe Sedrick, 25, of Mill Valley, worked as a nurse at Ellis Hospital. Sedrick's death is currently under investigation by the Marin County Sheriff's Department.

Sheriff Harold Marval, in an official statement to the press, said there was no apparent connection between the two deaths.

No connection, my ass, she thought as she turned back to the front page and stared at the photos. The whole thing made her sick, but unlike last year, she wouldn't write any letters to the editor about their bad taste in reporting. Her outrage went worlds beyond letters. It was now in the realm of—

Adele sucked in a breath so forcefully she choked. She closed her eyes and recalled the tall, lean silhouette in the window with Meg, and how she had almost hit the car in front of her when she'd pulled out—a Mercedes with a vanity plate: SITN PR T

Frantically, she turned to a photo of Aaron's car taken from the end of the driveway. Adele held the paper at arm's length, squinting unnecessarily to read the license plate.

Gripping the wheel, Adele did a U-turn and headed for San Rafael.

The Beast pulled up behind an unmarked police vehicle and was purposely put to sleep. Having noted that the white Toyota Camry was brand-new, Adele muttered to herself about wasted tax dollars and pork barrel spending, although she wasn't sure if pork barrel was a term that could be used for a cop car. She hoped the vehicle didn't belong to Detective Cini, or that if it did, he was either inside the bar getting looped or in the beauty salon next door getting a proper haircut.

Hugging the waxy carton of vegetarian wonton soup, Adele walked toward the run-down front of the Granary Bar and Grill, still trying to decide what tack she should take with Meg. Henry Williams's description of Meg's murderous rage had not surprised her; she'd always sensed that under the strange and quiet exterior, the woman was like a keg of dynamite waiting for a match. The one and only time she'd seen Meg animated had been during a locker room round of slap and tickle with Chloe, and even then there had been a frenetic quality to her playfulness.

Adele sighed. She'd wing it. She always did her best when she winged it.

Meg answered the door attired in a tired brown bathrobe. There was a minute flash of surprise followed by a look of dismayed disbelief. Her eyes, swollen and red-rimmed, made her appear even paler than she had that morning.

"What's going on?" she asked, holding open the door. "Why am I so popular all of a sudden?"

Uncertain as to whether it was an invitation or not, Adele stepped into the dark, narrow hallway, which smelled of cooked cabbage and incense. "I brought you some wonton soup. I know you and Chloe were close, and I wanted you to know that if there's anything I can do, or if you need a hug, I'm here."

The nurse's perpetually sullen expression changed enough to accommodate a small smile. For the first time in Adele's memory, Meg actually looked her in the eye. "Thank you. I . . . Come in."

Under the bright overhead light, the bleak apartment appeared cramped and dirty. Hastily decorated with cheap travel posters and battered furniture from the Goodwill, it felt and looked more like a homeless shelter than someone's home.

A red-haired man with the rugged good looks of an Irish farmer rose from one of the overstuffed chairs and smiled. Instantly she liked his smile; it wasn't every person who was comfortable with his smile—this man looked as though he lived in his.

"Oh, I'm sorry. I didn't know you had company," Adele said, sounding sincerely apologetic—she'd taken two years of drama in college.

Meg waved a finger in the man's direction. "This is Detective Ritmann from the sheriff's office. He's here asking questions about Chloe. This is Adele Monsarrat."

Ritmann's bear-sized hand seized hers in a sure, honest grip. "*You're* Adele Monsarrat?"

Adele laughed. "Why do you say it like that? Have I made national news or something?"

Tim Ritmann flushed, after the manner of redheads. "From Detective Cini's description, I expected the ogre's wife. You're a skinny slip—not the usual build for your run-of-the-mill 'difficult' type."

"I'm not skinny, nor am I difficult," Adele said, taken by his straightforwardness. "Mr. Cini tried my patience today."

Silence fell like a giant sequoia. Meg sat down looking unhappy and defiant, like a teenager who'd been dragged to some elderly relative's bridge party. Detective Ritmann tapped his pen against his notebook.

"Well, if nobody minds, I'm going to heat up this soup," Adele announced. Without waiting for Meg to direct her, she headed for a faded brocade curtain covering a doorless doorway, and stepped down into a kitchen which had most certainly been built with a small boat in mind.

She put the soup on low heat and reentered the living room as the detective asked Meg if she considered herself a close friend of Chloe's.

"May I use your bathroom?" Adele asked.

Annoyed, Meg pointed in the direction of another long, narrow hallway. "Off the bedroom."

Walking as slowly as possible, Adele strained to hear Meg's response.

"I liked Chloe," Meg answered tentatively. "She was a nice girl."

The bedroom, like the rest of the apartment, was claustrophobic and depressing. There were no wall hangings, no books, and no furniture save a stripped-down mattress and a Japanese tansu on which sat the obligatory bedside glass of water and a candle.

Everywhere, clothes and stray shoes lay at random where they'd been dropped or thrown. She retrieved a pair of soft leather high-tops from one pile. The soles were caked with mud. Lying next to them was a pair of black jeans, damp and muddy from the knee down.

She found the windowless bathroom a shade beyond deplorable. A thin wire clothesline strung from the shower nozzle to the opposite wall came close to garroting her as she entered. The smell alone—toothpaste and sewage—was enough to make her want to blow chunks.

Like any good American, she promptly opened the medicine cabinet. It held two condom packages, a prescription bottle of Tylenol with codeine, a bottle of ipecac, Aleve, Mylanta-II, and three unopened number twelve scalpels. With the exception of the condoms, her own medicine cabinet was identical.

She hiked up her skirt, looked at the dirt and scum collected in and around the toilet, and decided she could wait until she got home.

The detective was on the phone, not saying anything but nodding intermittently. After a minute, he cleared his throat and spoke in what Adele recognized as his Official Detective Voice. "Got her here right now." He smiled at Adele. After another silence he frowned, said thanks, hung up, and immediately turned to Meg. "One last question, Miss Barnes. Could you tell me what you did last night?"

Adele caught her eyebrows halfway to her hairline and returned them to their natural position on her face.

"Last night?" Meg pushed back a shock of disorderly hair and thought in earnest. "Let's see. I came home about five-thirty, made myself some dinner, did some

mending, then went to bed. I was asleep by eight-thirty."
The woman lied convincingly.

The detective made a note in his book. "When was the
next time you went out?"

"This morning when I left for work at six-thirty."

"Did you have any visitors last night?"

"No." Meg's tone turned decidedly hostile. "What's . . . ?"

The detective held her stare. "And you're sure you
didn't leave the apartment last night? Even to go to the
store or . . ."

In an attempt to break the building tension, Adele
offered Meg her soup. The woman ignored her.

"I'm sure."

"What kind of a relationship did you have with Dr.
Milton?"

"What the fuck is that supposed to mean?" The nurse
was off her chair so fast Adele jumped.

The detective seemed surprised by the outburst. "Miss
Barnes, I was only asking—"

"I'd like you to leave now." The veins in Meg's forehead visibly throbbed. "I'm really sick of this shit, you
know?" She stomped to the door and swung it open,
pointing at the man. "Out!"

Closing his notebook, the redhead casually turned his
back on the raging Meg—a risky thing to do, in Adele's
estimation.

"I'd like to talk to you," he said quietly. "Can we go to
my car?"

Keeping an eye on Meg, she shook her head. "I'm
really tired and I have to work tomorrow. How about
after work tomorrow?"

"You sure you're too tired now?"

Adele nodded. "It was a bad day and I'm—"

"I could put a hold on you, you know." The jovial blue eyes sparkled.

"I think you need to turn up your Miracle-Ear, Mr. Ritmann." She smiled like a stone. "I said I'm tired and I'm going home. I'll talk to you tomorrow."

Behind them, Meg pounded her fist into the hallway wall. "I asked you to leave! You too, Monsarrat. I can't do this right now. I want everybody out of here! I want you all to leave me the fuck alone."

Without meeting Meg's eyes, Adele picked up her purse and hurried past the detective and Meg. Ritmann followed so close he stepped on the back of her heel. At the last second, he tried to force his card into Meg's hand. "Call me in the next day or two," he said over his shoulder. "I'll need to ask—"

The door slammed behind them with such force a piece of green plaster fell from the hallway ceiling and shattered into several pieces at their feet. From the other side of the door came the sound of angry weeping.

Out in the street, the detective bit his grin into submission. "Nice car," he said out of the corner of his mouth, taking in the Beast.

"When it's not trying to kill me, the Beast is a wonderful car, Mr. Ritmann." She glanced at the rusty CB antenna and blushed.

The man got into the Toyota, laughing. "Sure you don't want to talk to me now?"

Adele smiled. "Detective Ritmann, if you knew what my day was like, you wouldn't even ask. Believe me, whatever I have to say will keep until tomorrow."

He started the car, then fished around in his pocket for a business card, which he handed to her. "The way you people are dropping, I wouldn't be so sure about that, Nurse Monsarrat."

Her smile faded at the truth of his words. "Don't worry about me," she said. "I'm . . ."

What? Too mean to die? Tough as nails? The owner of a homicidal automobile and a cowardly dog who's having a mental breakdown?

"I'm determined," she said finally.

On a hearty chuckle, the man pulled away, leaving her alone on the curb.

Nelson had burrowed into the corner of the living room to get away from the disagreeable smell of the human. A vegetarian since puppyhood, he shied away from the offered square of raw meat, which lay untouched on the kitchen floor; it smelled to him like something that needed to be dropped into Her toilet.

The intruder moved from room to room, searching through drawers and cabinets, pausing now and then over bits of paper, and writing things down in a notebook. The sense of Her momentary arrival caused Nelson to whine and bark suddenly at the front door. He wanted to warn Her something was wrong.

"Good dog," said the intruder, and picking up the uneaten scrap of meat with a cloth, exited through the kitchen door.

"One for you and one for me." Adele gave Nelson the larger of the two rawhide chews and bit the end of the other, holding it firmly between her lips like a cigarette.

Feeling for the fifth time for the Colt under the pillow, she lay back, and for a fourth time, methodically went through the file of papers and photographs provided by Dr. Collier.

When she could no longer fight her eyelids, she turned off her light and gazed out the window. Across the water, San Quentin was lit up like a castle.

A fortress of murderers, a collection of the violent and the insane. Them and us.

"I mean, just what *is* the difference between them and us?" she asked her imaginary group of friends who had gathered around the bed to watch her sleep.

Not much. A thin line. They get better food, and have much better social programs available at no cost to themselves, thanks to the bleeding-heart liberal Democrats.

"Hey! *I'm* a Democrat and I'd never go so far as to say . . ."

Realizing she was about to have an argument with her imagination, she turned onto her stomach, felt around under her pillow, and let the gun slip into her hand.

SEVEN

NETTIE WECHESKI WAS ONE OF THOSE GRAVEL-voiced down-home fifty-something gals who belonged to a Golden Girls Club and a bowling league, never shaved their armpits or bleached their mustache, drank cheap beer, and lived with their mother forever. That the woman was eager to talk didn't surprise Adele; Nettie Wecheski's reputation among Marin nurses was that she knew everything about everybody and loved to tell it all.

It also didn't hurt that Nettie had spent some time as a patient on Ward 8. Only a few highlights from the experience stuck with Adele, like the tuft of hair strategically placed on a tattoo on the woman's back, a horrendous tummy-tuck scar that was worthy of a malpractice suit, and the huge doses of IV Demerol needed to control her pain.

The expression "Just because someone is a character doesn't mean they have any" fit Nettie Wecheski to a T. In the deserted hospital cafeteria, Nettie displayed marginal talent by talking, smoking, drinking coffee, and snapping gum all at the same time.

Adele had to work at being pleasant; she'd forgone her morning run in order to be at Bellevue before Nettie got off night shift—plus, she didn't think the woman would take to being told how closely she resembled a cretin.

"I'm taking a criminology course." Adele decided on a direct lie approach. "And I've chosen to do follow-up research on the murders last year for my semester project."

"I didn't know there was a crime course given around here. My nephew would love that. Which school's it at?"

"Ah . . . it's a home study course through . . ." Adele glanced at an empty milk carton left on the table. ". . . Palmitate University."

The operator yawned, showing off molars whose size shocked Adele. "So what kind of things do you want to know, babe?"

Adele flipped back the cover of her notebook and licked the tip of her pen. The odd gesture unsettled her momentarily; she'd never licked a pen before in her life. "Were there people who called Dr. Ganet on a routine basis on the nights he worked?"

"Just his wife and Sonya. The hoot of it was that they'd always call within minutes of each other. But then again, Mrs. Ganet called every ten minutes anyway. What a friggin' pain in the keester *that* one was." The woman shook out another cigarette and lit it off the last one she'd smoked.

"Most of the docs' wives are paranoid, but she was the worst about keeping tabs. If I was married to a doc, I'd be totally paranoid. Philanderers every one. They've all got extra on the side—you'd be surprised who fools around." Nettie sat back with a sly smile, waiting for her to ask who was fooling around with whom.

Adele held out.

"So, you didn't notice any unusual calls at all during, let's say, the week or so prior to Dr. Ganet's murder?"

Nettie looked into her coffee cup and shook her head. Moving only her eyes, she suddenly threw a piercing glance at Adele. "Is it true that Helen Marval murdered that young nurse?"

"Where did you get *that*?" Adele was honestly stunned.

Nettie hawked out the raspy laughter of a heavy smoker. "Hey babe, I *am* the switchboard operator, you know. I hear it all.

"So, is it true or not?"

Adele maintained her poker face.

"C'mon babe—just gimme the basics. I mean everybody's going to know about it sooner or—"

"Nobody knows for sure what happened. We think she got the wrong drug from pharmacy."

The phone operator put out her cigarette, watching her closely. Adele had just opened her mouth to ask the next question, when Nettie took hold of her arm. The moist heat from the woman's fingers caused her to squirm.

"Okay, so here's a real Nettina Wecheski exclusive— you'll get an A in the course for sure." The woman looked around conspiratorially and leaned close enough to Adele to make her feel as if she were smoking too.

"Johnny boy got a few calls from a lady that had one of those mushy voices, like when women are in heat? I'd ask who was calling and she'd say, 'Tell him it's his friend.' "

The woman shrugged, twisting the brittle ends of her bleached hair around her finger. "I knew it wasn't Sonya, so I figured this one was a new side dish. There were dozens of 'em that called for him. It's amazing he didn't get his head blown off years ago.

"The last time this mushy voice called was a couple of days before the slice-o-matic demo. I put the call through to his sleep room, but before I could unplug, Mush Voice is singeing back his nose hairs."

"Do you remember anything she said?" Adele's gold eyes rounded with excitement.

"She said, 'Fuck off, Ganet, or I'll cut your god-damned balls off.' That was about it, except for her call-ing him every name in the book. The woman had a real foul mouth on her."

Nettie took on one of those self-satisfied expressions, as though she'd laid the golden egg.

"What did Ganet say?"

"He didn't. He got to laughing like she was doing a stand-up comedy routine. The more she ranted, the harder he laughed."

"Did you tell the police?"

"I told you this was an exclusive, babe." Nettie gulped her coffee, swallowed her gum by mistake, then tried to cough it up the way a dog might try to rid itself of a fox-tail. When the wad came up, it flew out onto the table, landing close to Adele's elbow. Nettie picked it up and, to Adele's secret horror, stuck it back into her mouth.

"The way I figured it," Nettie said, resuming the chewing of her cud, "they weren't ever going to find the call anyway 'cause it was local. If the cops hadn't been such uptight pricks, I might have told them, but they were, so I said screw 'em."

"Anything else you can think of that wouldn't have showed up on the investigator's report?"

The woman yawned again. Adele looked away.

"Only that the reports about the time of John's death are totally wrong."

Adele squinted. "Excuse me?"

"The police reported time of death to the newspapers as six-ten or later. The fact is that it was five-forty."

"How do you know that?"

"Psychic vibes, babe. At exactly five-forty that morning, I felt a sharp pain across my throat that left me gaspin' for air."

Adele stopped writing. "That's it? That's how you knew? Psychic vibes and a pain in your throat?"

Nettie nodded and laughed, mistaking Adele's disappointment for awe. "Yep. Psychic vibes, babe. It's all any of us got to go by."

Rain upset the Beast—like an old man with rheumatism in his joints. In the five miles between Bellevue and Ellis hospitals, the Beast went to sleep six times. The last time it went to sleep, a half-mile from her destination, it stayed asleep.

Under the backseat, Adele found a red and white fold-up umbrella—an old Goodwill acquisition. She ignored the Sapporo Beer advertisements printed on each of the nylon panels, grateful for the protection.

Twenty yards into her journey, a car pulled up and crawled alongside her. Through the steamed glass of the white Camry she heard raucous laughter, before the passenger window slid down enough to reveal Cynthia's wildly grinning face. Behind the wheel, grinning like a madman himself, Detective Sergeant Ritmann had his arm slung familiarly over Cynthia's shoulder.

Adele sighed. Cops and nurses—would the age-old coupling between the two professions never end?

The particular spotty flush on her friend's neck was a sure sign of infatuation and new lust. The vacant stare of Detective Ritmann was an even surer sign that his mind had been sucked right out the end of his dick.

She shook her head, partially from envy, more from wonder. Not that Cynthia fit the same category as Sonya Martin; Cynthia's parade of men seemed more like the sampling of a twenty-pound box of assorted chocolates by a woman who allowed herself one chocolate per month.

She sometimes—not very often—felt sorry for Cynthia's men, who eventually all felt as though they'd been hit by a Mack truck.

"Want a ride?" Cynthia asked.

"Sure." Adele stepped off the curb toward the car.

"Well, you can't have one." Cynthia waved, the window slid up, and the Camry sped away.

Adele laughed the rest of the way to the hospital.

Freak-out City on Ward 8.

Gayle Mueller did not show up for work—alcoholic or not, it was a first for the head nurse, who had entered the unit between 6:45 and 6:48 each and every workday for the last ten years.

When the calls to her house went unanswered, Detective Ritmann dispatched a squad car to her home. No Gayle. No automobile.

By 8:30, an APB was issued.

Adele had been appointed temporary charge nurse, a job no one in her right mind would want. Making sure the whole unit ran smoothly in addition to having one's own patient assignment was not humanly possible. That Meg had waited until the last minute to call in sick, and the replacement nurse was a nurse's aide with two hours' worth of training, was bad enough, but when Helen and Skip got into a high-volume argument over who was going to take the next admit, Adele adopted Gayle's demeanor: Stern Mother Bitch.

At 10:30, she slipped away from Mr. Salucci and the gang to the sanctuary of Gayle's office. On the wall over the desk, she found a cartoon depicting a patient talking on a psychiatrist's couch. Behind the couch, the doctor's chair is empty and the office door stands open. The caption read: "I'd like to discuss my abandonment fears . . ." She didn't laugh.

Above that was a framed group photo she had seen several hundred times, but never really noticed. Looking more closely now, she saw it was taken at the county health fair, in front of the Women's Clinic booth. Some fifteen nurses and doctors crowded into the frame. Everyone was smiling except Gayle, who had been caught with her eyes closed and a plastic cup halfway to her mouth. Dr. Ganet and Sonya stood close to each other and slightly apart from the rest. They were grinning, as if to say, "Ha ha, the joke's on you!" She wondered if Mrs. Ganet ever saw the photo.

Chloe and Dr. Milton were laughing. Skip was also laughing, one arm flung over the shoulders of Gina Ducke, a nurse who'd left Ward 4 a year before to work in Oakland. His other arm rested around another nurse Adele vaguely recognized, and his chin rested on the head of another nurse, who was completely unfamiliar to her.

Unlocking her memory, Adele recalled that not long after Gina Ducke left Ellis, a man identifying himself as her father had come into the unit showing her photo around, saying she was missing and had anyone heard from her?

She was trying to summon the names of the other two nurses from memory when the door opened, and before she could turn around, ice-cold hands circled her throat.

A whiff of Paloma Picasso perfume saved Cynthia from a fractured rib and a broken kneecap a nanosecond before Adele struck.

"Are you nuts!?" Adele shouted, furious at her friend's stupidity.

Undaunted, Cynthia clasped her hand and sat heavily in her lap. "Yes! I'm crazy. I'm crazy, insanely in love!"

Unimpressed and still fuming, Adele rolled her eyes. She'd heard the same speech a thousand times before from these same full lips.

"Who's the victim *this* time?" she asked dryly.

"Oh Del, the most wonderful thing happened after I got home from the gym." Dreamily, Cynthia looked off into the dead space of Gayle's office, speaking rapidly. "Timothy Ritmann called to ask if he could come by and ask some questions that Detective Cini hadn't covered? I said sure, and he showed up, and asked some questions, and then I made us something to eat and one thing led to another and the next thing we knew—"

"Stop," Adele said. "Let me ask you one question—what were you wearing when he stopped by?"

"My jammies."

"Your green silk jammies?"

Cynthia nodded and Adele shook her head. She'd seen Cynthia in her "jammies"—it was a sight sensuous enough to arouse a eunuch.

"Timmy wants to know if you'll talk to him now."

"Timmy?"

Cynthia smiled, the dreamy look revisited.

Adele sighed. "Yeah, okay. Sure." She pointed to the two women in the photo and said, "But first—do you remember these nurses' names?"

"That one is Clairissa Rittenhouse." Cynthia squinted, although her vision was perfect. "And the other one is Kathy Kern. Clairissa worked in labor and delivery here, and Kathy worked L and D over at Bellevue."

"You know anything about either one?"

"Clairissa moved to Sacramento and got a job at Sac General. I think Kathy got a divorce and moved with her kids to Kansas City. Why?"

"Just look at this photo, Cyn. What strikes you about it?"

Cynthia's smile faded after a minute of intense examination.

"Oh my God." She turned to look at Adele. "Everybody who's been murdered is in there."

In unison they whispered, "Shit. Gayle."

Adele thought for a moment. "You know, I once saw Gayle muscle her way into a movie queue—her aggression was impressive.

"All I can say is I hope she didn't suffer."

* * *

A half hour before shift change, Adele was taking report from Helen when Cynthia pulled her out of her seat and into the nearest patient room. Amerigo Salucci, lost in a thick Haldol haze, did not notice their presence.

"Tim said they just found Gayle's car in the parking lot outside Max's Cafe in Larkspur," Cynthia whispered urgently.

Adele held her breath.

"She wasn't in it," Cynthia added. "There wasn't any sign of a struggle or anything like that. The doors weren't even locked."

"Have they asked around to see if anyone saw her?"

"I don't think so. Not yet."

Adele walked to the window and looked out at the rain. In the parking lot below, two young boys skateboarded between the cars. The thought crossed her mind that one of the cars might be that of the killer. Inside a trunk, Gayle could lie dead or dying.

She shuddered as Cynthia came to stand next to her.

"How did your interview with Tim go?" Cynthia asked. Beyond the question was the question "Do you approve?"

She thought about his short and efficient interrogation. The man had been straightforward yet nonaccusatory. He'd zeroed in on her relationship with Aaron—it had been reported that they'd been seen in the chapel, "intensely engaged." When it came to the issue of Aaron's call to her home, she told him that she had saved the tape of her phone messages, and that she'd been with Douglas Collier that evening. At this piece of information, he'd raised his eyebrows and chuckled in a wait-till-the-boys-down-at-the-station-hear-this way.

He'd wanted a word-for-word account of her preop visit to Chloe, which she gave him freely, but his questions about Helen and Meg brought out a certain closed-mouth protectiveness in her.

Some internal alarm stopped her from telling him any more than the bare basics. She had, however, given him the names of the three nurses in the group photo and asked him to check them out—as a favor to Cynthia's best friend.

"He's very nice, Cynthia." Adele opted to answer the unspoken question. "Maybe you should think about sticking with this one for a while—it might prove to be beneficial to your health."

When she got home from work, she found Douglas Collier, tired and drawn, sitting on her front steps. Inside, Nelson barked, whined, and growled like a dog gone off his trailer hitch. When she tried to calm him, he backed away from her, his hackles going up.

It was, she guessed, a territorial thing. The dog had been the man of the house since Gavin left—another male coming onto his turf was going to make him jealous.

Embarrassed by his macho behavior, Adele locked him into her bedroom with his Mickey Mouse rug and a helping of tabouli and kidney beans. She'd deal with him when he came to his senses.

While she and Douglas talked, she flitted around the kitchen, preparing the meal she'd invited him to share with her. He sat on one of the stools nursing a beer, until she handed him a cutting board, knife, and a half-dozen carrots. Automatically he set to work, slicing the vegetables in a French peasant soup style—exactly what she wanted.

"Do you think Gayle is dead?" she asked.

"I don't kn—" He paused at his task, keeping his eyes on the carrot. "Yes. Yes, I do."

She closed her eyes as the confirmation of what she knew was true sank in. "Why?"

"The woman who owns Max's saw her drive up about five-thirty and get out of her car, dressed in her nurse's uniform. She thought Gayle was going to be her first customer and went in the back to start the coffee. When she didn't hear anyone enter the café, she checked to make sure the door was unlocked. Gayle wasn't anywhere around.

"She'd left her purse under the front seat and the car was unlocked, which meant that she wasn't planning on going very far for very long. Her neighbor told the police she leaves at six-fifteen sharp every morning, and this morning she left early. The owner of Max's said she'd never seen Gayle before." He stopped chopping and studied her.

"Obviously she went there to meet somebody," Adele said. "Someone she knew."

Neither of them said anything for a time. On a whim, she asked, "Don't you have *any* clue as to who might be doing this?"

Her question caused a silent reaction in him.

"Christ on a bike, Douglas—*do you?*"

"No. I mean, I don't know for sure. Right now, I can

only . . . Aw, Adele, forget it." He came close to her and took her by the shoulders. "I need to be very careful. You're going to have to trust me."

She pulled easily out of his grasp. "But you do suspect someone in particular, don't you?"

"Suspicion is my trade, ma'am." He smiled sadly.

Narrowing her eyes, she studied him, shrugged, and handed him two potatoes and an onion, which he placed on the cutting board.

"Do you know who Aaron was seeing?" he asked, deftly slicing into one of the potatoes. "Seems our good doctor had a very good time shortly before he died."

"I think so," she said. "His car was parked in front of Meg Barnes's apartment the night he was killed. I went by there on my way home from dinner with you."

He stared at her. "Did you tell Ritmann that?"

"He didn't ask," she said. "I thought I'd save that one for you."

"Pretty impressive tidbit. What else did you come up with?"

Adele recounted for him her discussions with Nettie, Henry, and Chloe's sister. That she had asked Tim Ritmann to check out the three nurses in the photo, she kept to herself. No sense instigating any professional jealousy.

"Under no circumstances"—he laughed—"tell anyone you're going to see Chloe's sister. It would fry the Sheriff's Department's collective nuts to the grill that you're going to see her before they do."

She added the carrots to the soup stock. "What else did *you* come up with today?"

"Relentless, aren't you?"

"Yup." She did not return his smile.

"Well, I don't think Helen Marval is going to escape interrogation this time. There are witnesses who named her as being the last person near Chloe. She was seen that morning by three nurses hovering over Chloe in surgical day care, and"—he clucked his tongue—"the lady's prints were all over the IV, which the lab confirmed was tampered with. It was almost pure calcium chloride. There are three vials that can't be accounted for missing from Ward Eight stock.

"Marval will try to hold Ritmann at bay for as long as he can, but that isn't going to be long.

"Another interesting point." He took the lid off the pot, slid the potatoes and onion in, and spooned out some broth for a taste. "Roger Wynn paid a visit to Chloe right before Helen got there. He says he was on his routine rounds, but the recovery unit nurses said he rarely if ever stops there.

"I was at the station when he was being questioned. He was so nervous he was sweating bullets and stuttering. If you knew Rog, you'd know that wasn't normal behavior."

He opened his mouth to continue, paused, then changed his mind. "Nah. Never mind."

"Don't do that," Adele warned. "It's one of my Bad Things in Life listings."

"Okay, but I don't want you even *thinking* about this with the light on."

"Tell me!"

"The postmortem on Milton indicates he didn't die right away, and there was evidence of a brief struggle in the car. That translates into the fact that whoever killed Milton would have gotten pretty messy—their clothes would have been soaked with blood.

"I drove home from the office just after one A.M. When I went by the rectory, I noticed Roger had a fire going in the fireplace . . . a big fire. I almost stopped to find out what the hell he was doing."

"Maybe he was cold."

Douglas shook his head. "Roger *never* has fires. The rectory chimney was declared unsafe two years ago and it hasn't been repaired. There isn't even any firewood for it.

"The car has been impounded, of course. The lab is still going over it." He chewed up a bit of carrot and shrugged. "Maybe the infrared will turn up some fibers or hair.

"In any event, I've contacted both PDs of the towns Roger worked in before he was transferred to Marin. They're sending his files."

"How soon?"

"Tomorrow." He moved against her again, slipping his hands around her waist. For a moment she allowed herself to go on the roller-coaster ride of the hormone rush.

His eyes penetrated her with an intensity that caused her to shift her gaze to the floor. She snorted and then laughed loudly.

Douglas looked down.

The paper covers he had used to protect his shoes during the autopsy still covered his feet.

"Oh hell." He laughed, pulling them off. "I'm so damned tired you'd better make sure I don't drown in my soup."

"Don't worry about that," she said. "I can't lose you now."

Adele opened the bedroom door and saw that Nelson was not only on her bed, he was *in* it—under the covers, his Mickey Mouse rug balled up beside his head.

She flicked on the TV. At the noise, Nelson whined and scrambled toward her. A paper scroll dangled from his collar.

Adele gaped, then automatically looked toward the bedroom windows. The one behind the curtain was open, its screen knocked out. The breeze gently moved the drape in a sort of dance.

She closed the window and locked it, then got the Colt and laid it securely in her lap while she unwound the scroll and read it out loud to the dog:

" *'Wife—This is my replacement? A balding, pencil-necked dork isn't your style, Charlie. I could break him in two with one snapback. Do you still remember how to do those? Or, I suppose I could slit his throat.*

" *'You've let the mutt get fat and undisciplined. Guess I can't leave for five minutes that you don't fall apart on me.*

" *'What am I going to do with you? I'll think about that and let you know. In the meantime, better stay on your toes—the worst things happen when you least expect them. Your loving,* very present and accounted for *husband, Gavin Wozniac'* "

An almost forgotten apprehension about being alone at night crawled over her. She turned her gaze to the TV, where images flashed on the screen, one after the other: coroner's deputies carrying Aaron Milton's body on a stretcher, a photo of Gayle, Gayle's abandoned car in Max's parking lot, Ellis Hospital, Harold Marval, a photo of Chloe, Sonya, and John Ganet.

The montage brought the horror home.

EIGHT

IN THE PASSENGER SEAT CHLOE REMAINED
silent, answering none of her questions. Adele was astonished by the weight of the toaster-sized box which
the young mortician's apprentice at Chapel of the Hills
had solemnly placed in her arms. It had to be a good
ten pounds. When the Beast had traveled no more than
three miles, Adele turned onto a tree-lined street and
pulled over.

"Hey Chlo?" She pulled the plastic box onto her lap
and snapped open the flaps. The pale tan ashes were littered with small bits of bone and a pearl-white tooth here
and there. Half buried in the ashes was an engraved brass
tag: "Chloe Anne Sedrick."

She closed the box, placing it carefully on the seat
beside her, and gazed through the grimy windshield. It
was the promise of a beautiful San Francisco day.

"Okay, Chlo," she said, waking up the Beast. "Let's go
put you to rest."

The morning-commute fender bender on the Golden
Gate Bridge caused her to arrive at Lesa Andreason's

home only minutes before they were to leave for Chloe's memorial service.

The shock for which Adele had prepared herself didn't come on sight as she had expected. Other than a few familial resemblances, Lesa didn't look much like her sister. The rest, however, was a study in genetics—the same mannerisms, the same voice, and, Adele imagined, the same laugh, although Lesa wasn't laughing at the moment.

Parking in a deserted rest area off Highway 1, the small group of friends and family, none of whom Adele knew, filed solemnly down the rocky path leading to the ocean. Once assembled on the beach, each of the mourners committed a misdemeanor by throwing a handful of Chloe's ashes into the Pacific.

Adele got through Lesa's my-little-sister eulogy and the frail aunt's rest-with-God-now-darling speech without crying, but when the youngest of the two children dutifully threw his tiny handful and yelled, "Bye-bye, Auntie Chlome! I love you," she sat down on the sand and wept her way through the remaining mourners' goodbyes.

Only when she heard the last mourner's voice did Adele raise her eyes.

The Reverend Roger Wynn, real tears streaming down his face, threw his handful of ashes into the sea and delivered "God's most beautiful child" into the hands of the Lord.

Lesa poised the pot of tea over Adele's cup. Adele glanced at Chloe's cameo ring, satisfied that it had found a rightful and permanent home. "They all worked together at the Women's Clinic," Lesa continued. "That's how Chlo got her job at Ellis. Gayle was clinical coordinator of the abortion clinic when Chlo did her student rotation there. Gayle was so impressed she offered her a job in Ward Eight as soon as she graduated."

"So that's where Dr. Milton knew her from?"

Smiling sadly, Lesa nodded. "He used to tease her about being shy. She'd call twice a day just to tell me the outrageous things he'd say to her in front of the patients."

Adele blew on her tea. "Did you know the man at the memorial service today, the one who went on about the innocent child of God?"

"You mean Roger?" Lesa sighed wearily. "Didn't Chlo ever tell you about her 'fling' with Reverend Wynn?"

Eyes wide, Adele shook her head.

Lesa shrugged. "Yes, I know—they make a strange couple. But what was even stranger was the way he took to her—like gangbusters."

Adele mentally snorted. Nothing strange about a man who had a history of child molestation being interested in a woman of twenty-five and as innocent as a six-year-old girl.

"He was the leader of the Marin Right-to-Life Organization at the time Chlo started her community rotation at the Women's Clinic. I don't think Chlo cared much for him at first—he'd literally tackled her and knocked her down one morning as she walked into the clinic. But you know Chlo—she wouldn't say anything bad about anyone unless she was, well . . ."

"Drugged." Adele finished the sentence, fondly remembering her presurgery speech.

"Exactly. When she didn't react with threats or foul language, he assumed Chlo was some guileless creature who'd been led astray against her will by the pro-choice brutes. He was determined to convert her to the Rush Limbaugh way of thinking.

"I don't think he ever realized just how pro-choice Chlo was." Lesa finally laughed. On sound alone it could have been Chloe sitting next to her. "But Chlo let him bend her ear for hours. He tried every trick in the book to make her quit the clinic.

"Chlo would just smile that sweet smile of hers and the next morning she'd be right back in the clinic. It didn't matter—he fell in love with her anyway. They went out a few times over the course of about two months, then he asked her to marry him, and she told him she was in love with someone else. He never tried to see her after that."

Adele sipped her tea. "Was she? I mean, in love with someone?"

"You didn't know?" It was Lesa's turn to look surprised. "I thought you would have guessed—Chlo has been in love with Dr. Milton since she was nineteen years old."

Adele left off breathing for a second. "Did Aaron know that?"

"God forbid. She would've been mortified."

"Didn't she have other boyfriends?"

Lesa nodded. "She dated a guy in high school, and then there was that awful business with that nurse a couple of years ago, but Chlo really wasn't much for dating or—"

"What awful business?" Adele sat back, fully expecting to hear some mild version of a story about Meg's amorous attentions.

"Oh, that guy on Ward Eight with the Coke bottle glasses—Skip somebody?"

"Skip Muldinardo?" she said, incredulous. "But he's . . . I mean, I believe he's . . ."

"Gay?" Lesa made a face and nodded. "Yeah, that's what Chlo thought too when they started hanging out together—like friends? But apparently he's AC-DC, because he became obsessed with her. You know—looking in her windows, calling fifteen times a day, dropping off gifts every day. It turned into a nightmare. I don't think he meant her harm, but I finally talked her into getting a restraining order. He backed off immediately.

"It upset her for months. She really liked Skip." Lesa hesitated. "But then again, Chlo liked everyone."

No one said anything for a while. Adele could see Lesa had moved to a distant place within herself. After a while, she began to cry.

"None of this seems real," Lesa said finally, when Adele put a comforting arm around her shoulder. "It hasn't hit me yet."

"You're lucky," Adele said, looking past her, out the patio doors to the backyard, where the children were playing in a homemade sandbox bordered by used automobile tires. "Try to put it off for as long as you can."

Radio blaring, the Beast headed north on Highway 280 toward San Francisco at a smooth seventy-two miles per hour. Her mind was going double that.

Skip's reaction to the news of Chloe's death suddenly made sense. She was trying to remember how Chloe had interacted with Skip. All that came to her was that she *hadn't*. Skip and Chloe almost never worked together.

She realized at once that it had been by design. Certainly Chloe had gone to Gayle, who in turn never scheduled the two together.

Skip mostly kept to himself, but when he did speak up, it was usually to complain. She tried to imagine the pale, bespectacled man as an ardent pursuer—one who peeped in women's windows—and couldn't. She *could*, however, picture him looking in men's windows.

"Do you think Chloe ever told Lesa about Meg's infatuation with her?" she asked the imaginary lesbian sitting in the backseat. Adele envisioned her as having a buzz cut, lots of moles on her face, and wearing baggy overalls without a bra. Her left nipple was pierced. On her forearm was a tattoo of a vagina with a little sailor hat perched on top, and two tiny legs. The woman's name was Andie.

Sure. They're sisters, man. The woman made the thumbs-up sign. *Sisters of blood or sisters of the sisterhood. We trust each other, because we are one. Take men—them suckers are lost because they aren't themselves . . .*

The phrase "brutal murders" came from the radio. Adele immediately dismissed the imaginary and pedantic Andie and let up on the gas as if to hear better.

Gayle—or Gayle's body—had not yet been found. Officials were unwilling to share their comments on the case, but if anyone had any information about her whereabouts, please call the Marin County Sheriff's Department at . . .

Disgusted, Adele checked her watch and accidentally swerved into the left lane. If 19th Avenue traffic was light, she would still have time to pick up Nelson, then make it to their appointment.

A series of thoughts, starting with the Colt tucked neatly under her car seat, led her finally to the invention of uniform accessories for the staff of Ellis and Bellevue hospitals. Blade-proof dickies and steel wristbands would sell like hotcakes.

Adele checked the rearview mirror. Nelson was so intensely happy she imagined him grinning, his head filled with nothing more than *I'm with Her I'm with Her I'm with Her I'm with Her* . . .

She cooed, coaching him not to be too hostile while Helen cleaned out his poor damaged chakras. Nelson didn't take much to strangers, let alone weird ones. She hoped he wouldn't create a scene, or worse yet, attack the woman. This thought caused her a moment of anxiety until she realized that Helen would surely know how to handle one antagonistic dog after thirty years of dog breeding.

The Marval house was a spacious split-level, nicely framed by picturesque woods and a barn which was twice the size of the house. According to Helen's directions, it was "set back a tiny bit" from the main road. Helen's "tiny bit" worked out to be a full mile of freshly paved driveway. It was, Adele thought, a shameless display of Harold Marval's reported corruption. The man had been accused more than once of receiving bribes and kickbacks from various land development agencies. A "driveway" like that had to have cost somebody—more than likely the taxpayers—a bundle.

As she stepped out of the car, the cacophony of barking and howling coming from the barn drove Nelson to cower in the backseat, his Mickey Mouse rug clenched firmly in his jaws.

"Get out of the car, Nels. They're your own kind."

Nelson laid his head on his rug and groaned.

Adele was pulling the canine to the edge of the seat when the front door of the house opened. Helen, still in her nursing uniform, stepped out onto the stoop. Pointing at the dog, the woman whistled softly. "Come on, Nelson honey. Let Nana Helen love you up."

Adele barely had time to move out of the way before Nelson dropped his rug and charged from the car into Helen's waiting arms.

Before Adele was allowed entrance to the house, Helen plucked all the roses from the gift bouquet and handed them back to her with the explanation that red roses were the Devil's flower. The calla lilies and fern, she accepted without a thank-you, although she did touch them tenderly, cooing and smiling at them as though they were infants.

Without fanfare, Helen got right down to business, conducting her "inner puppy" exam in the same gruff military manner as she did her nursing. If smelling the insides of Nelson's ears wasn't disgusting enough, Helen touched her tongue to each of his paw pads. For the next thirty minutes she sat with eyes closed in front of the animal, stroking the length of his back to the tip of his tail and talking in a language Adele would later describe to Cynthia as half Lithuanian and half lithium.

Adele had a hard time believing the dog across the room was hers. It was disconcerting enough that Nelson sat mesmerized, staring into Helen's face as though he'd met his Maker, but when he began obeying commands he'd never heard before, such as "Lift your ears" or "Sing," she went in search of a bathroom.

Mostly, Helen kept a meticulously neat and boring house. The bedroom paralleled any other middle-American bedroom, with nicely framed studio pictures of normal-looking family members and cute children (*his* side of the family, no doubt) on the dresser.

Displayed in the kitchen were the usual doggie's-head oven mitts, a "World's Best Cook" (Adele seriously doubted it) spoon holder, and various other doggie bric-a-brac. Strangeness, however, did reside right next to the oven mitts.

Rows of jars containing various powders and dried vegetable matter lined the shelves. And the inside of the refrigerator wasn't at all like other American refrigerators. Old mayonnaise jars filled with brown or green liquids also housed wormlike fungi tied into bunches with wrapping string. In the door were a few limp stalks of what smelled like cannabis packaged suspiciously in plain brown paper.

In the freezer were two jars, a dead mouse in each.

The dinner tray scene from *What Ever Happened to Baby Jane?* unpleasantly skittered into recall, and that decided her right there—if Helen asked her to stay for dinner, she'd just say no.

Leaning over the gleaming set of almond-colored Maytags, Adele got a full view of the freshly painted barn through the laundry room window. Ever so gently, it called to her to come and check it out.

Checking first on her dog and Helen, she found them both deep in trance. Nelson's front right paw was placed

squarely in the middle of Helen's forehead, and Helen's
left hand rested lightly between the dog's ears. It seemed
to her they were both chanting.

Adele took a mental photograph of the scene for future
comedic monologues, then made an announcement, sotto
voce, that if no one minded, she was going to slip out to
the barn to visit the kennel.

No one seemed to *have* a mind, let alone mind anything she might do.

To use the word "barn" to describe the interior of the
building was a misnomer. "Ethan Allen showroom" was
a more accurate choice. Converted to luxury living quarters for humans and dogs alike, over a third of the downstairs expanse had been turned into gourmet kitchen,
dining area, and living room. Upstairs was a bedroom
loft, complete with full bathroom, outside Jacuzzi, sitting
room, library, and office.

Adele bit her bottom lip as she rapidly checked out
each nook and cranny of the kitchen. Cupboards and
refrigerator teemed with foods one might associate with
an overweight middle-aged couple—marshmallow crème
and chocolate syrup, cream, Cheez Whiz, eggs, coffee,
bacon, blocks of sweet butter, pork chops and steaks
marked "Us" (as opposed to "Them"?), double-fudge
ice cream, chips, frozen pizzas, cookies, Cool Whip, and
Breakfast Pop-Tarts.

The other two thirds of the downstairs barn had gone
to the dogs, so to speak. The tiled floors of each of the
dog quarters were freely littered with cushions, doggie
beds, warm blankets, doggie toys, and chew bones. The
first of the four kennels housed golden retrievers of

various ages and colors; next were the Bouviers, then Labs, and finally boxers. In all, she counted twenty-six healthy, happy, flea- and odor-free dogs and puppies.

Nelson would froth at the mouth with envy.

During her adoration of the two black Labrador puppies, she noticed a room off to the side that appeared to have once been a tack room. The door was open and the light was on. Drifting inside, she found a mini canine Price Club; every kind of dog supply imaginable lined the shelves floor to ceiling.

She made note of the brands of food and pet vitamins, and was about to check for prices when she spied a small makeshift door behind the stack of doggie beds still in their plastic wrappings.

Pushing the beds aside, she flipped the light switch at the side of the door and pulled the handle.

The door's spring hinges creaked like in a horror movie. Inside, the old-fashioned cloakroom smelled of patchouli incense and candle wax. The odor momentarily transported her to the seventies—a time when the San Francisco Bay Area was permeated with the same smell.

Above the coat hooks, a row of white candles—looking like so many soldiers at attention—ran the length of a narrow wooden shelf. Crucifixes and crystals hung suspended from the ceiling, casting eerie shadows over the pentagrams and other symbols painted on the walls. Barbie and Ken dolls, most of which were dressed in handmade scrub uniforms, hung two and three deep from coat hooks by their necks. On the shelf above, a Ken doll in a gray suit had a miniature toy snake one might expect to find in a Cracker Jack box fused to his hand. Under him lay a Barbie unclothed from the waist down. Her plastic neck had been cut almost through.

Adele began to perspire, her mind going the Stephen King–esque route. "Helen is crazy as a loon," she said, uttering a wild giggle. She looked again at the maimed nurse dolls.

"It's the Richard Speck Memorial room," she said to Barbie.

And then some, sister! said Barbie and Ken in unison.

The table in the far corner held a triangle configuration made from six number twelve scalpels. Written along the outside edges of the form were the words "The New World Cometh!" Inside the triangle was a ball of hairs all shades and thicknesses, and several scraps of fabric. On closer inspection, she recognized the scraps to be from various scrub uniforms worn at both Ellis and Bellevue. Around the perimeter of the table, several miniature doll beds had been placed alongside miniature teacups holding what looked like congealed clots of blood.

Her eyes traveled up the wall and came to rest on the same group photo that hung in Gayle's office. Except in this copy, Chloe's face had been colored over with gold crayon, and Gayle's eyes had been poked out. The faces of Aaron Milton, Sonya, and John Ganet had all been blacked out with Magic Marker.

An atmospheric pressure change, as when a door opens in a well-sealed house, coincided with an immediate eruption of barking. In panic (God only knew what Helen would do if she caught her in the Richard Speck Memorial), she backed out of the room and switched off the light. Grabbing a package of pig ears, she leapt for the door.

Helen and Nelson stood on the other side, suspicion heavy in their eyes.

"Oh, hi guys." She waved the bag of ears, praying the smell of wax hadn't clung to her. "Thought I'd give the dogs some treats. They're all so sweet I—"

Helen snatched the bag away from her. "They have to work for their treats." She walked to the kitchen, Nelson following close behind. "They've been taught not to take anything from strangers."

Nelson turned and tossed her an accusing glance. *Yeah,* Adele imagined him saying, *what kind of a mother are you, anyway?*

"Nelson's a very terrified little boy," Helen said, squirting an orange ribbon of Cheez Whiz on the remaining section of her blueberry Pop-Tart. She sounded much like a child psychologist giving bad news to the worried parents.

The very terrified little boy sat near Helen, the model of dog perfection—he was not whining, begging, biting himself, scratching, or passing gas.

He's been drugged, Adele thought, taking another sip of the best decaffeinated coffee she'd tasted in years. The Pop-Tart with Cheez Whiz wasn't so bad either, although she'd deny under oath that she ever let such a thing touch her mouth.

"You need to spend more quality time with this child," Helen continued, carefully cutting her second tart in two with kitchen scissors. "Stop treating him every time he breathes—that's about *your* guilt, not his accomplishments. Nelson wants discipline—it shows him you care."

Helen gave a forlorn sigh. "He's badly sleep deprived, Adele."

Adele snorted into her napkin, covering it with a pretend sneeze.

"Go ahead and laugh." Helen's expression grew sullen. "I don't think you'll find it at *all* funny when you come home one day to find this animal dead from worry and exhaustion."

"I'm sorry," Adele said, actually feeling some remorse. "I believe you. And you're right—I don't discipline him, nor do I spend enough time with him. What you said about the treats is true too.

"I'm not so sure about the sleep deprivation, though. I mean, what could possibly . . ."

Helen put down her Pop-Tart and went for Adele's hand, forcing it around the crucifix she wore on a heavy silver chain. The faraway look fell over her eyes like a velvet theater curtain.

"It's the evil thing the animal's worried about, Adele. It's close to you, sizing you up. This dog can smell Its stench."

Helen looked over her shoulder—toward the supply room. There were tears in her eyes. "Please don't be next. You're the only one left I like. I need you for the New World, Adele."

In spite of herself, Adele felt a lump of pity rise in her throat. "I'm not going to let anything bad happen, Helen, but you have to trust me enough to tell me who It is."

Helen drew back, shaking her head. "Oh no no no no . . ."

"Okay, okay, okay. Can you just tell me if this person is a man or a woman?"

"Both," Helen muttered finally, with a resigned slump of her shoulders. "It likes to fuck everybody."

She ignored Helen's last statement; the one thing she'd learned in psych rotation was that once crazy people fixated on sex, it was difficult to change the subject. Adele moved her hand out of the woman's bosom to her shoulder—which she squeezed reassuringly.

"It likes to hurt people," Helen said flatly. "Dogs and children too."

"Did It hurt Sonya and Dr. Ganet?"

Helen again gave a slow sideways glance in the direction of the Richard Speck Memorial and nodded.

Adele waited. Getting concrete from a fluff weaver was going to be hard. "Is It like an imaginary spirit, or is It a real person?"

No answer.

"Is It a living person, Helen?" Adele had to pause to remove the impatience from her voice. "I know you know what I'm asking. Is this It thing someone who eats pizza and has a phone number?"

There was an imperceptible nod. Yes.

Adele sat back in her chair, trying to stay calm. "You saw It kill Sonya, didn't you?"

Helen crooked a finger, beckoning Adele closer.

Adele moved her chair until they were knee to knee.

"She made sex noises," Helen mouthed—all that was audible was the working of her lips and tongue. "She was quiet for a while and then it started up again. Except then It killed her for good. It didn't want any more of her. It got sick of her sex." Helen drew away, eyes huge and luminous.

"Did It know you were there?"

More nodding. "It knows where I am at all times. That's why I've got to be careful. You too, Adele." She put both arms around her, clamping so tight Adele thought she was going to suffocate. "No one can know besides us."

This time Adele did the nodding. The woman's strength was awesome. "Did you see It kill the others?" she croaked. "Were you there?"

Helen's breathing grew rapid. Throwing her hands over her ears, she rocked back and forth. Released from her grip, Adele took in a deep breath and repeated her questions with urgency.

"Stop it!" Helen hissed. She ceased rocking, and clenched her fists. "I hate you when you keep asking and asking and asking and ASKING!" She ripped at a clump of red hair and stood. She'd begun to yell, which set the dogs off barking.

"You think you're the smart-set nurses, you and Cynthia, but you're all stupid! I'm so sick of everybody asking questions all the time. Harold, Adele, Gayle. You all want me to tell so then I'll be dead too. You all want me dead! You WANT ME DEAD!"

Seeing that the woman's frenzy was headed toward the fringes beyond her control, Adele instantly dropped her head to the table and pretended to cry. The shock value ploy worked. Helen went silent, watching her in utter amazement.

"Don't be mad at me," Adele sobbed, peering through the slit between her fingers. "I'm scared. If I knew who It was, you and I could take Its power away. We could stop It from—"

"Shhhh." Helen stroked her head, the same way she might have petted one of her dogs. "When the time is right," she whispered. As her last word died, Helen pulled Adele out of the chair and pushed her to her knees.

Kneeling down beside her, Helen joined their hands. "We must meditate on the spirits of the New World," she said in a clear voice. "They'll protect us . . . for now."

Nelson, perfectly behaved until that moment, scratched, whined, and passed some particularly noxious gas.

By the time Nelson arrived home, he had normalized only enough to sniff at the half-chewed piece of plywood and bark—as if to say, *What bad dog dared to do this?!* He did, however, revert to begging for treats.

"You've gotta work for it, remember?" Adele stretched her left hamstring and Achilles tendon. "You're going to escort me on my run and keep me safe from attackers."

Nelson executed a long and complicated series of whines.

"Tough," she said, hitting the answering machine's replay button. She switched to her right hamstring. "If I can do it, so can you. Just do it. Remember?"

Nelson's reply whine was interrupted by Cynthia's recorded message. Did she want to go with her and Timmy to the Tuck and Patti concert at the Great American Music Hall? Call back before seven if so.

Adele checked her watch and switched to toe gluteal stretches, breathing through the lump of disappointment which surfaced. She loved Tuck and Patti. Then again, she hated being the third wheel . . . especially when it was with Cynthia and one of her new boys. There was so much syrup and blatant lust she always ended up feeling like a diabetic nun.

It was just as well—she had to work the next morning,

and Cynthia didn't; that meant not getting home much before—

A moderately heavy breather and a hang-up came next.

Another breathing and hang-up, which caught the beginning of a man whispering "Fuck." She rewound and played it over six times before she gave up trying to figure out who it was.

Call four was from Cynthia again, giving her one last chance to go to the concert, and then in a teasing voice asking if she was not answering because Douglas was there.

She rolled her eyes and switched to squats and back-stretch mode.

Five was a third breathing and hang-up. In the background a car honked.

Cynthia calling again. Giggling. Last last chance.

Seventh call was Douglas Collier, announcing himself as "Douglas Collier here"—as if she wasn't going to know which Douglas would be calling her. It was anal retentiveness at its working best. Would she like to meet him tomorrow for dinner? He was eager to speak with her. There was new information.

Adele fitted the pepper spray canister under the left strap of her jog bra, leashed Nelson, set her watch, and ran.

It was too dark to run Baltimore Canyon or the Mount Tam trails. *That* lesson had been permanently learned the time she'd ended up lost on Mount Tam at two o'clock one icy, rainy January morning after going on a late-evening run. The Magnolia Avenue route was for the most part lit and populated.

After Nelson's mandatory stop at the Silver Peso, Larkspur's one and only biker bar, for his rough petting and extra-large cornmeal biscuit, she set her pace at an easy eight-minute mile and tuned out.

Blissed, Nelson sniffed and ran, easily keeping up with Her. The abundance of smells and sounds kept him in hyperalert: dogs calling to him, things slithering in the grass, pee (human, dog, cat, and fox), bad food, deer and jackrabbit pellets, the hum of the phone wires, and the human behind them who was matching Her pace exactly.

Halfway through the only section of the route that was isolated, the human behind Her moved closer until Nelson caught the scent of pursuit and anger.

He broke the pace and whined his warning noise, pulling on the leash. Adele mentally closed the door on the Richard Speck Memorial and returned her mind to the present.

Nelson cried and barked twice.

Instinctively, she sped up and fine-tuned her ears. Twenty years of running lonely trails and back streets had provided her with an acute sense of everything near her. The person behind her sped up and gained on her. It was a man, and he was most certainly a runner . . . a strong runner at that.

Despite the adrenaline rush, the idea of conducting a survey as to what percentage of murderers were physically fit came to mind.

Calculating the man's rate and stride against her own and the remaining distance to safety, she gave up on the idea of beating him. Slowing, she readied the canister, stopped dead, twisted around, delivered an abortion of a defense kick, stumbled backward over Nelson, and fell on her ass screaming at the top of her lungs.

In direct response to Her barking, Nelson could not stop himself from going into barking delirium. The male human was making that grating sound humans made when they were happy, but Nelson sensed more aggression than happy.

"Nelson, settle!" He yelled in the voice that instantly triggered memories of puppy training: rolled-up newspaper against the nose, a spray bottle of ice water, and the worst—the hackle-raising sound of a can half full of pennies.

Nelson stopped barking, and like a child who has to choose a parent in a divorce, looked from Him to Her, then sat down next to Her.

While Nelson whined, Gavin stood over her laughing. The green beret was tucked military-style into the band of his running shorts. The combat knife was in its leg sheath under his sock.

"You jerk!" Adele was on her feet and in his face. "What is wrong with you? What do you think you're trying to prove?"

In one rapid, faster-than-the-eye-can-see move, Gavin had her in a hold, her arms and legs immobilized. He was no longer laughing.

She forced her body to go limp in order to lessen the pressure of his grasp. He was still physically faster and stronger—like a machine, she thought. His same dull expression, however, reminded her she still held the mental edge. "Release me, Gavin. I'm not in training anymore. I'm not married to you anymore either, and this is an extremely politically incorrect assault."

He cocked his head, as if she had spoken too fast. "Politically incorrect?" he snorted lamely. "How about emotionally incorrect?"

"What are you talking about, Gavin?"

"You didn't even give me one extra day over the legal limit before you filed for a divorce, Charlie." He released her, giving her a slight push toward the dog. "Didn't you even miss me?"

"Miss you?" she said, rubbing her wrists. "You mean after you worried everybody sick by disappearing? After your mother and I got hauled into the morgue to view every unidentified male body that floated up out of San Francisco Bay or was discovered in some men's toilet in the park?"

She sighed, shaking her head. "Miss you? I wanted to wring your neck with my bare hands. You think I enjoyed watching your mother lose her mind with grief? Did you think—"

She stopped and regarded the man with disgust. With Gavin it was always best just to cut to the chase. "Oh for Christ's sake, Gavin, you knew the marriage was over even before you pulled your Disappearing Fruitcake number on us. It was only a matter of time before we filed."

Adele glared at the smooth baby face, wondering what she'd ever seen in him. Intellectually, he ranked closer to Nelson than human, and it sure hadn't been sexual—she'd never found him particularly physically appealing.

Their sex from the beginning had been the worst combination going: unsatisfying and rare.

"It's over, Gavin. Notify the police and then go see your mother. You almost killed her with this stunt."

"Don't you even want to know why I left or what I've been doing?"

Gavin's childlike question brought out in her a momentary flush of pity, which immediately turned to apathy. "No, Gavin, I don't. Stop spying on me. I'm *not* your wife. Get out of my area code. Move on, get a life—just get out of mine."

Nelson whined and pushed his cold nose into her leg.

"And my dog's."

"*Your* dog?" Gavin narrowed his eyes. "I'm the one who insisted we get the goddamned animal in the first place, Adele. You didn't even want him in the fucking house, but you don't remember that, do you, O humane nurse?"

"I remember." She placed a hand on Nelson's head and smiled into his dark brown eyes. "I also remember staying up all night every time he got sick, and carrying him out of that ridiculous survival camp you set up for us in Death Valley the night he cut his artery on somebody's broken beer bottle. You called me hysterical for wanting to take him to a vet—the vet who said he would have bled to death if I hadn't brought him in."

Adele adjusted the tension on her shoelaces. "I remember a lot of things, Gavin, and that's exactly why I want you out of my life."

The man removed the knife from its sheath and casually began cleaning under his fingernails. "Resign yourself, Charlie—I'm not going to let you slide out of this.

"You've gotten harder." He chuckled. "And you're a self-righteous bitch. But you're *my* bitch. I didn't spend all that time and energy training you so you could go off with some ball-less dickhead."

Knowing it was useless to argue, Adele turned to run. Before she went an inch, he blocked her and raised the knife to her neck. A sudden terror went through her; what did she really know about this man now? Anything could have happened to him in two years. Maybe his Green Beret years had caught up with him, or maybe he was having post-traumatic stress breakdown. After all, he *had* killed people in Nam. Once, she'd witnessed him on a training course go from white-bread Gavin Wozniac of New Hope, Wisconsin, to a crazed killer who had to be pulled screaming off a dummy after he decapitated and then stabbed it 107 times.

"Don't fuck with my head, Charlie," he demanded, growing more intense. "I missed you—every town or city I passed through, I'd find my way to a hospital just to see the nurses come out in their scrub dresses. I'd remember all the times I waited for you after work and we walked home." Gavin slid an arm around her waist and pulled her close. He let his hands rove over her body, lingering over the taut muscles of her buttocks. "I need you, Charlie. I need to talk to you the way we used to. I've got to tell you things—things about me and what's happened. You can't leave me now. I won't let you go."

She studied his eyes for a second. The image of Nicole Brown Simpson lying in a pool of her own blood was all the incentive she needed to deliver a bilateral elbow jab to his pecs and solar plexus.

"I'm going on my run now, Gavin," she said firmly. "Go see your mother and then a psychiatrist. Leave me alone." She gave Nelson the signal to go ahead of her, then ran a few steps backward, away from him. Intuition at full volume, she turned and looked up into the night sky, waiting.

Behind her Gavin laughed. "Sure, Charlie. Don't hold your breath, though. I'll get what I came back for."

NINE

WARD 8 WAS HEAVY INTO CHAOS BY 9:00 A.M. Adele assessed the general mood as one of poorly re-pressed panic and not so repressed fear. Other than adopting the buddy system for almost every activity, most of the staff had taken to whistling tunes as a method of always being *accounted* for.

Marsha Geekas, General Nurse Supervisor, was a size 18 Cindy Crawford. A nervous, high-strung woman, she spoke in a staccato rhythm, her body in constant motion.

"You'll do it then?" she asked, crossing one arm over the top of her breasts and biting her thumbnail. "You'll act as temporary ward supervisor until Gayle gets back?"

"Gayle isn't coming back," Adele said dryly. She was fond of Marsha. Unlike the other nursing supervisors, she was pro-nurse, pro-human, pro-compassion. She was known to lie and cajole when it came to protecting the nurses and the patients—a rarity in the time of man-aged care.

"All I'm agreeing to is working a few more days a month and playing charge nurse when I'm here. I'm not doing any paperwork except scheduling. I strongly sug-gest, however, that you post Gayle's position as available immediately. I'm sure there are plenty of full-time people who'd love to score Gayle's job."

Marsha opened her mouth and eyes, then scrunched them down into a grimace as she shifted her weight from foot to foot. "Ah, negative. Nobody . . ." The woman tossed her head and fumbled with her bangs. ". . . in their right mind . . ." She crossed her other arm over her bust and bit that thumb. ". . . would want her job." Marsha pushed back the hair from her face and rubbed her neck. "Especially since . . ." She hitched up her scrub pants and fiddled with her stethoscope.

Adele was getting tired.

". . . the nurse manager of Ward Eight . . ." She scratched her head and pulled on the other side of her neck. ". . . will be managing Wards Seven . . ." She wiped away some infinitesimally small bit of eye gunge, rubbed her lower back. ". . . and Four as of the first of next month."

Maybe Gayle didn't get abducted, Adele thought. Maybe she'd simply taken the opportunity to disappear. "When the hell did *that* get decided, and did Gayle know about it?"

Marsha did not pause in her toe raises. "Gayle's the one who suggested the restructure—sold the board of directors on it in less than five minutes. It saves them about a hundred thousand dollars a year. Of course, it costs three full-time nurses their jobs, but . . ." She searched her pocket and came up with a Kleenex with which she proceeded to clean the insides of her nares as if she were polishing the silver. Lowering her voice, the supervisor spoke in a whisper. "They'll be downsizing the wards within six months, which means about seventy percent of the nurses will be getting their pink slips anyway."

Adele's face hardened momentarily. "Christ on a bike in hell. Three nurses are out on the streets living in their cars with their kids while managed care makes the hospital corporate bosses and the insurance companies richer. Meanwhile, nurses get replaced with untrained people off the street who don't know shit. Hooray for the new wave of health care—it's a killer."

"Gayle didn't seem to care," Marsha said. "The administration put her in charge of who gets canned on those three wards." The zoftig nurse handed Adele the patient acuity sheets. "I was at the meeting. You could actually see her head getting bigger. Power and control—it's like a drug."

The comment depressed Adele. "Yeah." She sighed. "Like they say—the higher a monkey climbs, the better the view of its ugly side."

Behind the supervisor, a group of needy people were assembling, waiting for Adele to solve their problems. Meg, recently liberated from an hour-long interview with Detective Cini, appeared angry and pale—she'd want to go home sick again. Skip wore his usual dour expression—he'd want to continue to complain about his patient load in hopes of getting it lightened. Mrs. Deputy, Helen's postop hysterectomy patient, had scores of the usual complaints about the food and Helen. Dr. Wollenberg, Meg's prostate cancer guy, wanted a private room. Mrs. O'Day wanted to grill her about what happened to her little Susie, and Detective Cini wanted to rake her over the coals.

On the rancorous side of an expanding bad mood, she

found herself no longer mourning the details of Gayle's fate. It seemed almost inconceivable that Gayle would have sold them down the river for control, or even a hefty raise in salary. She hoped Gayle's career decision had been made with a thought to saving as many good nurses as possible.

But—Adele shrugged—one never knew anyone until they'd walked in their shoes for a week. And Gayle Mueller's shoes were, at that moment, one place she most definitely did not want to be.

"What the fuck did you tell them, Monsarrat?" Meg sobbed, standing over her. "You've ruined me." The peculiar timbre of her voice, with its modulations of audacity and anger, fascinated Adele.

"Oh, don't be so dramatic, Megan. I didn't ruin you. I never told—"

Meg's neck veins visibly distended with her anger. "What were you doing sneaking around my apartment at eleven o'clock at night? You some kind of freak or something? What, do you get off on watching me . . ."

"Meg, I wasn't spying on you," she defended evenly. "I stopped that night to talk to you about Chloe. I was getting out of the car when I saw you walk by the window with someone, so I left. I didn't tell the police about seeing Aaron's car at your apartment. I told someone else who I thought I could trust, and that person told one of the detectives. I wanted to talk to you when I brought the soup over, but we didn't get a chance to be alone." She paused. "Look, I'm really sorry. I didn't mean for that piece of information to get passed on."

Meg sat down, looking a lot older than thirty-two. "I

didn't kill Aaron," she said. Her expression was one of contempt and challenge. "He was the first . . . man . . . I loved him. I could never have hurt him like that."

Surprised by the admission, Adele said nothing, hoping her silence would encourage Meg to keep talking.

"I know what you think."

"Okay, tell me what I think."

"You think I killed them." A smile flickered at one corner of her mouth. It had a chilling effect. "Sonya hurt me, but I didn't kill her or that slimeball she was screwing either. If you really wanted, you could make a case that I killed Chloe too."

Meg picked up a letter opener and began tracing concentric circles into Gayle's desk blotter. "Let me help you plug into some reality, Monsarrat—sweet Miss Chloe wasn't as virginal as everybody thinks. She came on to *me* at the beginning. Your 'innocent lamb' pursued me harder than a dyke in heat." Meg stabbed the blotter and laughed contemptuously. "She *wanted* it."

"She showed up at my apartment one night with a bottle of wine. One glass later, the little lightweight began asking questions that were making me blush. 'How did it feel? How did girls do it?' The typical curious first-timer shit.

"By the second glass, she was pleading with me to show her.

"I begged off. She pushed. I gave in.

"After that she treated me like I was invisible dogshit. She wouldn't even look at me—colder than the grave, man."

Adele hid her shock by freezing her face in impassiveness, the way Kitch had taught her. The unappealing image of Chloe and Meg locked together in the throes of physical passion, however, threatened to stick on her mental screen forever.

"That's how I first got involved with Aaron. Chloe was madly in love with him, and I wanted to hurt her as much as she hurt me—so I went after him." Meg laid down the letter opener. "I didn't expect to fall for the guy, but hey, weirder shit than that has happened."

Bored now with the drama, Meg walked to the door. "I didn't kill anybody, so fuck off."

"Wait." Adele blocked her path. "You were the last person to see Aaron alive. He was upset about Chloe. He must have said *some*thing to you."

Meg gave her a look and reached for the door. Her surliness tempted Adele to grab her by the scrub collar and slap her. Instead she forced herself to be calm. "Please, Meg, I'm trying to find some thread—anything that'll maybe give us a clue as to who's doing this."

"What is this? The Nancy Drew tryouts? Leave it to the cops, Monsarrat."

"I can't—they aren't going fast enough. Come on, Meg. You say you've got nothing to hide, so help me out."

"Why should I? What do I get out of it?"

"It might save your life or somebody else's. Aaron might have said or done something that you think is insignificant, but it could be pivotal. Don't you want them to find the person who killed him? Humor me on this, please?"

Meg shifted on her feet impatiently, the defiance never leaving her face. She swore under her breath and finally spoke reluctantly—angrily, as if against her will.

"Aaron was tweaked about something other than Chloe. I mean, he was upset because the coroner had asked a shitload of questions about who ordered the IV and if anything had happened during surgery that didn't get reported, but there was something else that really had him going. When I asked him what it was, he wouldn't tell me.

"That pissed me off royally, so I told him to go home. He didn't want to go, so he told me that Helen had called him and gone off about how she was going to kill him because he'd helped some evil spirit kill Chloe.

"It was a lie. I mean, she's threatened him before, and he's always laughed it off. As far as Aaron was concerned, Helen was a joke."

"What do you think was bothering him, then?"

The woman shrugged. "Fuck, I don't know. He wouldn't tell me. We got into an argument over it and I threw him out."

Meg started to say something else, choked it back, and opened the door.

Adele wanted to ask about the damp clothes hanging in her bathroom and the black shoes caked with mud, but knew it would set off an explosion of fury.

"I want to go home sick."

Adele shook her head. "No way. Bite the bullet like the rest of us. Concentrate on taking good care of your patients."

"Fuck the patients."

"Oh. Well then, if I were you, Meg, I'd concentrate on finding another job that didn't involve caregiving."

* * *

Harold Marval hated the man hanging over his desk. He'd smelled trouble the first time he laid eyes on the bastard a year before. Detective Sergeant Timothy Ritmann—the Irish-Jew snitch. Another hero who thought he could waltz into the department and take over. Did the sons of bitches at the DA's office really think his contacts wouldn't tell him about a mole planted in his own department?

Tim Ritmann repeated his question about interrogating Helen. Harold noted that the sappy smile on the man's face didn't change. That and the way he moved, like a man getting it regular. He was probably slamming one of the nurses at the hospital.

Nurses—sluts or nuts, every goddamned one of them.

The thought made Marval want to laugh. Instead he scowled and covered his mouth. "I'll run the questioning myself, with you and Cini present of course, when the old lady's feeling better. The shock of the Sedrick girl's death really got to her. You know how women can get, around the change of life. She . . ."

For a brief instant, he had the urge to say his wife had slipped off her tracks thirty years ago and might need a spot of electroshock therapy or a lobotomy before she could be questioned. He thought about the look that would produce on the pretty boy's face and bit down on his tongue to stifle the laughter.

". . . isn't thinking straight. A few days and she'll be up for it."

"A few days and you'll have her drugged and rehearsed, you mean?"

Tim Ritmann's icy blue stare made him uneasy.

"You're a cocksucker, Ritmann. Back off, or you might have an unfortunate accident in the line of duty."

The detective laughed. "Hey, that's pretty funny, Sheriff. You should audition for Comedy Central."

Ritmann seated himself on the corner of the desk. "Let me tell you something. While you've been out schmoozing with your rich politician buddies who got you elected, I've made some friends here. Seems nobody much likes you, Marval. Your own men call you 'Kickback King.' Far as I can tell, you haven't got one loyal man in the entire department. But see, I do.

"Anything happens to me, and you'll be at the bottom of the bay wearing a cement necklace. It'll be a race between the department and the DA's office to see who gets the pleasure of wasting you first.

"Meanwhile, we've got two hospital administrators and every nurse, doctor, and citizen in this and the surrounding three counties breathing down our necks. This time, *you* aren't going to be dictating anything about how and when your wife gets questioned."

Marval stood partway up, pointing to the door. "Get the fuck out of here before I—"

"Before you what?" The redhead put his hands on the desk and leaned over until he was a few inches from Marval's face. His smile faded. "You aren't that stupid, now are you, Marval?

"I'm not done, so put your fat ass back in that chair."

The detective didn't so much as blink until Marval sat down.

"*We* aren't going to question your wife. *I'm* going to question the notorious Mrs. Marval in the presence of

Detectives Cini and Chernin and anybody else I choose, including the fucking janitor.

"You . . ." Ritmann relaxed. ". . . are restricted. I'm not taking the chance of somebody saying there was collusion going on. And if you try and fuck with me on this, I promise you that there's going to be a leak to the DA's office about how the sheriff is protecting his loony wife, and then the DA will have to leak that to the press, and—oops—all the rats in the Marval Support Pack are gonna jump ship before you can say 'I'm fucked.'

"After that, you can kiss your six-figure salary and those kickbacks goodbye—along with your sorry ass."

For a brief instant Harold wondered how fast the cocksucker would change his tune if he knew that with one nod from him, any number of people would rub him out like a fly. He had connections. Big connections.

He shifted in his seat and scowled. Son of a bitch had him screw-fucked on that one too. This was Mr. Good Cop Mole from the DA's office. His reputation for being tough and honest—hats off to the flag, apple pie, and all the other happy horseshit—was becoming legend throughout the county.

There would be no question who set him up, and like the bastard said, he'd be put out of the game before he could even *think* "I'm fucked." He smiled tentatively, his watery brown eyes searching the face in front of his. "You've got a lot to learn, Ritmann." He didn't know exactly what he meant by that, but he wasn't going to knuckle under in front of the bastard, eyes or no eyes.

Marval picked up a pen and tapped it, glad that the steadiness had returned to his voice. "I'm still in charge of this department. I've dealt with Eagle Scouts like you before. You can push all the weight around that you want, and I'm still gonna be in charge in the end."

He turned his attention to a letter lying on his desk and picked it up, hoping Ritmann would go away. The letter was a personal note from the mayor of San Francisco, asking for financial support for the upcoming San Francisco Lesbian and Gay Pride Parade. He busily scribbled random phrases in the margins—"Suck my dick" being among them.

Still the bastard didn't leave. He could feel his eyes waiting for him. He didn't really want to, but he finally looked up. The eyes were there to meet his.

"In charge of parking meters, Marval." Ritmann smiled. "We'll get you elected as head meter maid."

Adele flushed, pulled up her scrub pants, exited the stall, and screamed. Waiting outside with arms folded, looking for all the world like Barney Fife, was Detective Cini.

"Jesus Christ on a bicycle in hell! Isn't this a little desperate, Cini, following a woman into the can?"

The detective jerked his head and reddened. "You've put me off long enough. I need some information."

Adele washed her hands. "Okay, go ahead. Ask."

The detective hesitated, muddled by her sudden compliance. "I need you to come to my desk."

"Nope. Either you ask me what you need to know now, or you can wait for another day or two until I have time to talk."

"I want you at my desk," he insisted. "Now."

"Can't." She pulled a large red brush from her purse

and began brushing out the midmorning tangles. The task seemed to fascinate him.

"I'm in charge of the ward and I've got patients. Unless you subpoena me or put me under arrest, you can't bother me while I'm working. I'm willing to talk to you right here, right now. If I were you, I'd take advantage of that."

Arms still folded, the man watched her brush the thick black hair, then, as if a spell were broken, snapped angrily, "Now you listen to me, lady, the only reason I don't charge you with interfering with this investigation is out of respect for Doc Collier."

She stopped brushing and clucked her tongue in annoyance. The rate at which the hospital/law enforcement grapevine passed gossip around was astounding. Even so, this particular bit of misinformation seemed to have worked to her advantage.

"I'm placing a hold on you. That means you don't go out of my sight without telling me where you're going. The second you're off duty, you're mine. You disappear, and there'll be a warrant for your arrest. Understood?"

Adele didn't answer immediately; she was carefully applying lipstick and lip gloss, an act which again took the detective's attention.

"I said, do you understand, Ms. Monsarrat?" He wished she was not so attractive; it would make it easier to be a hardass.

"Oh, I got it, Cini." She straightened her scrub top, gave her bra a slight adjustment, and ambled past him. "I'm a held woman, one step away from arrest."

*   *   *

Mrs. Daley's lungs sounded like a bubbling fountain. Adele injected the forty milligrams of Lasix into her intravenous line and put the bedpan under her. Adjusting the woman's oxygen to five liters per minute, she gave another two milligrams of morphine and put the call bell in her clammy hand. "Call me the second you urinate, okay?"

Mrs. Daley, too tired to answer, closed her eyes.

Next.

Mr. Salucci's transfer to radiology for his chest X ray went fairly well, with the exception of the discovery of a syringe full of insulin hidden among the sheets. Where it came from, or how it got in his sheets in the first place, was a mystery never to be answered. Adele guessed the old upstart had found the syringe and drawn it up himself. God only knew who he had planned on injecting.

Skip approached her a total of fourteen times to report each of his various crises: "Mrs. DeJacqua wants a private room." "Mrs. Smith is refusing her medications." "Megan is being hostile." "Mr. Turnbull's IV is infiltrated." "Miss Stone is having pain again." "Cynthia is daydreaming all *over* the place." . . .

His fifteenth gripe was the best. Sitting down between her and Tina, he dramatically ran his fingers through his hair. "I can't take this!" he moaned. "Every time I turn the corner, I expect to see Freddy Krueger with a scalpel. I swear I'm being watched, and I keep hearing strange noises outside my apartment door at night. Shit, isn't anybody else creeped out? I mean, I'm a guy, and I'm jumping out of my skin."

Adele almost said, "How can we be *sure* you're a

guy?" but didn't. Instead she thought of him with bin-oculars, stalking Chloe outside her apartment. It made her feel immensely sorry for him.

"I'm as flipped as you are, Skip. I just refuse to think about it."

Tell us another one, Adele.

"I've gotten so I don't want to go home." He pushed up the thick, black-rimmed glasses and absentmindedly pulled at some chest hairs which had strayed over the collar of his scrub top.

"So don't go home." Tina mimicked his whimpery voice.

"There's safety in numbers," Adele said more kindly. "Stay with friends."

"Have you got room at your house?" He asked the question directly, without a smile.

Adele employed laughter to keep from answering. It gave her time to evaluate the seriousness of his question. She decided he was what she and Cynthia called "kidding on the natch"—acting as though he was only kidding, but not really.

She continued to laugh until she was saved by the bell—Mrs. Daley's call bell signaling it was time for the First Emptying.

"What are you doing after work?"

"Going to jail. Why?" Adele edged her voice with incipient coldness. The silence from the other end of the phone told her Douglas Collier got the message.

"I see. Detective Cini has been to see you?"

"Oh yes. He followed me into the bathroom . . . waited for me outside the stall. He's put a hold on me."

"Why? Were you difficult? Did you refuse to—"

"Me? Difficult? No, of course not. I told him I'd talk with him after work, although . . ." Adele searched for the right amount of sarcasm. ". . . I don't know why he needs to talk to me. I think he got most of what I know from you already."

More silence. If he said he didn't know what she meant, she planned on hanging up.

"Ritmann needed that information, Adele," Douglas said, defensively righteous.

It was just like a cornered anal-retentive to get defensive, she thought. "Information that I would have told him, eventually."

"He needed to know sooner than you were going to tell him."

"Do me a favor, Dougie. The next time I tell you something—anything—talk to me first before you decide to broadcast it to the world at large, okay?"

"Okay. Promise."

There was silence, then his unsure, nine-year-old's voice: "Are you angry with me?"

"Not as much angry as feeling betrayed and reconsidering how much I can trust you or even like you."

There was a pause, then: "It's okay, Adele, you can tell me the whole truth. Don't hold back."

She laughed, glad for the broken tension.

"I'm really sorry," he said, finally. "Ritmann and I were going over the Milton investigation, and he was going on about where Milton had been, and I had to tell him. I didn't even think about whether you'd mind or not. I tried to call you last night to fill you in, but you weren't home, and you never returned my call."

"Okay, okay. So, did you want to see me after work?"

"Oh yes. Come down to my office after your interview with Cini. I want to hear about what happened yesterday, and I've got something I think you'll find interesting."

"Okay, but do me a favor?"

"Depends."

She smiled quietly to herself. His anal-retentive reserve was beginning to grow on her. "If I'm not down there by six, call the police. Cini's body can be found in the supply closet, and I'll be out of town."

He did not disappoint her. At two minutes after six he walked into the supply closet and broke up the battle of wills. Monsarrat versus Cini.

Much to the detective's frustration, the nurse had matched him question for question, and given only generic answers. In the end, he realized he'd been wheedled out of more information than he'd received. Instinct told him the woman was sharper than he thought. He guessed she knew more about the case than he did. It amused him and made him wonder—she had all the earmarks of a cop, fiercely holding on to what she knew and getting as much as possible without letting on.

Douglas nodded ever so slightly at the detective. "I'd like to claim my dinner date now, Mr. Cini. I'm hungry. I won't let her skip town, I promise."

His promptness and the ease with which he handled the situation elevated him a full ten points on Adele's Suitable Male Companion scale.

Enrico Cini rubbed his neck. "Heck, it wouldn't matter if she did bolt. She hasn't given me one straight answer yet." He stood and shook hands with Douglas. "Get her outta here, Doc, before my ulcer starts to bleed and I have to have her as my nurse."

They were halfway to the closet door when the detective found it necessary to call after her, "All kidding aside, Ms. Monsarrat, I'm not done with you yet, so don't go too far."

It was, they remarked to each other in the stairwell, like something right out of the movies.

He'd sent out for Chinese, ordering all meatless dishes and requesting no MSG. He spread a plastic tablecloth over his office desk, but provided linen napkins with the Ellis Hospital logo imprinted along the edges. The sake, he heated on one of the lab's Bunsen burners and served in ceramic specimen cups. The rhubarb-strawberry pie, he said he'd made himself—a fact which astounded and pleased her. When she insisted he tell her how he knew it was her favorite, he would only give a Mona Lisa smile and hum.

Despite the three cups of sake, she did not tell him about her run-in with Gavin or her confrontation with Meg. The story of her visit with Helen and the Richard Speck Memorial was still to be told; she was waiting for the sake to loosen him up.

"So, Roger went to the memorial service," he said, pouring them their fourth cups of sake. "How clever."

"Clever?"

He sipped from his cup, burned his lips, and pulled two huge manila envelopes from his briefcase, which she guessed he'd probably kept pressed protectively between his feet the whole time they'd been eating. He probably had trouble with constipation, she thought.

Each envelope produced a dark blue file. Carefully brushing away several runaway grains of steamed rice from the dissection counter, he placed them side by side in front of her.

"These are copies of Roger Wynn's police records from Oregon," he said. His hand lingered over the tops of the two folders, as if he were still debating about whether or not to let her see them.

Adele pulled one out from under his hand and opened it. Two mug shots of a younger, unkempt Roger Wynn stared at her from the page. The man looked decidedly sinister, but then again, she supposed even Margaret Thatcher would look that way in a mug shot. There was probably some special camera lens the police used to make all those who were booked appear diabolic and guilty as hell.

Douglas sipped his sake as he watched her, his eyes constantly darting from her face to the folders. "His records go back to 1986 for a total of ten arrests for aggravated assaults against healthcare personnel who worked or volunteered at abortion clinics, twenty-one unlawful-assembly charges in or around women's clinics where abortions were known to be performed, and three for brandishing a knife."

She slowly turned the pages. At the top of each page of each report was an official-looking letterhead with the logo of the police department and the date of occurrence. Under that was a brief description of the incident followed by details of interrogations and interviews of various witnesses, experts, or victims.

Each new report had a separate mug shot. Adele noticed

that in every one, the chaplain wore the same sinister, though vacant, how-the-hell-did-I-get-here? stare. She wondered if he and the photographer developed a sort of bond after a while. She picked up the second folder with the more recently dated reports and skimmed through them.

"There's a six-page confidential report from a psychiatrist which says Wynn's history of violence directed toward medical personnel developed soon after an incident in which he watched his mother die in an emergency waiting room from complications of a self-administered abortion. It seems the nurses and doctors misjudged the seriousness of her condition, although she registered with the complaint she felt—quote—'a little dizzy.' Nothing about the abortion, nothing about bleeding.

"Unaware that the woman was bleeding to death, they tended to other patients first."

He got up and slowly paced the room, still sipping the hot rice wine. "Roger saw another psychiatrist a couple of weeks later," he said hesitantly. "The reports from those sessions present a personality profile of a very twisted man. They're chilling."

Adele turned the pages faster, searching. "I'd like to read those. Where are they?"

"I have them at home. Stayed up until two this morning going over them, then couldn't sleep. I kept thinking of things he's done and said in the past that now make sense in a sick kind of way."

He sat down, drank off the rest of his sake, and poured himself another full cup. "I thought I knew the man."

From his expression, Adele thought he was going to

cry. She touched his shoulder. "Does Tim Ritmann have both of those evaluations?"

"Only the first psychiatric evaluation. I briefly mentioned that I had more information on Wynn, but I want to finish going over the second report before I talk to him."

She reached for her cup as Douglas slipped an arm around her waist. Pulling her to him, he kissed her deeply.

Her initial gut reaction was to push him away, but Adele stopped herself, partially out of curiosity about what kind of kisser he was (fair to middling) and whether or not he could ring her chimes (not so much as a clang).

Ashamed of herself, she wrestled with the notion of prostituting herself a bit—as long as he was lusting after her, she could be assured of receiving information. She gave him a full minute—until he began breathing hard— then pulled away, hiding her face against his shoulder. "This isn't a good idea, Douglas," she said, curbing the desire to spit and wipe her mouth.

He came back with the usual "Why?" and the rest of the conversation read like a soap opera script:

(The bleeding organ music begins in the background.)
SHE: *(turning away from him, obviously upset)* I don't want to get romantically involved right now.
HE: Why not? I like you, Adele. It's been a long time since I've felt this way about someone.
SHE: *(turning back and smiling sadly)* I like you too, Douglas, but it's too soon for this. I have to know you better. *(drops eyes and stammers)* I've . . . I've made some mistakes before, and I don't want to make any

with *(raising eyes to his)* you. I . . . I . . . don't want to be hurt again.
(The background music changes to soft violins.)

She wished there would be a commercial break soon.

HE: I would never hurt you, Adele. I've been looking for someone like you for a very long time. Everything about you is perfect.

SHE: *(smiling beatifically, a woman adored)* Oh Douglas, I'm not perfect. *(pulling away and laughing)* Let's wait for a while and see where time takes us.

She wanted to gag and blow chunks. Instead she downed the full cup of sake and preoccupied herself with cracking open a fortune cookie.

HE: *(smiling, resigned, and bashfully giving her hand a final squeeze)* Okay, whatever the lady says.

"Listen to this," she said, squinting to read the fortune; she was still vain enough to refuse to wear bifocals. " 'You will meet many mysterious and interesting people.'

"Which," Adele said, pouring the remains of the sake into his cup, "reminds me of my adventures with Mrs. Marval and Richard Speck yesterday."

Douglas raised his eyebrows and his cup at the same time. "Do tell," he said. "I'm as anxious to hear about that as I am to see where time is going to take us."

TEN

ADELE PULLED INTO HER DRIVEWAY AND parked behind the white Toyota Camry. No one appeared to be in the car, nor did she see Detective Ritmann on the front steps. For the second time in two hours, instant blind anger struck her like a hot flash.

The first fury had come during her sojourn through Whole Foods, where only the most self-actualized of the coolest of the cool of wealthy yuppies were allowed to grocery-shop. The haughty attitudes of both patrons and clerks (*How* dare *you shop in my presence?*) had her blood pressure soaring before she even got out of the produce section. That, plus the added injury of shameless price-gouging, which cost her one-third of her weekly salary for four bags of basic groceries, sent her cursing into the evening.

And now this! Cynthia's latest squeeze or not, Ritmann had some kind of gonads to be poking around uninvited. Wrestling with her notoriously obese purse and two of the four bags of groceries, she slammed the Beast's door hard enough to send the automobile's nonfunctional CB antenna wobbling on its sturdy magnetic stand.

Immediately, two heads popped up in the front seat of the Toyota.

Through the back window, Adele glimpsed Tim Ritmann and Cynthia struggling to pull on various articles of clothing. Shaking her head, she walked to the house and let herself in feeling slightly jealous, amused, and suddenly very fond of the couple.

By the time they showed themselves at the front door, sheepish as caught thieves, she had loved up and fed Nelson, changed into running garb, poured three glasses of sparkling water with lime twists, and was making a crushed-garlic-and-cream-cheese-on-cracker, prerun, carboload snack known as Natasha's Breath.

Every so often she would invite nonrunners to run with her. She enjoyed observing how different people handled the process. Tim Ritmann, more than likely still stinging with embarrassment over having been caught with his pants down, accepted the invitation with pure Irish-Jewish machismo. Full of false enthusiasm, he fetched his gym bag from the car.

Cynthia, a moderately strong runner herself, was accustomed to being made a partner in this particular one of Adele's addictions.

She was more excited, however, at the prospect of running her new man into the ground.

No Steve Prefontaine, Detective Ritmann started getting into trouble at the top of the second mile. Cynthia, ignoring the runner's first commandment—"Start off like a turtle and finish like a hare"—seemed bent on staying at least eight feet ahead of him. If he showed any evidence of closing the gap, Cynthia was sure to widen it by speeding up.

Nelson, happy to have lots of humans to play with, would wander, disappear, and then reappear. Each time, he would give them a look as if to say, *Sure, you only got two legs, but boy, are you guys* slow!

Adele brought them to, then kept them at, a relaxed nine-minute-mile pace by telling them about Chloe's memorial and a few of the lighter, funnier highlights of Nelson's visit with Helen. Even though it made them lose their breathing rhythm from laughing, it took their minds off the numerous small pains of running.

"I've got Mrs. Marval set up tomorrow for an interview at her house at two," Tim wheezed. "The sheriff has to be at the groundbreaking ceremonies for the new safety building around the same time. Hopefully we'll be able to get somewhere with her without the old fart hanging over us."

Adele snorted. "Good luck, buddy. She'll never talk to you in a million years."

"She'd better," Tim said with a stubborn jerk of his head. "Because if she resists, we're going to bring her in and book her on suspicion, and that could get reeeeal ugly."

They ran along the College of Marin soccer field in silence except for the clinking of Nelson's tags, the measured breathing of Adele and Cynthia, and the wheezes-turned-gasps of Detective Ritmann.

"It's actually the reason we stopped by tonight," Tim said finally. "Cynthia tells me you handle Mrs. Marval pretty well. Got any tips on how to approach her?"

"Try to think like a crazy person. Play to her moods, and whatever you do, try not to rile her." Adele thought for a minute. "Then again, I suppose you could rile her and see what happens, but I think she'd do her drop-the-curtain routine on you."

"What's that?"

"Oh, she kind of goes away mentally. She zones out when she doesn't want to deal with anything she finds unpleasant—or too close to reality."

"Does she zone out enough to have brutally murdered four people and not even know she'd done it?"

"I don't know. Sometimes I think she's crazy enough to do anything, and then sometimes I get the feeling she wouldn't hurt a fly on purpose." To herself she added, *unless it bit her.*

They crossed College Avenue against the light and headed toward Ross Commons. A bus with only one passenger—a bespectacled Chinese girl reading a book—roared past them. Adele turned her face away and held her breath until she was sure she would not inhale the exhaust fumes.

"Have you guys turned up anything on Roger Wynn?" she asked.

Cynthia turned around to exchange a secret glance with Tim. "Tell her about the car," Cynthia prompted.

"Jesus, Cynthia," Tim muttered under his breath. "You weren't supposed to repeat that." He gave Adele a sheepish look.

"Small mind, big mouth," Adele said. She hoped he might spill a little information. Granted, she wasn't sharing his bed, but she knew that cops sometimes leaked details as bait for larger fish.

"The owner of Max's Cafe called me this morning," he said. "She remembered seeing the tail end of a 'boxy,'

light-colored car pulling out of the parking lot a few minutes after the Mueller woman pulled in."

"Guess who drives a light beige 2002 BMW?" Cynthia
piped up cheerily.

Adele dodged a fire hydrant situated in the center of
the sidewalk.

"Roger Wynn. So why aren't you guys raking him over
the coals? Shit, all you've got to do is look at his police
records to see that the guy is—"

Tim shot her a look and Adele bit her tongue. The last
thing she needed was to have the cops on Douglas's back
for giving out information.

"What I mean is, everybody knows he was accused of
molesting a couple of kids up in Coos Bay and that he
was arrested for antiabortion demonstrations.

"There must be police records on him or maybe a
psychiatric evaluation on file with the local authorities?
Didn't your department contact them?"

She left her hook dangling in the night air.

"We're checking it out," Tim said cautiously. "I talked
to the shrink involved in the child molestation case."

"And?"

The detective laughed. "Uh-uhn. Confidential police
information, Ms. Monsarrat. Loose lips sink ships."

Frustrated, Adele playfully punched his arm and called
him a rat. They'd run another half-mile before his breathing began to even out.

"About those nurses in the health fair photo?" He kept
his voice low.

"Ayuhn?"

"Detective Chernin made the same connection with the
Women's Clinic when Ganet and Martin were hit, but

Marval pooh-poohed it as too much of a long shot, so we were forced to drop the idea. As soon as Milton got pithed, even the Old Man had to agree there was a link."

Cynthia giggled in spite of herself. "Oh God, Tim. Pithed? That's gross."

"The department was aware of the Ducke girl's disappearance. I mean, you'd have to be a moron not to link the Ganet-Martin murders, since they all came right around the same time.

"We tried tracing the girl, but there wasn't so much as a whiff of a lead. Boyfriend was the prime suspect until the East Bay department found out he had an airtight alibi.

"Kathy Kern moved to Missouri with her three kids. I talked to her this morning. She says she hasn't had any kind of problems. The other nurse . . ." He hesitated, searching for a name.

"Clairissa Rittenhouse?" Adele volunteered.

"Yeah. I talked to her mother last night. Miss Rittenhouse also figured out the connection between the Women's Clinic, Gina Ducke's disappearance, and the murders. She split for Sacramento pronto.

"Three months ago, her apartment was broken into, and she started getting phone hang-ups. Four weeks ago, someone chased her around the underground parking lot of her building, but she outran them. Packed up two days later and split. The only person who knows where she is is her mother, and she wouldn't even tell *me* where that might be."

"Smart girl," Adele said.

They came to the Natalie Coffin Greene Park entrance sign: OPEN FROM SUNRISE TO SUNSET. Adele suggested they turn around and head back. Without hesitation, Tim did a sharp turnaround. He was limping slightly.

"So, what's the consensus?" Adele asked. "I mean, do you think this is a pro-life radical or what?"

Tim didn't answer right away, although Adele wasn't sure if that was because he was winded or he was thinking. "Whoever it is, they're pretty damned clever," he said finally. "Cini, Chernin, and I have been brainstorming the shit out of this case. Even on our days off, we're talking about it."

"You can say that again," said Cynthia. "He left his seat at the concert six times to call Cini or Chernin and run something by them. The people sitting next to us were ready to kill him."

"Until I let them see my shoulder holster." Tim smiled.

None of them spoke for a while, and Adele guessed the subject was closed. She was tempted to push for more, but decided that what she needed from Tim would eventually come through Cynthia or Douglas.

Then, as if he'd read her mind, he said, "So, I hear you and Doug Collier are doing the horizontal bebop routine."

"We are *not*!" Adele glared at Cynthia.

Nelson felt Her sudden change in temper and barked.

By the light of the streetlamp, Adele saw Cynthia zigzag ahead, pretending to choke herself with her own two hands.

"Don't listen to her," Adele said, miffed not for the first time that Cynthia was so eager to hook her up with some man that she would fabricate and exaggerate the merest hint of romantic possibilities into major relationships. "Cynthia thinks if I'm even in the same room with a man, I'm engaged to him."

* * *

Adele finished the monologue detailing all her encounters with Detective Cini, Helen, and Douglas, and glanced beyond Cynthia's chartreuse face masque at the clock: 2:00 A.M.

The half-eaten lime Popsicle froze her bottom lip as she held it steady while shaving the remaining "throwback" ape hair from her large toe. She was glad she didn't have to work in the morning.

Tim, completely hobbled by the end of the run, had begun to show classic signs of what they as women called the Wounded Male Pride/Crybaby in Crisis syndrome. The man's grimaces, jaw clenching, and deep, funereal statements of "It isn't funny!" and "Hey! This really hurts!" sent Cynthia into an eye-rolling nurse's impatience. Dealing with sick mates not being the nurse's strong suit, she'd sent him packing within minutes and invited herself to stay overnight.

Adele and Cynthia's overnights were infrequent enough to be an event both of them savored. It gave them the time they needed to talk through layers of concerns and emotions until they got to the heart. It was the place where each woman felt comfortable, knowing she would not be attacked or judged by the other.

That Cynthia had to work the next morning concerned neither of them, since the younger woman claimed—and proved on a regular basis—that she could thrive on less than four or five hours of sleep every twenty-four.

Nelson, hoping for a low-flying treat of dropped Popsicle, sat on his Mickey Mouse rug between the two women, staring hard at the food in hand.

"He put his bare tongue in your mouth?" Cynthia said,

making a face, thus cracking her mud masque. From expression alone, one might have assumed that she had taken a swallow of straight lemon juice.

"His *bare* tongue? You mean as opposed to wearing a tongue condom?"

Cynthia giggled. "He's such a nerd. I mean, he's so . . ."

"Anal?" Adele finished the sentence.

"Yeah." Cynthia looked away and fidgeted with the Popsicle stick she'd deposited in the ashtray. "Did I ever tell you about when I was eight and we lived on a military base in Germany?"

Cynthia didn't wait for Adele to respond. "There weren't any kids my age to play with, and we couldn't have pets, so I was superbored. Out of desperation I'd dig up earthworms, take them home, give them each names and then a warm bath in the sink.

"After they were all nice and clean, I'd put them in my bed and sew outfits for them and dress them up . . ." Cynthia paused. ". . . like dolls."

Torn between howling laughter, pity, and incredulity, Adele's face went through a variety of expressions. "You dressed them . . . you mean like in tiny tube dresses?"

"Oh yes." Cynthia smiled sadly. "And tiny, one-legged pants and shirts for the guys."

"How'd you know which was which?"

"I could just tell." Cynthia sucked her Popsicle stick clean and balanced it on Nelson's nose.

The intimate knowing that came out of fifteen years of friendship tipped Adele off that Cynthia had purposely changed the subject. True, the story about dressing worms was one she hadn't heard before, but it had come out of left field (or garden) just as the subject of Douglas Collier arose.

"What aren't you telling me, Cyn?"

"Nothin'."

"Come on, Cyn. Who do you think you're lying to here?"

"You'll hate me."

"I already hate you."

Cynthia smiled. "You'll lecture."

"Probably." A thought suddenly crossed Adele's mind. She stopped sucking on her own bare wooden stick. "Oh shit. You're pregnant and don't know who the father is."

"Psssh no!"

"Well, what then?"

"I slept with Douglas Collier when I was in mort training." She gave Adele a sheepish sideways glance, as though she expected her to haul off and hit her with a two-by-four.

Adele chuckled. "Oh yeah? Well, how was he?"

"Um, kind of nerdy, actually."

"Nerdy."

"Yeah. I mean, he wasn't the worst screw I'd ever had, but afterward, he scrubbed his prunes down with bacteriostatic soap and a nail brush."

"Scrubbed his . . ."

"His balls. He went into this whole explanation about women's bacteria and testicular growth and how a woman's bacteria could travel up the man's urethra and damage sperm. I thought it was so rude, I said I just wanted to get laid, not have a biology lesson about the hidden sinister properties of a woman's crotch."

She picked up the jumbo-size emery board they'd been

using on their toenails and ran it over a scab on her knee. "Which is probably why he never asked for another date."

"Well, you know how those medical-science types are, Cyn—at the first mention of sex or erectile tissue, they have a tendency to turn the whole lovemaking process into an *Animal Kingdom/National Geographic* special. Why didn't you tell me this before?"

Cynthia wagged her head and picked up one of Nelson's paws. She began giving the dog a manicure.

Nelson looked to Adele. His expression was one of infinite patience, but his message was clear: *She's your friend, babe—can't you control her?*

"You're sweet on the boy," Cynthia answered. "I didn't know if you'd get upset over something like that or not."

"Once and for all, I am not sweet on Douglas Collier. He's a nice guy, but I don't have a heart-on for him. Something's missing. He's too anal, too intense, and still too hung up on the ex-wife. He gets a facial tic at the very mention of her."

"Yeah, well, Dana was as weird as Doug." Cynthia sighed. "He brushed his balls—she pierced her nipples and shaved her head on occasion. They were the perfect San Francisco couple with the usual kinky practices— bondage, various fruits, and ice cubes."

Cynthia traded Nelson's left paw for his right, going at his nails with zeal. "There's something else too," she said, without looking up.

Adele, studying her face in a triple magnifying mirror, picked off dried pieces of her rose-colored masque. "Ayuhn?"

"Tim would kill me. I promised on my future children's lives that I wouldn't tell you."

"Tim will never know, Cyn. Besides, you hate kids."

"True." Cynthia scratched her chin, causing several chunks of chartreuse clay to fall into her lap. "Except, he didn't really give me any details at all, so . . ."

"Cynthia, if you don't tell me what he said, I'll tell him about that time at the Castro Street Halloween parade when you—"

"Okay, okay. All he said was that Meg had been in trouble a few years ago. Her family went to the police and demanded she be charged with murder."

Adele jerked forward, dropping the mirror. "What?!"

"Honest. The DA's office charged her with second-degree murder."

"Who'd she kill?"

"Get this." Cynthia stopped filing, to Nelson's relief. "Her mother."

She waited until Adele closed her mouth before she continued. "Her mom was some wealthy socialite muck-a-muck who was related to one of the old San Fran money families like the Spreckles or the Hearsts. That's all he told me."

"And you didn't demand details?" Adele asked, irritated. "Christ on a bike, Cyn, you're slipping."

"Wait! There *is* something else." Reproachfully, Cynthia pointed the emery at Adele. "I asked if there was a will involved. He said the old lady divided the estate between Meg and her brother. Fifteen million dollars."

"Holy Christ on a Harley in hell."

"The case was dismissed because of insufficient evidence."

"How was she supposed to have killed her mother?"

"That was the part he wouldn't tell me."

"Oh come on, you mean to tell me you couldn't have cajoled him a little?"

Cynthia rolled her eyes. "I tried. He still wouldn't tell me. What do you expect—he's a cop. Collier will know the case—ask him."

Silently, they both picked at dried facial mud for a while.

"Why the hell does she work?" Adele asked, her mind indulging in numerous fantasies about what she'd do with seven and a half million dollars.

"Work?" said Cynthia. "Shit, why would anybody with seven and a half million—not including the interest it must be earning—live in a disgusting hole over a bar?"

Answerless, they returned to mining their facial incrustations, their minds wandering elsewhere.

"Hey, all you shoppers!" Cynthia suddenly shouted after the manner of a television barker. "Come on down to Ward Eight and do your freak-shopping now! We got 'em all—nymphomaniacs, stalkers, psychos, control freaks, a complete line of the sexually disoriented. Heck, folks, we even got murderers and pedophiles.

"So, for a complete selection of oddities, freaks, and other human aberrations, come into Ellis Hospital today or call one eight hundred weirdos . . . that number again is one eight hundred weirdos."

"Hand me that phone, Mabel," Adele said, laughing. "I want to order me up one of them there sexually discombobulated pedophiles."

Cynthia waved a hand. "Shit, Dolores, all you gotta do to get one of them is go to church."

Together, they laughed themselves into a run for the bathroom.

Helen, kneeling before the Table of Common Spirit, flicked her fingers to keep the evil spirits away. Three new figures had been prepared and added to the Avenue of Death Lights: a witch doll with its mouth gouged out, sitting on a tiny broom; a fat candle in the shape of an old country doctor with both hands melted off; and an angel doll complete with wings of white satin.

Before her, several of the tiny monsters played ring-around-the-rosy inside the Triangle of Swords. She wished they would go to their beds. Not that they had been very effective in scaring Adele away.

Adele had snooped. It had enraged her to the point of considering immediate execution, but when It didn't come to hurt her or the dogs, that meant Adele wasn't a tattletale. That meant she might be able to trust her.

Helen crossed herself and reached for the angel princess, kissing the tip of each wing. "Oh my baby girl, I'm so sorry. You know I didn't want to execute you, don't you? When It says it's time, my power is frozen, baby. There isn't any sassing back. You know that now, don't you, Princess?"

The kennel phone, outfitted with an amplified-volume ringer, pierced the peace of the New World Room. The noise, coupled with the lateness of the hour, brought forth a swell of fury. Ripping at the doll's head and hurling it to the floor, Helen bolted from the room as though she were on fire.

She'd told Harold she was not to be disturbed for any reason. If it was him ringing to say he wanted another ice-cream sandwich from the freezer, she would take the meat cleaver, march to the main house, and cut off his g.d. head.

She pulled the phone to her ear with such violence she smashed herself in the mouth. "I TOLD you, Harold, NOT to—"

Someone said her name.

She screamed and dropped the handset. Immediately, she saw what she had done and snatched it up from the floor. After a gasp for air, she closed her eyes and answered in the smallest voice she could make.

Unable to bring herself to orgasm, Megan Barnes took her hand off herself and stared at the wall next to the mattress. An oblong gouge had been made in the plaster under a long, curved crack. It looked like an eye. It had been made by one of her lovers the day Clinton signed the Defense of Marriage Act. She couldn't remember the woman's name—not that it mattered anymore.

Her eyes moved around the room. Everywhere she looked, all she saw was Aaron's face: Aaron's face smiling. Aaron's face as he moved inside her. Aaron's face when he told her she was a pearl of a girl. Aaron's face when she told him to get out.

It was the hurt behind the eyes that stopped her—like those of a child who had been punished unfairly. Tears slid down her temples and fell into her ears. How could he not have known it was only a small tantrum and that more than anything she wanted him to hold her and love her until it passed?

She punched the mattress with her fist and turned her face into the pillow. Again, she had been unwilling to give in or let up. She didn't *want* to say the things she said, but she couldn't stop herself. She'd never been able to stop the rage once it started. All the people who had ever loved her had eventually left her because of it.

Such a willful child! her mother used to complain to her friends while reporting all the Terrible Temper Megan stories. She liked to shock new acquaintances with her favorite, about how, as a child of three, her daughter had attacked her seven-day-old brother with a pair of scissors for having soiled his diaper. *Peter, show our guests where Terrible Temper Megan stabbed you.*

They'd laughed at her mother's Terrible Temper Megan stories, never really believing them . . . at least not until the last one—the one they told in whispers among themselves.

Monsarrat knew about her temper. As good as she'd gotten about hiding it, Monsarrat could see through her.

She heard her own voice, cool and in control, say she hadn't killed anyone. Had Monsarrat seen the lie? Did she know about all the people she'd hurt? Had she heard the worst Terrible Temper Megan story?

Oh Mommy, why did you make me so mad? It was the anger, Mommy. It was that Terrible Temper Megan . . .

She crawled off the mattress and opened one of the tiny drawers of the Japanese tansu. The red capsules would make her sleep. They would make her not care about Aaron or Chloe or any of the others.

Swallowing two of the pills dry, she dressed in black to prepare for her nightly pilgrimage. Tonight she would sleep there in the cold, and wait to be delivered to the only kind of peace she knew.

ELEVEN

AT 3:30 A.M. THE PHONE RANG TWICE AND stopped. Adele, in the first stage of hard sleep, registered the disturbance with a snort and a hypnic jerk which connected with Cynthia's left calf muscle. Her subconscious cleverly incorporated the noise into a dream about Mr. Salucci urinating on his call bell and causing it to short out.

At 4:42 A.M. the phone rang four times and was picked up by the answering machine, which recorded a dial tone. At this time, both Adele and her guest realized the phone had rung, were too tired to care, and returned to REM sleep.

With the 6:07 A.M. call and hang-up, Adele groaned and turned over. Gayle could take her extra shift and— At 6:08, heart pounding and fully awake, she ran for the answering machine, which was empty of messages save for one lone dial tone.

Fourteen minutes and no further calls later, Cynthia rushed through her morning toilet, while Adele threw together granola with walnuts, bananas, and apples. It was her California Special—full of flakes, nuts, and fruits.

Also for Cynthia's benefit, she brewed up a pot of super-caffeinated coffee-mud.

"Who the hell was on the horn all night?" Cynthia poured her coffee over her granola, swallowed a mouthful, and nodded her approval at the flavor mix while Adele gagged.

"Nursing office probably," Adele said, although she was worried it might have been Douglas with news of another murder, or—almost as bad—Gavin.

"I'll warn you, Cyn—the ward is minimally staffed today. You're marked to be charge. Scheduled on with you are Abby, Skip, Meg—who will more than likely call in sick—and Nancy Morales, who's an LVN. They'll probably pull the rest of the staff from housekeeping and food service."

"Great," Cynthia said dryly, rising from the table. Adele's scrub pants, the legs of which she had rolled into cuffs, still hung over her shoes and draped onto the floor. "Should be as much fun as a mass burial. Want to go in for me?"

"I'd rather be one of the buried, but give everyone my regards."

"And what will the lady of leisure possibly do to fill her empty and meaningless day?"

Adele held up her foot, already clad in racing shoes. "Go to church."

"Ah." Cynthia kissed her friend and Nelson farewell and headed toward the sound of Tim Ritmann's car horn announcing his chauffeurial presence in the driveway. "While you're up there, say one for me and the other fools, would you?"

Adele did not answer the phone when it rang at 6:58,

nor did she stop to worry about all the things she wanted or had to accomplish in the course of the day. The only thing that mattered at the moment was restoring herself to full mental and spiritual well-being, which meant getting to her church as fast as she could.

A born agnotheist, Adele found herself stuck in the unpopular niche between quasi-believing in some nebulous higher power and severely disbelieving in any and all religions and their various absurd heroes, rituals, and icons.

She had come to know her peace in the spiritual world soon after arriving at a retreat in a remote area of an Arizona desert. She was told in no uncertain terms that the only way she would be allowed to remain at the retreat was to profess a belief in a power greater than herself. Having already taken the time off work and paid the non-refundable admission price for a week's stay, she knew she'd have to come up with something, even if it was Santa Claus.

She took a long walk out into the desert to think about it. After four miles of silence and heat, as she watched the sun rise out of the endless sand, the truth of the matter hit her like a ton of cactus. Her higher power was, and had always been, the earth—Mother Nature herself. At the most painful moments in her life, she had, without fail, turned to a bird in flight, a tree, a river, a glimpse of sky, for solace.

Six miles from the sound of her ringing phone, Adele ran past Phoenix Lake and worked her way up Shaver Grade to Five Corners. She toe-ran Little Motherfucker Hill, sprinted to the top of Horse Ring Bluff, and then to

Yolanda Trail, which skirted the back side of Mount Tamalpais.

Coming to a curve which jutted out over a valley of redwoods and green meadows, she stopped. In the distance was the endless expanse of the sea. Taking in a deep breath, Adele stretched out her arms as if to embrace it all.

Her church—the earth—was in session.

It was 10:03 A.M. when she allowed herself to answer the ceaselessly ringing phone for the first time.

"Hello?"

There was a hiss at the other end of the line, like the ballast release on a hot-air balloon, and then a human's tortured wail. In the background was the din of frantically barking dogs.

"Helen?" Adele asked cautiously. "Is that you?"

Lying beside her on the couch, Nelson stopped chewing his rug. His ears twitched.

"It's angry," Helen whimpered, breathing rapidly. "It doesn't want me to talk to those deputies. It said if I told, It's going to kill me. It's going to get me and my dogs. I don't know what to do. What's going to happen to the New World, Adele? What'll I do? Oh no no no no . . ."

"Stop, Helen," Adele said firmly. "Calm down and tell me what happened."

"You're the only one left who can save me. It's going to eliminate me. I'm so scared, Adele. Please, please, please, you've got to come now." Helen cupped the mouthpiece. "I can't talk on the phone. It listens to everything I say and think."

Adele pushed a fussing Nelson off her arm and sat up.

"Tell me exactly what this person said to you, Helen. How did—"

Helen's whimpering at once changed into low, hoarse respirations. What Adele heard next caused her to go to gooseflesh.

"Youuuu taaaalk toooo themmmmmm and I'llll killlll youuuu, youuuu psychoooooooo BITCHHHHH."

Helen moaned. "It said it just like that, Adele. I don't know what to do. You have to come now. I'll hide until you get here, and then I promise I'll tell you what you asked about before. I'll take you to the New World and show you everything. I'll tell you . . . I'll tell you and nobody else. Just you."

"What will you tell me, Helen?"

"I'll tell what I know."

"Tell me right now."

"It'll hear."

"No It won't." Adele had to fight to keep her voice steady. "I have a special scanning machine that tells me when others are listening. We're clear now. I want to know who It is."

"It takes different forms," she answered, then hurriedly added, "We've got to get to the New World and then I'll tell you."

"Give me Its initials."

"I saw It with Sonya on the day of the snake. It was around Chloe too, the morning she went away. It made an evil sign over me and said what I had to do." Adele could hear Helen shudder, her voice breaking. "Please come, Adele. I've got to hide now—in case."

"All right, but you've got to tell me the name of one of the human forms It takes. If you don't, I won't—"

A sound like the phone being smashed into a wall and then the screaming caused her to pull the receiver away from her ear. Nelson barked furiously. She made out a few isolated words and phrases: "Stop . . . Kill you . . . Mad . . . G.d. . . . Tell . . . New World . . ." The rest was a ball of tangled shrieks and the beating of the phone. Adele waited for the noise to be replaced with the harsh sound of panting.

"Come *now*." Helen gulped air. "Or I'll be dead and you won't ever ever know."

Adele thought the woman might have a point there. "Okay, you go hide, and I'll get there as soon as I can. I'll honk my horn three times so you'll know it's me. We'll go in my car somewhere where we'll be safe and then you can—"

Helen's whimpering escalated again. "No. No. No. I can't leave my dogs. It'll kill my dogs. It wants blood to drink. I've seen It drink blood before. Don't you understand? It *needs* to kill."

The woman's words chilled her; she didn't think Helen could have come up with blood-drinking on her own. "Okay, then I'll stay with you. I won't let you be alone. It can't kill us both at the same time." She hesitated. "Can It?"

"Come right now," Helen said a final time, and hung up.

The handset wasn't fully in the base charger when the phone rang again. Adele lifted it to her ear. "I said I'll be out as soon as I can. Just give me a few minutes to get Nelson fed and—"

There was no hysterical Helen—not a sound from the other end of the line.

"Oops, sorry. Hello?"

"Charlie, I need to see you."

Adele's mouth tightened. "No. Go away, Gavin, we're over. Did you see your mother yet?"

"Yeah, I saw my mother. She gave me a lot warmer reception than you did. Who are you in such a rush to get to, Adele? That needle-dicked bugfucker you had over the other night?"

"None of your business. Look Gavin, I'm not even remotely interested in—"

"Charlie, please." Gavin was begging, and she knew it had to be killing him. "I need to see you. There's something I've got to talk to you about."

She opened her mouth to protest but he cut her off.

"It's about me. I've got to tell you something that I haven't told anyone. You're the only one I can tell."

Adele snickered in spite of her contempt. "Christ on a bicycle, what the hell is going on around here? Suddenly I'm the only one anybody can unburden their soul to? Maybe I should charge a fee."

Tracing the infinity symbol in Nelson's fur, she weighed the pros and cons of allowing Gavin to get a toe in the door. After a moment, she sighed. "Sorry, Gavin. Go tell it to your mother or hire a shrink." She heard him take a preargumentative breath and quickly added, "I've got to go now. Goodbye."

"Put me through," Adele said in her most assertiveness-trained tone. "This is an emergency."

Douglas Collier's secretary, an older, fiercely loyal woman, dug in her heels. "Sorry, Dr. Collier left explicit instructions that he not be disturbed."

"Look, he called two minutes ago," Adele lied. "He's frantic about losing his wallet. I just found it under my pillow. He must have put it there last night before we had wild sex."

The secretary sucked in a breath and the next sound she heard was ringing. Douglas answered on the fourth ring, irritation lacing his voice. "What is it, Mrs. Cohen? I told you—"

"Helen just called. She's convinced this It person is going to kill her. Wants me to come out to the house. I think she's ready to tell me what's going on.

"I believe her, Douglas. She's really freaked. I want to get out there before Tim and his cowboys get to her."

"Don't you *dare* go out there, Adele!"

She went silent, shocked by his tone of absolute command. Her respect for him as a man with balls—brushed or not—soared.

"Helen Marval is a dangerous psychotic who's on the edge of cracking. There's no telling what she might do. Let me put in a stat call to Ritmann. He can be out there in half the time."

Adele almost tripped over her tongue. "If you call the cops, I'll never talk to you again, Douglas. I'm the one person left she thinks she can trust. If you send Ritmann out there, she'll really go nuts. Not only will she not talk to them, she'll never talk to me again, and we'll never know what information she has.

"I appreciate your concern, but Helen isn't going to hurt me." Adele laughed. "Besides, any nurse who works Ward Eight values her days off too much to be devoting her free time to something as unpleasant as murder."

There was a pause, and then he said skeptically, "Okay,

but carry your gun. Do you know how to conceal it properly?"

"You're talking to Combat Connie, remember? You insult my weapons intelligence."

"And make sure you bring your minirecorder. It won't be admissible evidence unless you can get her to state on tape that she grants you permission to tape her, but it's still evidential."

She frowned briefly. "Will do. I'll call you as soon as I get home."

"Ritmann's supposed to go out there around two-thirty, so if I haven't heard from you by two, I'm going to come out there myself and get you."

"Okay," she said, brushing aside the well-intentioned warning. "Hey, tell me something—how did Megan Barnes's mother die?"

"Who?"

"Meg Barnes, the nurse from Ward Eight?"

She could hear him trying to make the synapses connect. Brain death had visited the coroner.

"The one who was doing Aaron Milton? One of the suspects? Hello?"

"Oh yeah, Megan Barnes. Sorry. It's been a hard day. What about her mother?"

"I heard that Meg was charged with second-degree murder in the death of her mother a few years ago. The mother was from old San Francisco money. Whole thing was kept hush-hush."

"I remember. The mother's name was Elinor Ellingham-Barnes. Went down a long flight of stairs, headfirst. Punctured a lung. Lacerated liver. Concussion. She expired some hours after the initial injuries, but wasn't found until the next morning when the maid came in as scheduled.

"It was established that mother and daughter had had an argument, but it couldn't be proven whether the daughter pushed her and fled the scene, or whether the mother fell accidentally and the daughter fled without trying to help her, or if she fell after the daughter left the house."

"No polygraph was done?"

"No polygraph. She was dismissed."

"Well, okay, thanks. Gotta go. I want to get out there before Helen goes any crazier. Talk to you later." She touched the Colt stuck down the back of her jeans, and started to hang up.

"Adele?"

She brought the phone back to her ear. "Ayuhn?"

"No matter what, stay the hell out of that damned Richard Speck place."

Confused, Nelson looked at Her as She entered the same door She had exited from less than sixty seconds before. He sensed Her level of stress and whined in commiseration—a noise he had perfected.

Adele hastily ravaged the phone book and came up with a number.

An older, kind-voiced woman answered. "St. Hilary's Rectory. Mrs. Muten speaking."

"Hi, Mrs. Muten, is Reverend Wynn around?"

There was a sigh like the rustling of ancient leaves. "Oh dear, no," breathed the wavery old voice. "The good Reverend has gone off in a whirlwind. He's a busy man, you know, dear. I'm the housekeeper—perhaps I could take a message?"

"Did he say where he was going?" Adele heard the pushiness of her question and backed off. "What I mean is that I wasn't sure if we were supposed to meet this morning at the church or not and I didn't know if perhaps he was headed over there now or if . . ." Adele trailed off.

"Oh, well, I don't think he'll be meeting you at the church, dear. He must have forgotten your appointment. I believe he's gone off to Seattle." There was a slight pause, then: "Or someplace like that up north."

"Thanks very much. Glad I didn't go to the church without calling first."

"Can I have him call you, dear?"

"No, I'll call him when he gets back. Do you know when that might be?"

"Ah, let's see . . ." There was another pause, then: "My memory is just terrible!" Mrs. Muten fussed, making clucking noises with her dentures. "You'll have to forgive me. I, ah, I believe it wasn't for very long. Overnight? Or maybe two days . . . I'm sorry. I can't remember now. I'll have to look."

The housekeeper teetered nervously and Adele could hear the shuffling of papers. "I'm afraid I'm getting too old. Now you just wait a minute. Here it is. . . . Yes, tomorrow evening around six-thirty. You call then, all right, dear?"

Adele smiled. There was such a lovely calmness about the elderly. "Yes, thank you, I will. Goodbye now."

"And you have a nice day, dear."

Bargain-priced department stores meant for the multi-childrened, poor, starting-out, starting-over, blue-collared, colleged, and the imitation yuppie depressed her. Partly it was the smell of cheap hot dogs and popcorn grease and the noise of screaming, ill-behaved children and parents. Mostly it was the atmosphere of desperation and poverty, which was exactly where, she believed, the Republicans wanted to drag middle-class America.

From the look and sound of the grossly overcrowded store, the Republicans were winning.

She automatically headed to the left rear of the store. In every store of its kind, the electronics department was always in the left rear. She passed health and beauty, children's active wear, books, office supplies. In the left rear, she found electronics?

Not.

Women's lingerie.

A young adult male, pale and pimpled, was kneeling at the base of one of the brassiere racks, working over a box of newly arrived bras.

"Excuse me, can you tell me where the electronics department is?"

The boy paused in his efforts of pulling slinky green satin bras from the box and slowly looked up as if he was thinking.

Adele blinked. Spread across half of the youth's face and neck, like a grape juice spill, was a port-colored birthmark. Immediately, she shifted her gaze to the unmarked half of his face.

"To the right of the checkout stands," he answered in a cheerless monotone. "In the front."

Every instinct told Adele to smile and say thank you and go on with her business. Instead, she clucked her tongue and said, "That's a strange place for electronics, don't you think?"

The boy flushed on the unmarked side of his face. It was impossible to tell whether the color of the other side had changed, since he'd turned back to removing more brassieres. "To the right of the checkout stands," he repeated, sulkily. "In the front."

"Say, you wouldn't be a Young Republican, would you?" Adele asked, and without waiting for an answer, walked back to the front of the store.

There were five different minirecorders, ranging in price from $19.95 to $129.99. Her hand, well trained in such matters, immediately reached for the lowball special, stopped, and reconsidered.

She should have something that would last, a piece of equipment that would perform in a superior fashion without fail. What if Helen was right at the crux of her confession, and it broke down? Worse yet, what if Helen got hold of the thing and tried to destroy it? Plus, hadn't her mother taught her to go for quality when purchasing anything meant to last?

She picked up the $129.99 model and examined it through the plastic bubble which housed it. There was nothing on the package that indicated whether or not batteries were included. She pulled open the bubble and was in the process of trying to pry open the battery compartment when she felt someone grab hold of her purse strap.

"The second she walked into the store, I said, 'There's trouble.' " The clerk with the birthmark snickered as he yanked her purse off her shoulder and quickly began to rifle through it. A thinner young man wearing a name tag that read "Bill—Here to Serve YOU!" stood directly behind the clerk, looking at her with an expression she'd seen on the faces of special task force police when riled. It was the Nazi Gestapo look.

Indignant, she pulled her purse out of the clerk's hands.

"What do you think you're doing?" she asked, glaring. "Have you lost your mind?—assuming you started out with one, that is."

Before he could answer, "Bill—Here to Serve YOU!" yanked the recorder out of her hand. As he did so, the machine slipped out of its bubble house and smashed into several pieces on the tiled floor. Batteries were not included.

"That's it," said the clerk, taking a firm grasp of her upper arm and giving her a rough shove out into the main aisle. "Call security, Bill. Tell them to call—"

Adele screamed at the top of her lungs, and kept screaming until a small crowd of shoppers gathered around them. A toddler, sitting in his mother's cart, put his hands over his ears and began to cry. The clerk— whose name Adele now saw was "John—Here to Serve YOU!"—looked between Adele and the toddler, momentarily flustered.

Taking her chance, Adele looked out over the crowd and addressed two reasonable-looking women, both standing behind carts laden with clothes. "Will someone please help me?" To her own ears, she sounded surprisingly calm. Without forethought she added, "This man has attacked me. I think he's dangerous and needs psychiatric attention."

A woman with her cart full of evening dresses and spike-heeled shoes directed her gaze at the two clerks and pointed a finger at the hand grasping Adele's arm. "I'm an attorney. That's assault and battery, gentlemen."

"You take your hand offa her," commanded the toddler's mother in a scolding voice.

"Yeah," said a teenage girl digging for a piece of bubble gum stuck in her braces. "Let 'er go, creepo. She didn't do nothin' to you."

The attorney came to stand next to Adele, handing her a business card as she did so. "You can bring a suit against this store and these two employees. We can claim unlimited damages here. We have witnesses."

A short, sturdily built black woman approached the throng, perspiring and out of breath. "What's the trouble here?" she asked no one in particular. "What's going on?"

His hand still grasping Adele's arm, "John—Here to Serve YOU!" stammered, "She was acting suspicious." His face had turned a uniform crimson. "She swore at me and then she . . . she was taking a piece of merchandise out of the package and she was—"

"Excuse me," Adele broke in, wondering if by swearing he was referring to her use of the word "Republican." "But I was simply checking to see whether or not the minirecorder I was about to purchase included batteries. The outside package didn't say, and I didn't want to have to come back.

"This . . ." Adele paused. ". . . young man . . ." She said "young man" with as much incriminating distaste as she could muster. ". . . assaulted me bodily and then had the nerve to rifle my purse!"

A murmur of shock and disapproval rippled through the crowd, which had grown by another ten or so shoppers— mostly women.

"Sue the damned store!" shouted a white-haired woman at the back of the crowd.

"That's what *I'd* do," said a bald man wearing a work shirt from a carpet-cleaning company. In his cart was a leaf blower.

Much to Adele's pleasure, someone made the comment that the store was going to the dogs.

The black woman's gaze settled on the clerk. "You never touch the customers, John," she said evenly.

The clerk dropped Adele's arm and stuck the offending hand in his pocket.

"If you have suspicions," continued the woman, "you call main security. You have no business with the customers except to help them find merchandise and answer questions."

In the same breath, she turned to Adele, saying, "I'm very sorry, ma'am, for the misunderstanding. I hope you'll forgive Mr. Belfiore."

Immediately, she turned to the clerk and issued a simple command. "Apologize, John."

Without any preamble, "John—Here to Serve YOU!" turned to Adele and mumbled "Sorry," then disappeared through the crowd in the direction of the brassieres. His accomplice had already slipped away without notice.

The attorney, smelling the stench of a disappearing fee, stepped up to the black woman. "What about damages here? This woman has been assaulted, publicly slandered, and held against her will by your incompetent staff." She turned to Adele. "You have plenty of grounds for a suit against this establishment."

"No," Adele said resolutely, looking at the manager. "An apology is sufficient."

"I'd really have to advise you not to settle for something so weak as a . . ."

The crowd—bored by the lack of violence perhaps—was dispersing rapidly. Adele, acutely aware of passing time, hurriedly thanked the lawyer for her concern, waved to her other supporters, and took another minirecorder off the shelf—along with several packages of batteries and some micro tapes.

Forsaking her cart, the attorney followed Adele to the cashier.

"I must advise you that we have a clear-cut case of assault and battery, false imprisonment, slander, and negligent infliction of emotional distress. You stand to make some money here." The attorney lowered her voice. "What does it matter to them, anyway? Do you know how much this company pulls in in one day's retail sales?" She leaned back. "Millions. One tiny lawsuit won't make a dent. I work for a percentage of what you win in court."

"I appreciate your concern, but it's no big deal. If I sued every time I'd been verbally or physically assaulted, I'd be a billionairess." Adele laughed, hoping the woman would leave. Instead, she seemed to grow even more intent on selling her a lawsuit. Adele was relieved when the cashier ("Carmen—Here to Serve YOU!") took the minirecorder and batteries and asked—with some amount of surprise—if that was all for today.

Adele answered that she'd had quite as much as she needed for the day and turned to the lawyer.

"Tell you what." Adele wrote out a check for the amount of the purchase, making sure to keep her thumb over her name and address. "Let me think about it and a few other potential lawsuits I've got, and I'll give you a call. Maybe we'll do lunch next week and talk all of them over."

Giving in, the woman shrugged. "What do you do?"

"I'm a nurse."

It was as if the lawyer had come upon a suitcase filled with unmarked bills. Smiling broadly, she dug in her purse to produce an inch-high stack of business cards. "Here." She shoved them at Adele, who took them and put them in her jacket pocket. "Hand these out to your patients. Put a few in the emergency room waiting room."

Adele nodded absently and ran to the car. It was 11:47. Helen would be coming off the ceiling of the Richard Speck Memorial by the time she got there.

The commotion of the dogs baying and howling was audible a mile away—literally. At the beginning of the Marval driveway, Adele first heard the distant howls and immediately had a vision of Helen wringing her hands and pacing in front of their cages, ranting on like a maniac. It would be enough to upset the dead, let alone a few dogs with brains the size of kumquats.

As the house and barn came into view, the uncharitable thought came to mind that the idyllic setting was lost on Helen. The scolding-mother part of Adele's psyche slapped her hand and reminded her that one never really knew what went on in others' minds. For all she knew, Helen might meditate daily in full lotus position in that very yard.

She honked three times, waited a moment, then went to the house and rang the bell. As she expected, both front and back doors were locked. She set out for the barn, fingering the recorder hidden neatly in her pocket. She hoped it would not make too much of a noise when the tape ran out; she doubted Helen would take warmly to the idea of being recorded.

Although no one could have heard a bomb drop over the din of the dogs, Adele knocked before entering the barn. Inside, the noise was deafening. Her impulse was like that of the toddler in the store—she put her hands over her ears and commanded the dogs to be quiet.

Of course, they didn't obey. All she accomplished was to make them more agitated. It was useless to call out; she'd need a bullhorn to be heard over the noise. It would have to be a game of hide-and-seek. Although she knew exactly where Helen would be hiding, she checked the upstairs bedroom and office suites first, searching the closets and even under the bed. No Helen. No dust either.

Downstairs, the outer door to the storage room was closed. Adele knocked and called out before stepping inside the dark room. Immediately, she was assailed with the smell of candle wax. The cloakroom door was outlined by the unmistakable glow of candlelight coming from within.

She knocked. "Helen? You in there?"

There was no answer, but she caught a movement through the crack near the doorjamb. "Helen? It's okay, it's Adele. Can I come in?"

There was another movement. Thinking it was Helen coming to open the door, she leaned back.

The door stayed closed. Arms raised, she flailed around in search of the light's pull cord. Unable to find the thing, she gave up and turned her attention back to the cloak-room door. She pulled it open a hair.

"Helen? I'm coming in."

The movement, which she now saw as a large shadow, shifted slowly.

"Helen?" She opened the door four more inches but could not bring herself to look inside. Instead, she turned her ear to the opening. "Helen?"

There was a peculiar creaking sound, a sound that brought up memories of old Westerns and episodes of *The Twilight Zone*. She pushed her head through the crack and unconsciously stopped breathing after the first whiff of something foul.

Helen's left hand grazed her cheek.

For a moment, her brain refused to put the pieces together.

Helen's hand. Hanging down.

Raising her eyes, it took her a second to see beyond the soft dazzle of the host of lit candles and perceive the reflected image in the mirror over the coat hooks: Helen, swinging slightly at the end of a dog's leash which had been attached to a light fixture in the center of the narrow ceiling. Her head was bent at a grotesque angle, a pur-plish tongue protruding from between dark, swollen lips.

Flashback to Mrs. Mau's third-year clinicals. The nurs-ing student's Golden Rule: *A nurse acts without delay in all critical situations. Emotions are considered and handled in the aftermath.*

Given superhuman strength with the instant surge of adrenaline, Adele righted the overturned step stool at her feet. Stepping up so her head was level with Helen's, she shouldered the woman and lifted up, released the clasp on the leash, and climbed down with her burden. It was the first time she'd done an assessment on a ladder.

The eyes were half open and bloodshot. Contrasting strangely with the woman's red hair, the bottoms of the ears, the lips, the double chins, and the area above the leash were a deep purple. Below the neck, everything was pale gray except the feet and lower legs, which matched the purple on top. From the smell and the wetness of Helen's stockings, she realized Helen had soiled herself.

Automatically, her fingers sought the carotid pulse, but found that the neck was too rigid to be moved backward. The nurse in her grew frantic when, determined to begin CPR, she found she could not pry open Helen's mouth in order to give mouth-to-mouth resuscitation. Pushing aside the woman's underpants, she felt for the femoral pulse and found nothing but the cold, unyielding feel of dead flesh.

She stared at the cotton panties with the pink fleur-de-lis design, then up at the frizzled red hair. Without wanting to, she looked at Helen's face. The pupils were fixed and dilated. There was no pulse, no breath sounds. School was out forever.

"Time to blow this pop stand, girl," she said—the words she usually used to signal the end of a code. Ignoring the need to call 911 immediately, she sat back on her haunches and surveyed the body, thinking how appropriate it was for Helen to have hung herself in the Richard Speck Memorial—along with the rest of her crystals.

The inexplicable urge to laugh came over her. Try as

she might, she was unable to stop herself. She laughed until her sides were sore, never knowing that by this very act (one which she would later consider a form of clinical hysteria, but would never share with another living soul), she had saved her own life.

TWELVE

IT (IT REFERRED TO ITSELF THIS WAY EVER since Helen had bestowed the name) stopped halfway across the supply room and lowered the scalpel, perplexed. The dark-haired bitch's sudden outburst of laughter was not the reaction It expected; it made her worth a moment of consideration.

Perspiring, It ran a gloved finger along the scalpel's handle. She wasn't one of the Sinful, nor was she supposed to be one of the Retribution Offerings to the Master. It would not kill her for her minor transgressions, but she was still a bitch, a man-killer, vermin of the earth, a whore, a sinner, and especially, a sister to the killers of innocents.

But still, to laugh at the sight of a dead sister was curious. Perhaps this one . . .

The pain in Its upper arm, where the fat whore had bitten, caused the muscles to spasm. The fat thing had held her breath forever, fighting the ether. It hadn't expected the savage strength of that flaccid, useless body—hadn't expected her to fight at all, for that matter. She'd been so perfectly subservient.

And the massive weight! It had taken longer than planned to get the sow up the ladder. It had to give her a second dousing of ether, although It was careful not to give too much. It still wanted to enjoy the death struggle.

The extra work had been worth it, for the performance was splendid, the way the obese neck had snapped and the eyes and tongue protruded. The waste of flesh had urinated at the same moment her neck broke. And the seizures! Three . . . four of them, one right after the other. It had been brought to a glorious orgasm when the bowels released.

How badly It had wanted to rip open the belly and remove that sacred organ so foolishly bestowed by the Master on these worthless whores. But this Holy Womb was not to be part of the Offerings; this one would be sacrificed for—

The strange black-haired one suddenly stopped laughing and got to her feet. It pulled back into the darkest part of the room and decided It would kill her if she moved first to the right—the hand of curse—but if she moved to the left—the hand of blessing—It would let her live. This time.

The whore swayed slightly, as if she was going to faint. Then she jerked her head up and staggered to her left.

It jumped behind a stack of dog food a second before she stepped out of the execution chamber. Instantly, she stopped and turned slowly, searching for the presence It knew she felt.

She pulled a gun from the back of her pants. It tightened Its grip on the scalpel, then eased up as she ran from the room and to the wall phone by the door of the barn. It smiled in the dark, glad now that It had cut the barn's phone wires. The bitch would have to go to the main house and break in. That would provide the time It needed to leave unobserved.

Pleased, It opened Its mouth and silently laughed.

THIRTEEN

BY THE TIME SHE CRAWLED INTO BED WITH Nelson, she felt like she'd had major surgery on a vital organ—like her brain—and been sent home much too soon. She checked the clock and yawned until her jaw popped. It was only seven o'clock, and yet she felt as though she'd been without sleep for days. Nelson yawned too, which caused her to smile—cross-species power of suggestion.

Adele wiggled out of her tight girdle of Catholic morals and gave herself permission to go to bed early, which, according to the doctrines of the religion-straight-from-hell, carried with it the stigma of slothfulness and the temptation of evil. The nuns' invention of "Early to bed with idle hands and do the Devil's bidding" stuck stubbornly in her mind, no matter how she tried to convince herself of its absurdity. She neutralized the peccadillo with the rationalization that she had to work the next day and didn't want to kill anyone because she wasn't thinking straight.

Laughing out loud, she kept a close watch for the crazy ring she'd heard when kneeling beside Helen's body. Opening the doors on her brain theater, she started the reel of the day's events, beginning with Cynthia's question about who the hell had been calling all night.

"Helen," she said to the light fixture.

Obviously, the light fixture breathed.

"She was hysterical and afraid—concerned about herself and her dogs," Adele continued, speaking now to the headboard. "The woman was concerned about getting killed . . . *not* committing suicide. She was so sure that someone was going to harm her she insisted I get out there immediately."

Nelson put his head on her shoulder and licked her neck. She slipped her arm under his body. Resting her head against his, she cringed with embarrassment at her overall clumsiness at the scene.

Kitch would be so *disappointed in you,* sighed one of the judges on the amateur sleuth panel, all of whom now sat at the end of her bed.

"But I knew instinctively that someone was in the tack room," she pleaded in self-defense. "Just like I knew Helen was forced to commit suicide—or was murdered outright."

Pfffth. Pure mumbo jumbo, said another of the judges, who had a slight lisp. *It'th the other thingth, Adele, like the clueth you totally mithed? Red and crimthon flagth flapping in your fath, honey, and you didn't thee any of—*

"Okay, okay," she grumbled. "Enough already . . . I'm already lower than a speed bump. I don't need my imaginary critics to run me down too."

It was true, though—she *did* miss all the goddamned flags. Tim had seen the muddy shoe tracks the moment he arrived at the scene, and within two minutes noted the absence of a suicide note. Douglas had had to point out the faint blue linear abrasions above the two prominent wrist bones—rings of possible forced restraint.

She'd been questioned for the better part of three hours by Tim and then Detective Cini. Even if Douglas hadn't been caught up in doing his job, he couldn't have rescued her from that.

Later, Harold Marval had to be forcibly restrained from coming into the barn, his bellows of anguish echoing over the property. It was Douglas who, in the midst of all the chaos and horror, had the presence of mind and compassion to make arrangements to fly Marval's sister in from Dallas. Taking his lead, Tim contacted the county police-dog trainer about finding someone to care for Helen's dogs. Adele, taking both their leads, called the nursing office and told them that Helen would need to be replaced for the remainder of the schedule. And then some.

She gazed out the window toward San Quentin and shivered. The murderer had been within inches of her. So close.

It was when she was trying to break into the main house to use the phone that she'd heard the distant sound of a car motor starting on the far side of the woods behind the house. How stupid she'd been—taking the time to run for the fire road, knowing the vehicle would be gone long before she even reached the edge of the copse.

Neglecting 911, she'd called Tim Ritmann directly. She hadn't had the balls to call Douglas, just as she hadn't had the balls to call him when she returned home. In her present state, even his most meager offer of kindness would not be turned down. It was a certainty that her

need for comfort and his need for her would lead them to
a round of scrotal brushing.

She hadn't listened to even one of her seventeen phone
messages, nor did she sort through her mail. She switched
off the ringer, put a thick towel over the answering machine so as not to hear it click, locked all the doors and
windows, and crawled under the covers with her dog.

She'd deal with it all—tomorrow.

"What a miserable wimpette I am," she sighed in
Nelson's ear, which flicked reflexively, hitting her in the
mouth.

"Think about it tomorrow, Scarlett," she answered herself in her best imitation of Nelson's human voice.
"Tomorrow is another day."

Douglas watched her lights go out, waited five minutes, and slowly drove on. He wondered if she'd tried to
call, or if she'd gone straight to bed. To bed, probably;
she'd had a hard day.

He stopped the car, debating whether or not to go back
and knock. The tightening in his chest and groin caused
him to circle the block again. His protective juices
flowing, he saw each shadow as a possible danger to her,
so that every car, every person within sight underwent his
sharp scrutiny. The thought that he could have lost her
distracted him from his work—to the point where even
Mrs. Cohen asked if he was getting enough sleep.

But it had been so close. Too close.

He slowed as he approached her house again. It remained dark. He envisioned himself knocking, and her
answering the door in a white cotton nightdress. She

would invite him in. He would love her like she'd never been loved before. With her he'd be different. There would be no mistakes this time. She'd never leave him. She would be his lover, his queen, his wife, his child's mother . . .

His erection grew uncomfortable. Adjusting himself, he glanced at his watch and his mind changed gears. There was a meeting in thirty minutes. He couldn't be late.

Looking a last time at her house, he kissed the air. "Sleep, Adele, my love. Sleep in peace. No one will hurt you now."

A Gideon Bible in one hand and a photograph of Dana Collier in the other, Roger Wynn lay naked, staring at the ceiling of his motel room. He'd stopped crying, though the pain still stabbed at him. He knew now for certain that there was no going back, there would be no more pretending, no more hiding.

Holding the picture above him, he stared at the pretty woman in the flowered straw hat. Behind her, a large wave was breaking on the rocks. Shading her eyes despite the hat, she smiled shyly into the camera.

"Oh dear God," he addressed the picture, "what have I done?"

In his mind, images of Chloe and Sonya joined Dana on the beach. Each woman stared at him. *What have you done to us?*

A wave of nausea passed over him, making him retch. Still holding the photograph and the Bible, he lunged off the bed and bolted for the bathroom. Leaning over the toilet, he vomited first bourbon, then bile.

In the bright bathroom light, Dana's expression seemed

more joyful. He remembered her touching his face, wearing the same smile. He remembered Chloe's childlike laughter and the feel of her small hand clutching his. He remembered Sonya's seductive low voice and the way her mouth felt on him.

He made a fist and punched himself in the stomach. He retched again, but did not vomit. Readying himself for another blow, he saw his razor on the sink rim. He picked it up and looked at himself in the mirror. The sight disgusted him. He was tired of hiding. He would let the world see what a repulsive atrocity of a wretch he was.

He pulled the razor across his cheek, leaving a trail in his beard. He rinsed the razor and repeated the same action until the tender skin began to bleed.

Megan Barnes pulled off the black watch cap and let the mass of blond hair fall over her shoulders. Sitting cross-legged on her mother's grave, she faced the white marble headstone.

Elinor Ellingham-Barnes
Beloved Daughter, Wife, Mother

Atop the stone was a magnificent statue of a woman with a child at each side. A small boy, and a slightly taller girl. The woman's head was bent gracefully toward the girl.

Since the first time she saw the stone, and every day since then, Meg imagined the statue's expression to be one of motherly disapproval.

Stop sulking, Megan! It is so unbecoming to a young lady.
Stop carrying on so, Megan. What will people think?

Stop, Megan. Help me.

Stop, Megan. Where are you going?

Stop, Megan. Don't leave me here to die.

Facedown, head pressed against the stone, Meg hollowed out a small hole in the earth—in line with where she knew her mother's ear to be. She placed her mouth over the hole.

"I need to tell you so many things, Mommy. I . . . I don't have anybody anymore, just like you said. Terrible Temper Megan made them all go away."

Megan lay flat against the ground, her arms stretching and pulling in, as if she were trying to hug the earth.

"Remember how you said I'd have to face my retribution someday and it would be hell on earth? You were right, Mommy. I live in hell.

"I wish I'd never told you about liking girls. I wish you hadn't run away from me. I wish I hadn't left you alone."

She began to cry, her tears falling into the dirt. "I didn't think you were hurt that bad, Mommy, honest to God I didn't. I was so mad, I didn't know what I was doing. I just wanted you to love me.

"Don't hate me, Mommy. I promise I'll try. I promise I'll . . ."

She got to her knees, bent toward the hole, and whispered one last thing before she stood. Studying the face of the mother statue once more, she kicked dirt into the hole and ground it down with the heel of her shoe.

FOURTEEN

AT 5:30 A.M. ADELE REMOVED THE TOWEL FROM the face of the answering machine and discovered the seventeen had grown to twenty-two. She fortified herself with another spoonful of yogurt and hit the replay button.

Four hang-ups, four calls from Cyn, five from Douglas— the last of which was his warning that he was leaving the house to check on her in person—one from Nelson's vet reminding her to make an appointment for his booster shots, two from the nursing office, three from Tim with additional questions about Helen, one from Gavin's mother, two from Gavin—one tearful, one angry.

She pulled out of her running shoes and peeled off a sweaty running sock. Nelson eyed the filthy gray thing with great longing. Outside of his Mickey Mouse rug, one of Her dirty socks was the best security/suck toy life had to offer.

While she made vegetarian stew and rice for Nelson's breakfast, she mentally reviewed all twenty-two phone messages and wrote a single note to herself to call the vet on her lunch break (if she got one) and make an appointment.

* * *

"I'm so sorry, Amerigo." Adele stroked the side of the old man's face.

Mr. Salucci chuckled weakly, though he did not take his eyes off the ceiling.

Pumping up the blood pressure cuff, she slowly released the valve, allowing the mercury to fall until she heard the faint thud of the man's heart. His blood pressure had been steadily dropping for an hour, and his pulse had turned erratic and weak.

A part of her wanted him to slip away with peaceful dignity. She also wanted to take the medical warrior's gamble of cheating the natural process of death out of a victim—except there was always the chance that he would then become a victim of medical technology. Either way, she decided, he would lose.

Meg appeared in the doorway looking for her.

"Put a call in to Dr. Greenwald," said Adele before the other nurse could speak. She returned her hand to Mr. Salucci's and let him hold on to her. "Tell her he's crashing. We need a code status, stat."

The old man lifted his eyes to hers and spoke quietly in his native tongue. She interpreted the words to mean, "I am dying. I don't like dying."

She adjusted his oxygen canula and smiled gently. "I know, and I'll stay with you, little clown. I'll see you to the door."

He nodded and patted her hand, bringing it to his ancient dry lips for a kiss. In that moment her throat caught and locked in a lump. She returned the kiss on the back of his weathered hand.

"No family. No insurance. No code," Meg said from the doorway.

Adele nodded and asked her to shut the door.

Meg hesitated, giving her a searching glance. "You're in charge, Monsarrat. We're nuts out here. We've got four admits coming up, and Tina said you've had three calls from Dr. Collier. That Detective Ritmann left another message that he'd be here at noon to talk to you, the supervisor wants the acuity reports, Skip is being a total asshole about his assignment, and Cynthia needs you in room eight-oh-two as soon as you're done screwing around in . . ."

Adele stopped listening. Never taking her eyes from Mr. Salucci's, she clasped his hands and, because she knew the sound would calm him, began reciting the fairy tale of the Lion and the Mouse.

At the moment the lion was freed from his trap, the old man's eyelids fluttered slightly and he was gone.

An entire apple gripped in her mouth, Adele made swearing noises from the back of her throat. The lock on the supply closet was a bitch to get open. She would call the maintenance man before the day was out and have the damned thing changed—it had been sticking for nearly seventeen years.

The lock released as a glob of saliva spilled from the side of her mouth, around the apple. Wiping her chin, she switched on the light and headed to the rack where the morgue packs were kept. The jingle of a belt buckle and a giggle stopped her in her tracks. She looked in the direction of the noises and gaped. The apple fell from her mouth and rolled across the floor.

In Detective Cini's makeshift interrogation room, on

top of the desk, Tim Ritmann and Cynthia were, again, involved in playing around with physical passion.

"Christ on a bike, don't you two ever just *talk*?"

Rapidly, Tim—with his back to her—adjusted his clothes. His neck had turned beet-red. "I don't know how it happens, Miss Adele," he said in a heavy Southern accent. "This here's one hot tomato. Can't never keep her hands to herself."

Cynthia left off smoothing down her scrub top long enough to punch his arm. "Yeah." She chuckled. "I can't stay away from his gun."

"Well, you'll have to restrain yourself, Cyn, because I assigned you two of the new admits and one is waiting out in the hall for you."

While Cynthia alternated between groans, complaints, and snorts of laughter, Adele searched down the rack of small paper bags labeled "M Pack." Taking one off the shelf, she broke the seal and checked its contents: blank toe tag, adult diaper, and a length of thin gauze to tie the arms together so they wouldn't fall out from under the covers. There was nothing more upsetting to visitors and patients than to see a covered gurney rolling down the hall with an escaped arm flopping about.

"And if *you*"—she pointed at Tim—"need to talk to me, I can spare you five minutes right now if you don't mind playing orderly and helping me get a patient ready for cold storage."

"It's fine with me," he answered, smoothing back his hair. "As long as there's no body fluids involved, and I don't have to do CPR on some drooly old guy."

"Can't guarantee you there won't be fluids, but it's

way too late for CPR." She paused, glancing down. "But first, I think it'd be a good idea to zip up your fly."

The moment Adele released the retention balloon, the bloody urinary catheter slipped out of Mr. Salucci's bladder and down his urethra like a worm down a waterslide.

A drop of blood dripped from the end of the dead man's penis, causing Detective Ritmann to shudder and look away. There was a large smear of Cynthia's lipstick on his right jaw.

"Ever lived in a cockroach-infested place?" he asked.

"Not yet. Why?"

"When you turn up the heat in the oven, they scatter out from underneath. Seems our Reverend Wynn has scurried from the heat."

Adele raised her eyebrows as if it were news to her, and went on washing Mr. Salucci's hands over a basin of warm water.

"We found his muddy shoes at the bottom of St. Hilary's clothes-donation box. Wynn's housekeeper identified them as his favorite shoes. A match for the prints out at the barn.

"A United ticket agent at SFO gave a positive ID on him. He took a two P.M. Chicago flight yesterday under the name of Glen McMartin. Paid cash."

"Chicago?"

"Busiest airport in the world. It's a great place to get lost."

Adele asked him to hold Mr. Salucci's arms together while she laced the gauze strip around the thin forearms, which were covered with old intravenous sites—blue bruises that looked for all the world like ink stains.

"Boy," she said, desperately trying to sound nonchalant, "I'd love to see a psychiatric evaluation on this guy."

"There was an evaluation in his files, but it's useless—the guy asked these ridiculous questions like, 'Do you think of little boys when you masturbate?' or, 'Are you jealous of Michael Jackson?' "

Adele controlled her voice with the mastery of a seasoned actress. "I worked on a psych ward in Seattle for about a year once. I wonder if it's the same shrink who evaluated all the child molesters there."

Tim pulled the diaper under Mr. Salucci's cold buttocks and fastened the tabs. "Maybe. Wilmont is used a lot up there as a court expert in child abuse cases."

Adele frowned and shook her head. "Wilmont? No. I don't think that was the name." She pulled the sheet up over the body. "Oh well." She sighed. "At least we know Helen didn't do it."

Tim cocked his head and repeated a phrase Kitch frequently used: "In this business, don't be too sure of anything."

He scrubbed his hands at the sink. "There's no doubt she hung the contaminated IV that killed the Sedrick woman—"

"She may have hung the bag, but anybody could have spiked it," Adele protested. "Helen told me somebody—this 'It' entity—told her to do something to Chloe. She admitted it was the same person she saw kill Sonya."

"Or," Tim said, drying his hands, "maybe *she* was the 'It.' She was a bona fide psycho—she didn't need a motive for killing anybody."

"And I suppose she staged her own suicide to look like

a murder?" Adele shook her head. "That's too weird, even for Helen. Besides, she was too freaked out about getting killed. That hysteria wasn't any act."

"Maybe. Let's just say I'm not ruling her out. I'm taking everything into consideration. She was crazy enough to do anything. However . . ." He paused to look at himself in the mirror. "Right now I've got my money riding on Wynn."

Discovering the lipstick smudge, he instantly wiped it off. "How about you? Want to place any bets?"

"Naw." Adele shook her head. "I'm going to wait to see who else crawls out from under the stove."

Together, Adele and Cynthia raced for the sanctuary of Gayle's office, where line three was lit and ringing. Adrenaline pumping, Adele could not believe that she'd managed to pull off such a major coup. Now all she had to do was make sure she didn't screw up.

Tina had done her part by obtaining Dr. Eugene Wilmont's number and leaving a message he was to call Dr. Christine Klien's office regarding a former patient of his, Roger Wynn. The number she gave was Gayle's private line.

The psychiatrist had promptly returned the call.

Cynthia answered in her best secretary voice, put him on hold, and handed the phone to Adele.

"Dr. Wilmont? Yes, well, thank you for returning my call. My name is Christine Klien and I'm the clinical psychologist working with Internal Affairs at the Marin Sheriff's Department and DA's office.

"We've got a multiple homicide case here and I'm doing an internal investigation on a man who was a former patient of yours—Roger Wynn. He's on the run and I need some input from you in order to do a background on him."

Adele listened for a moment, nervously tapping her pen on Gayle's desk blotter. "Release?" she said, then in convincing dismayed surprise: "You haven't received it yet?" For effect she pulled the phone away and spoke to the imaginary secretary in the invisible other room. "Janice? What day did we mail out Mr. Wynn's release to Dr. Wilmont?" She paused, then a disappointed, "Oh, I see."

She would not look at Cynthia, who was sitting on the floor, laughing hysterically and hiding her face in a balled-up sweater.

"I'm sorry. It seems the release didn't go out until yesterday. I thought it went out before that." She covered her unoccupied ear so as not to hear the muffled gasps coming from the sweater. "It should be in your mailbox no later than tomorrow. But I've got a meeting at the DA's office this afternoon, so I need this information now. Perhaps you could forgo the . . ."

Without further prompting, the psychiatrist began to spew information while Adele chased his words with her pen. Every once in a while she'd nod and repeat a phrase while writing it down.

"Yes? Father's dominance, mother's submission. Uhn-huh. Fluctuates between being codependent victim and aggression? I see, of course he's conflicted . . .

"So, this is not fitting the profile of a child molester. . . . Well, yes, it is obvious, isn't it?" Adele looked at Cynthia, who had abandoned the sweater and was now listening with interest.

"Ah, of course. How typical. The mother of the two children allegedly molested was militantly pro-choice and coerced the children to lie. Hmmm, I see, and . . . The knife was planted on him by the same woman? . . . No? Oh gee. So it was another activist who wanted him out of the . . ." She laughed. "My, what an assertive bunch!"

She grabbed Cynthia's hand, and shot her a glance that read *Bingo!*

"I see. Well, like you say, Dr. Wilmont, he certainly doesn't fit the profile of a murderer, but now what about the aggression toward health care workers? I believe it was mentioned somewhere in your report about this being fostered by the incident wherein the mother died waiting for medical attention in an emergency room?"

Adele took a few more notes, thanked the doctor, and got off the line. She read over the notes she'd just taken, completely confused.

"I don't get it," she said, disbelieving. "Doug lied about the psychiatrist's report."

"Why would he lie?"

"I don't know," Adele said, rising from her chair. "But if this Wilmont guy is giving me the straight dope, Roger didn't have any reason to blow town."

With a quick gesture, she turned to Cynthia. "You busy tonight?"

Cynthia shrugged. "Nothing special. If Tim can get away from the office, we're going to the movies to see—"

"Wrong. As soon as you give me report, you're going to call Tim and tell him that you've got a horrible migraine. Then you're going to go home, get something warm and dark to wear, and come to my house for further instructions."

"Why something warm and dark?"

Adele smiled. "Does the term 'stakeout' mean anything to you?"

"John—Here to Serve YOU!" froze with the price sticker machine in one hand. "Oh shit," he moaned under his breath. The task of putting neon-orange "SALE! $8.99! SALE!" stickers over the old white $12.99 stickers was completely forgotten.

The *Best of Patsy Cline* CD slipped out of his other hand. Adele caught it on its way to the floor. "Howdy. Do you carry pager/beeper devices?" she asked lightly. She was the type to let bygones be bygones, Young Republican or not.

John Belfiore flinched at the sound of her voice, as if it verified for certain it was really her and there was going to be more trouble. "Aisle ten," he said, forgetting they were standing in aisle 10.

Adele looked over the clerk's shoulder and saw the glass case at the far end of the aisle. She assumed that the pagers and beepers would be in the case locked away from the hands of suspected thieves such as herself.

"Do you think you could help me? I need some kind of device that will allow two people to send messages to each other without using a telephone."

The clerk, in actuality, knew more about women's bras and panties than electronic devices. The only thing he could think of that sounded like what she wanted was the two tomato cans and five yards of string he and Chris

Conover had stretched between their bedroom windows during the summer before he entered the fifth grade.

He wondered if he should suggest such a thing, saw a glint of Woman on a Mission in her eye, and decided not to. He'd ignored the glint in his first encounter with her—rarely did he make the same mistake twice.

"I, uh, can open the case and you can look. I don't, uh, know too much about pagers."

Conscious of the fact the kid looked positively freaked by her very presence, Adele slapped her forehead. "Oh, I forgot! You aren't the pager expert—*you're* the expert on interplanetary missiles."

"John—Here to Serve YOU!"—born humor-impaired—couldn't believe she had actually insulted him . . . again! He felt his face burn, knowing it would make the port-wine stain (his mother had often referred to it as his Red Badge of Courage until he punched her lights out one day when he was sixteen) more prominent.

At his side, his hand bent into a claw of steel.

She turned and headed for the case, chattering on about needing a small and not too heavy device, preferably something quiet that wouldn't cost a million dollars, but wasn't cheaply made either. She was going to do some undercover work, she told him, and she wanted something reliable that would take a secret code.

The whole time she spoke, she was totally oblivious of his hand clutching the air where her throat had been one nanosecond before.

The Beast fell asleep on the way home. It chose its place and time carefully—the middle lane of the Lucky Drive exit off Highway 101, in the thick of commuter traffic, which in the Bay Area was continuous between 6:00 A.M. and 6:00 P.M.

Long since accustomed to the glares and prolonged honks of passing motorists, Adele flicked on the hazard lights and read the operating instructions included in the set of pagers she'd just purchased. It seemed simple enough—even for Cynthia, who was sometimes dithered by mechanical contraptions.

A loud screech of brakes behind the Beast barely warranted her raising her head. When the blue smoke from the BMW's tires had cleared, and she failed to respond to the profane oaths and gestures hurled at her, she checked to see if the Beast was ready to give up its temper tantrum and carry on.

The Beast coughed, wheezed, and with a metallic shriek of reluctance, woke up.

Like a petulant child who lets go of his bladder in front of the bathroom door, the Beast went to sleep again at the end of the driveway.

Letting sleeping Beasts lie, Adele gathered her purse, her gym bag (her workout clothes hadn't been washed for a while and were evolving), and her new electronic devices. The sun had set and the light was in the deepest stage of dusk. It was the time of day when Adele's eyes, like her car, simply shut off.

From memory alone, she found her way up the driveway, tripped over the edging, and went sprawling headfirst onto the lawn. The contents of her purse spilled out along with her body and the two electronic devices.

Turning onto her back, she stared at the darkening sky through the branches of the acacia tree and howled with laughter. Behind the embarrassment of possibly having the spastic movement observed by one of her neighbors was the worrisome thought that she really was losing her mind. Holding her stomach, Adele got to her knees, unable to see—not because of the failing light, but rather, because of the laughter tears blurring her vision.

The scene of herself merely walking to her front door and then suddenly being airborne and flying through the air to take a header on her own front lawn repeated itself in her mind, which set her off all over again. It was a reaction to the stress, she thought. After all, she hadn't cried since Chloe's funeral and God knew she'd had plenty of reason to cry.

She tried to stand, still howling, weaved a bit, and propelled herself toward the front door. There was an unnatural movement of branches in the juniper bushes to the right of the door.

"Adele." A man's voice came from the juniper.

Her gut reaction—to jump back and run—was impeded by her hilarity.

"Yeah . . . ?" She now saw herself talking to a juniper bush at the front of her house and wheezed out a renewed explosion of laughter. Her sides were beginning to ache, and she'd started with the wheezies.

"You've got to hear me out," pleaded the voice, which she recognized as Gavin's.

"Shoot," she said, which sent her into yet another round of hard laughter.

"I've changed, Adele. You're the only one who ever really understood me. I'm begging you . . . I need to reveal myself to you completely. I need you to know me as I really am."

Adele only caught half of what he was saying; she was concentrating on gasping for air. "Sure," she managed, limping for the door. "Just don't break any branches." As best she could with "silly hands"—hands made weak with laughter—she pulled the shopping bag–size purse close to her face and rummaged for her house keys, praying they had not escaped onto the lawn.

From the right edge of her visual field, just outside the handle of her purse, a foot and ankle appeared.

She sobered at once.

A black suede open-toed pump with ankle strap showed off the shapely foot and lower leg to advantage. Following the sheer black nylon upward, above the knee, she came to the hem of a flounced black taffeta skirt. The matching handbag was trimmed with iridescent black beads.

Before her stood Gavin in full drag. She thought he might have been blushing, but it was hard to tell through the fine chiffon veil which cascaded down from the wide-brimmed black hat and ended under his chin.

Stunned, her first impulse was to push up the spaghetti strap which had slipped off his shoulder. "Oh my God," she whispered. "You look great."

His smile shone from behind the veil. "Yeah? You really think so?"

Adele nodded in awe.

Gavin turned around, giving the taffeta shawl a delicate twirl. Adele had seen professional models do worse on Paris runways.

"When did you . . . How long have you . . ." She indicated his dress.

"I've been cross-dressing since I was twenty-two,

although I had to take a break when I served in the Green Berets. I've never had the balls to go public before. I wanted you to be the first."

Silently thanking Providence that he'd not sprung this on his mother first, she smiled uncertainly. "Well, I'm flattered . . . I guess. Were you doing this while we were married?"

"Oh, all the time!" Gavin bubbled. "My God, you had some fabulous dresses. Of course your shoes, skirts, and bras didn't fit."

It made sense, of course. She remembered the sweaters and dresses that would come up missing for a time, then suddenly, a week or a month later, reappear in her closet seemingly stretched out a size larger.

They didn't say anything for a moment. Then, because she didn't know much about the world of cross-dressers, she had a panicked thought. "Wait a minute. Does this mean that you're . . . I mean, are you . . ."

"Gay? Not even close, and I'll punch out anybody who says I am. Lots of cross-dressers are straights who just like getting gussied up in women's clothes. See, when I was . . ."

Behind him, she spied Cynthia's car slowly approaching. When she mentioned that Cynthia was pulling up at the curb, Gavin's first reaction was to step back into the juniper bushes. She grabbed his gloved hand and pulled him back onto the walkway.

"Stay here. You'll be more conspicuous hiding in the bushes. Pretend you're my next-door neighbor. Say you came over to borrow a clothes brush."

Cynthia waved as she got out of the car.

Gavin pulled his shawl tight around his shoulders.

"Promise me, Adele," he whispered. "Promise you won't tell her it's me."

"Sure, no problem." She couldn't wait to see the look on Cyn's face when she told her—it would be worth breaking out the camera for.

"Hiiieeee," Cynthia called cheerfully from halfway across the lawn, where she stooped to pick up Adele's house keys. They both waved back.

Walking past the couple, Cynthia fit the key into the lock and opened the door. "Hey Gavin, you're looking good," she said without pause, and entered the house, closing the door behind her.

"I'll get there as soon as I'm done talking to Douglas," Adele said. "I'll probably park a few blocks away and run to your car. Two people sitting in a car talking aren't as conspicuous." She picked up the small notebook from the kitchen table and handed it to her doubting friend Cynthia.

"Let's go over the pager codes one more time."

Cyn nodded and read down the list. "One means get the police. Two means everything is cool. Three means go to Ellis. Four—go to Reverend Wynn's. Five—go to Adele's house. Six—go to Douglas's. Seven—danger, proceed with caution. Eight means check my answering machine for a full message. Nine means stat. Zero means I copy your message.

"So one-nine-four-seven means call the police stat, go to Wynn's, and proceed with caution. Right?"

"Ten-four, babe."

"God, Tim would brain me if he knew I was staking out Roger's house."

"Yeah, well, I can't believe *they* aren't. I mean, if Roger is a major suspect, then why aren't the cops up there?"

Cynthia rolled her eyes. "Oh come on, Del. Even Roger wouldn't be that dense. He's on the run. The only reason he'd come back here would be if he *wanted* to be caught and punished."

"Well, if that's the case, then your boyfriend won't have anything to be upset about if you stake out Roger's, right?"

Cynthia hadn't thought of it like that. For a brief moment, the bad feeling she'd been harboring about the mission eased.

"Just remember," Adele continued, "don't get out of the car whatever you do. Park far enough away so you have a good view with the binoculars, but make sure you can't be seen. Try to park behind another vehicle, or across the street at a corner. Don't worry about my finding you—the Blessed Virgin Mary isn't exactly easy to miss."

Cynthia's automobile was an unreliable 1965 VW bug she'd baptized the Blessed Virgin Mary—Mare for short. Although Cynthia was an Un-Christian, the car's deep blue color reminded her of the robe the religious celebrity consistently wore in pictures and in stained-glass windows. And with the car's license plate—BVM 001—the name seemed preordained.

"Until I get there, take notes of everything that happens and keep the car doors locked. If anything significant happens, use the pager."

Cynthia saluted in affirmation, although she was still somewhat skeptical. It had begun to take on the flavor of a Lucy Ricardo–Ethel Mertz conspiracy, set in a *Texas Chainsaw Massacre* plot. She rubbed Nelson's rump with her bare foot, trying to ignore the weird feeling in her throat. Something, she thought, was backward—not quite what it was supposed to be.

Cynthia pushed the disconcerting thoughts to the Fibber McGee closet of her mind and locked the door. She'd learned over the years to trust her friend's judgment, especially when it came to fitting irregularly shaped pieces together. Why Adele had stayed in nursing was beyond her. Endowed with an abundance of intelligence and intuition, Adele was worthy of a more challenging profession; biochemical engineering or a doctorate in criminology would have better fit her personality.

She watched Adele carefully examine the inner mechanism of her pager so she would fully understand how the thing worked, and bit her lip. She wasn't so sure about staking out a house that was probably going to remain empty, but then again, Adele must have had a good reason for asking her to go there—she wouldn't send her on a wild-goose chase.

She opened her mouth to tell Adele about how something didn't feel right, and changed her mind. Intuition about those things wasn't her strong point anyway—those instincts were all in Adele's domain. She wouldn't want Adele thinking she'd taken up Helen's proclivity for prophecy.

"You okay?" Adele asked. Picking up on Cynthia's apprehension, she'd left off studying the pager.

Cynthia entered a code number and sent it to Adele's pager, which quietly vibrated five seconds later.

A red "2" flashed on the LCD window.

* * *

Cynthia O'Neil was glad she'd worn what she called her "sleuthing outfit": leggings, socks, shoes, turtleneck, face scarf, gloves, and beret—all black. It was an outfit she'd worn a dozen or more times in her years as an obsessive-compulsive, love-addicted woman who consistently fell for misogynistic men. During those years and those particular men, she'd learned what many an obsessed woman inevitably came to know—the excitement of spy-and-stakeout detail.

It would start out innocently enough with a simple drive by his house or apartment—just to see if he was home. Then there would be an escalation of drive-bys—once an hour, every hour of every day and night, until sleep deprivation became a problem.

Then there was the task of writing down all the license plate numbers of cars (including all pink vehicles, or other "suspiciously" feminine autos) parked within a block's radius of his residence and then having a cop friend run checks on each plate.

When that failed to turn up anything, the final step was the stakeout. The stakeout entailed borrowing a car—one he wouldn't recognize—and parking it in full view of his house. Camouflage in the form of wigs and dark glasses was donned, and then the house was watched (without blinking) for the slightest of movements.

Once, after the object of her attentions caught her spying, she invented the box trick. In the side of a cardboard box of appropriate size, she cut a hole in the shape of an arrow. Above the hole she printed "THIS SIDE UP."

Sitting in the front passenger seat, she would place it over the top half of herself, situating the sides so she could watch from the arrow hole. Her legs and lap were covered with a blanket, so to the casual passerby it appeared to be only a box sitting on the seat.

She was glad she hadn't thrown it away.

Sitting less than thirty feet from Reverend Wynn's front door, Cynthia moved the peep arrow so it gave her a clear view of the house and driveway. In the notebook in her lap, she blindly jotted down notes:

19:14—Squirrel on garage roof.

She momentarily considered crossing out the entry, but changed her mind. Adele did say to make note of *every*thing.

19:16—St. Hilary's Church (east—right side—of Wynn's garage) dark. Front doors to church locked (checked upon arrival).

Lamp on in front r. window of rectory. Newspaper inside plastic wrap lying on top doorstep. Wynn's car not visible. No cars parked near rectory except the BVM. Garage/driveway to r. of house. Spotlight over garage door not on. Garage door closed. No windows in garage. No sign of life . . . or death.

FIFTEEN

ADELE'S ANSWERING MACHINE BURPED UP three messages.

One: Gavin's mother tearfully repeating several times that she didn't understand why Adele was rejecting her son, and couldn't she please forgive "her boy" and try to start over?

Adele thought about it for two seconds and decided she didn't have enough clothes to start over.

Two: Douglas saying he had information on Helen he thought she would want to hear but he was going to the lab for a while and would be home later and what was going on that she had not returned any of his calls and was she angry with him and he hoped she wasn't and he hoped he hadn't said or done anything to offend her because she meant a great deal to him and would she PLEASE call him the second she got home and leave a message because he was worried and he was so glad she hadn't been hurt yesterday and maybe the next time she'd listen to him.

Fat chance.

Three: Henry Williams telling her he *had* to speak with her right away. He'd remembered something important about the day Uncle Milty got himself cut. He gave a number Adele recognized as a Marin City prefix and told her to call right away.

She dialed and got a busy signal.

The Salem chime clock on the mantel chimed the half hour although the face read 6:38. It reminded her she was ravenous. She would eat and then try Henry again.

Carrying his Mickey Mouse rug by a ragged corner, Nelson followed her to the kitchen. He'd been upset and whiny since she stepped inside the house. Usually he behaved particularly well when Cynthia was around, but tonight he'd refused to leave her side, despite Cynthia's presence. At first she thought it was because Gavin had been spooking around the house, but when he was still shadowing her long after Gavin had been sent click-clacking home on his high-heeled pumps, she put up her finely tuned antenna.

After giving the dog his spinach-and-garbanzo-bean surprise, she opened the cereal drawer, pulled out the puffed wheat, and dumped a layer on the bottom of a mixing bowl. On top of that went consecutive layers of rolled oats, rice bran, rice flakes, nonfat granola mix, and whole dried bananas. Over that she poured rice milk and a cup of plain, nonfat yogurt.

It was while she was topping the mixture with a layer of sliced apple and nutmeg that Nelson growled, his hackles up and bristling like a Marine's buzz cut. Slinking low to the ground, he crept into the hallway and stared intently at the bedroom door.

Adele whistled "I've Been Working on the Railroad" to cover the panic that was causing the hairs on her arms to stand straight up. In an attempt to make normal kitchen noises, she banged the knife on the side of the bowl, opened and closed a few drawers, dropped a spoon, and ran water in the sink.

Nelson growled again and crept closer to the bedroom door.

In a light singsong voice, raised to cover her trembling, she called to "Mommy's wittle-dittle wover bunny" to come and get his "nummy-num-nums." She figured whoever or whatever was in the bedroom would never suspect for a moment she would talk like that if she were panicking, or, she supposed, if there were another human being within earshot.

Just as she was beginning to think perhaps Nelson was an idiot and she was starting to feel embarrassed for herself, there was a creak of a particular floorboard which she knew after six years of tenancy was exactly ten inches from her bedroom door. It was the only squeaky board in the house.

"Amazing Grace" was hummed loudly, intermittently interrupted with baby-talk doggie praises. All the while gathering purse, car keys, and pager, Adele snapped on Nelson's leash, ran the water in the kitchen sink one more time, banged two or three pans, then noiselessly let herself and the dog out the side door of the kitchen.

The second she hit the driveway, she ran like hell for the Beast, praying to the Jesus she didn't believe in to please let the car wake up and start.

Adele patted the Beast's dashboard chest and said "I love you" several times to it and then to Nelson, who sat happily in the backseat, chewing on his rug.

She felt for the Colt and put it in her purse, then

removed it and slid it under the seat again. She wouldn't need it for now. She'd go to Douglas's and ask him why he'd lied to her about the shrink's report, ask what information he had on Helen, Meg, and Roger, and hope he'd let her join Cynthia in the stakeout without having to air some pedantic, anal-retentive reprimand. She also hoped he'd give her something to take with her to eat.

Cynthia's neck veins were beginning to bulge. She cursed the three cups of coffee she'd downed before she left Adele's. What had started out as a distant, gentle call of nature had turned into the raging scream of urgency.

She clicked on her penlight and looked down at the scribbled entries in her notebook. In order by exact times of occurrence were the descriptions of each of the three cars that had passed, the squirrel foraging for food in the side garden, and the whistling teenage boy who paused on the sidewalk in front of the house long enough to hitch up his jeans and give his prunes a good tumble.

Her bladder threatened her; she would have to either move quickly or deal with the consequences. She looked out the passenger window, measuring the distance to the curb. She could squat alongside the car. The act of micturition, from start to finish, would take less than forty seconds, and there hadn't been any activity in or around the house for over twenty minutes. The odds seemed right.

Slowly, she pushed the box over her head and set it in the backseat. Sliding out the passenger door, she crouched and began pulling her leggings down over her buttocks. As she was ready to let go, the glare of headlights abruptly reflected off her side-view mirror.

In fast motion, she swore with feeling, pulled up her leggings, and ducked back inside the car. Judging from the distance of the approaching car and the angle at which the VW was parked, she doubted she'd been seen, but wasn't sure.

The car slowed to a crawl as it came alongside the VW.

Cynthia broke into a sweat. What if she had been spotted bare-assed by a patrol car? She'd be cited for indecent exposure and then Tim would have something to tease her about forever. She'd never be able to show her face at any of the sheriff's or police department functions, or considering the way men gossiped among themselves, at the Firemen's Ball either.

The automobile seemed to come to a halt. She decided to sit up and wave a friendly greeting to the officer as soon as the searchlight went on. She could come up with a million excuses: she was sick, tired, dizzy, or someone slipped a diuretic in her coffee.

If those things failed she could always mention that she was a nurse and then throw on the charm. She'd drop Tim's name a few times, perhaps even call him her main squeeze. No cop would ever cite another cop's intended, let alone a nurse.

The headlights suddenly disappeared and the car sounded like it was going in another direction. Risking a peek, Cynthia saw the beige BMW 2002 move up the driveway at a snail's pace. The garage door automatically opened and swallowed the car.

Several minutes later, the Reverend Roger Wynn emerged from a garage side door carrying a briefcase and a duffel bag. He leisurely made his way to the front door, picked up the newspaper, and went inside.

Man, this guy's got some kinda pits inside those prunes! thought Cynthia. *Half the cops in California want to hang his ass, and he's walking around like he's Mr. Rogers going to do some gardening in his neighborhood.*

The house lights went on room by room as the scream of urgency threatened to crack the dam of her sphincter's resistance. Cynthia decided to kill two birds with one stone—she would relieve herself in Reverend Wynn's side yard while peeping in his windows.

Running as fast as she could on legs held together tightly at the knees, she found a bush and squatted. At three feet above ground level, Cynthia would recall later, it was like someone was breaking out of Auschwitz or a maximum-security prison. Wailing sirens cut through the night's silence as rotating red and white spotlights scanned the premises.

It figured. If anyone had a security system straight out of San Quentin, it would be someone like Roger Wynn.

As she pulled up her leggings, the waistband caught on a sticker. Ripping the entire branch off the bush, she turned to run, and found herself facing two round holes at the end of a double-barrel shotgun.

Halfway there, she suddenly realized the Collier address was in one of Marin's most elite areas. As it turned out, his was the largest house on Mount Tam's southwest ridge.

Adele parked the Beast in the driveway, and like the mother of a toddler, took great pains to noiselessly sneak from the car so as not to wake the sleeping dog in the backseat.

Peeking through the windows of the three-car garage,

which was attached to the house itself, she could see a large freezer (Unwritten Rule #53: Carnivores always own freezers), two mountain bikes with matching helmets, boxes and cans of various poisons and chemicals, a garden hose, gardening tools, a workout area with several pieces of gym equipment and free weights, a wall-mounted TV, cardboard boxes, a set of golf clubs (this item alone was prohibitive of any possibility of a romance), a basketball, and a workshop with saws, hammers, and other homeowner's tools. The only thing missing from this portrait of the American Professional Male's garage was his black Lexus.

She sat on the front-porch swing for five minutes playing with the pager, got bored, and did some stretches. When she grew tired of that, she wound her way to the back of the house, where a screened-in patio had been built around a kidney-shaped pool.

The patio's elegant wicker furnishings gave the space the feel of a luxurious verandah in the tropics. Delighted to find the screen door unlocked, she went immediately for the door to the main house, which, to her astonishment, was also unlocked. That someone like Douglas would leave his house open seemed extremely unanal and suspicious. For a moment she froze in place with her hand on the doorknob and considered the possibilities. He could be inside unaware of her presence, he could be inside and dead, he might be watching her to see if she would take advantage of the open house, he might be next door borrowing a cup of sugar, or he could really be at his office.

She knocked, then stuck her head inside the door and called out in a loud, neighborly voice.

There's no one home, answered the welcoming committee that had gathered to greet her. *But come on in and make yourself feel welcome. We're sure Dougie won't mind.*

She nodded in agreement and pushed open the door. Certainly Douglas wouldn't mind if she went inside to make a cup of tea, although it was sometimes hard to tell with anal-retentives what would and wouldn't be okay. In her experience, they transformed into passive-aggressives at the drop of a hat.

Throwing caution to the winds, she found herself in a gourmet kitchen right out of *Sunset Magazine.* Instantly, the idea of an innocent cup of tea was replaced with the less innocent but more attractive notion that it wouldn't hurt to take a quick look around—emphasis on quick.

Forging on uninvited, she assuaged her guilt with the thought that if she was going to consider dating him, she needed to know what kind of house he kept. Like going through someone's garbage or their medicine cabinet, it could give her as much information about the guy as a full six months of fooling around. The pragmatic way she chose to look at it, not only would she be saving them both a whole lot of time, but when one considered what he might lay out for dinners, gifts, gas, plays, ballets, movies, she was actually saving him money.

With the first step, the thick Persian rugs that covered most of the hardwood floors barked at her to remove her shoes. Most normal people who owned Persian rugs were anal-retentive about them—he'd be downright hostile.

She listened carefully for the sound of a car pulling up, heard nothing, and ascended the stairs to the left of the informal dining room two at a time. The second-story

hallway, lined with expensive antiques, was more elegant
than most living rooms she'd ever been in. Inside the first
door to her left, she found a large airy bedroom done in
shades of light salmon and forest green. Expensively
framed Currier and Ives hunt scenes hung on the walls.
The walk-in closet was filled with beautifully tailored
men's suits and shirts, while in the corner of the room
was a rack of shoe trees bearing several pairs of Bass and
Bruno Magli fruit. It was a room, she imagined, in which
Prince Charles might feel at home.

At the other end of the hall, the even more expansive
master bedroom took her breath away. Done white on
white, the decidedly more feminine room sported a massive canopy bed on a platform. Surrounding this altar
were huge round windows through which could be seen
parts of Mount Tam and the tops of several redwoods.
Facing the foot of the bed was a carved fireplace in
veined white marble.

The master bath—found at the rear of "his" and "her"
dressing rooms—unhinged her jaw. Two jade-green
marble columns stood on either side of a sunken open
shower. Beyond the shower was a set of steps leading to
a steam room of matching marble.

Fighting the urge to strip and take a shower, she rushed
back into the hallway. At the end of the hall she found a
third door, which was locked. She decided it led to some
sort of attic room reserved for storage . . . or the family
jewels.

Sliding down the banister, Adele went to the front of
the house, where the black, white, and crimson marble
front hall was lit by a massive crystal chandelier. The
foyer from *The War of the Roses* came vividly to mind.

After a logical progression of thoughts, she came to the question of what kind of investments the guy had made to be able to sit in the lap of luxury. County coroners couldn't make more than about seventy thousand a year, so the extra had to come from somewhere.

The idea of a having a romance with the man crossed her mind again. As she stared at the chandelier ten feet above her head, she had a vision of herself as Mrs. Douglas Collier, driving a forest-green Jaguar with tan leather interior to Whole Foods for her weekly shopping spree, and then poring over expensive catalogs in the privacy of her marble bath. Nelson would lie next to her in front of the fireplace, having his nails clipped and filed by the professional groomer who came each day to brush his coat and check for nasty, socially unacceptable fleas. His Mickey Mouse rug would have to go.

She took several strawberry gummie worms from a Waterford crystal jar on the entrance table. Nibbling the sweet, she meandered into what appeared to be the library/den.

"Very chic, darling," she said to Ramón, the imaginary interior decorator at her side. "Except I simply *must* have that chair recovered. Let's say a simple off-white linen with . . ."

Out of the corner of her eye, she caught sight of someone standing behind the door.

Whirling around she came face-to-face with a hideous old man.

"What are you doing?" Roger Wynn—or someone who closely resembled him—cradled the shotgun with shaking hands. The man appeared thinner, paler, and more haggard-looking than Roger Wynn. Where there once was a goatee and mustache now grew an ugly grayish brown stubble. Behind his puffy eyes was a haunted, savage gleam.

"I . . . I was driving by and I felt sick and thought I was going to throw up, so I saw your bushes here and I didn't want to throw up in the street and mess up your sidewalk, so . . ." Cynthia trailed off. It sounded ridiculous.

The man glowered at her.

"I was waiting for you to get home," she said finally.

"You couldn't come to the door like a decent human being? You had to go sneaking around like some kind of back-street filth!" Lowering the gun, he grabbed at her arm and yanked her closer to him, until she could smell his breath. The stink was what she called "nervous mouth"—as putrid an odor as nervous BO. Cynthia tried to pull out of his grip and found herself being yanked off her feet. His hand darted behind her back; she opened her mouth to scream, but no sound came out.

The last thing she felt before she blacked out was a sharp, stabbing pain above her left kidney.

The old man, whose name tag read "Jeeves," was someone's idea of an objet d'art. The full-sized wax figure had been dressed as a butler, complete with silver serving tray in his outstretched hand. His features were perfectly lifelike, yet somehow grotesque in their authenticity. The figures in *House of Wax* had nothing on Jeeves. It was, she thought appreciatively, a part of Douglas's sense of humor. Thank God he had one.

On Jeeves's tray lay a single ivory linen card. Printed

in elegant black script, the message read: "Teatime, you fuck pig."

Adele laughed out loud like a crazy woman. Again.

She had turned away from the figure, when curiosity climbed onto her back to nag her. This specific curiosity stemmed from the same curiosity that caused young children to automatically lift the skirts of a new doll to see what was under there.

Embarrassed that even her imaginary friends might see her doing such a thing, she surreptitiously turned her back to the dignified Jeeves and reached around to unzip his fly.

She reached in.

Instead of a flaccid wax penis, her fingers found a floppy disk.

Before she even opened her eyes, the nurse slid her hand up to the sharp, burning pain in her back and felt a sticky wetness through her sweater. Close by was the sound of a man's harsh breathing.

"Wake up! What's wrong with you?"

Cynthia felt herself being roughly shaken. Disoriented, she slowly opened her eyes, sure she would find herself in her own bed, Tim leaning over her. The stickiness on her back would be where she had momentarily fallen asleep or passed out at the moment of ecstasy on the wet spot.

Instead she stared into the face of the Reverend Roger Wynn, who had a halo of the full moon behind his head. Her first horrible impression was that she had had outdoor sex with the Devil and Reverend Wynn. Immediately she regretted it.

"Are you sick?" asked Roger in a tone of restrained impatience. "What should I do?"

She shook her head, the details of how she'd ended up on the ground falling back into place. "You stabbed me?" she asked, feeling for the wound. "Are you going to kill me now?"

Roger sat back on his haunches and ran a hand through his hair. "What in the name of Jesus are you talking about? Are you high on drugs?"

Cynthia sat up and lifted her sweater, searching for the wound in earnest. Roger pulled away the branch stuck to her and held it up. "A bougainvillea thorn. They're like the claws of the Devil."

He briefly examined her back and helped her to her feet. "Come into the rectory and wash off the blood. I can't see if the thorn is still in there. If it is, you'll have to go to the emergency room. That'll give you plenty of time to tell me what this is about."

Cynthia stopped in her tracks. "First, why don't you tell me where you've been?"

The rage returned to his face. "Me tell *you* where I've . . . That's none of your business! Who do you think you are, coming into *my* yard, spying on me with your clothes half off? For God's sake!" Roger threw up his hands, disgusted. "I'm not going to engage you any longer. I'm calling the police and having you arrested for trespassing."

"Oh sure, Roger." Cynthia put her hands on her hips. "Go on, make my day. Call the police. Do think I'm a moron? Half the police in Northern California are looking for you." She pointed in the direction of the house. "Go ahead. Call the police."

Roger looked at her as though she'd lost her mind. His expression made her hesitate. He seemed genuinely mystified.

Waving her away, he resumed heading for the rectory. "You're hysterical. I'm calling the police."

Snapping to, Cynthia grabbed him by the arm. "Hey, wait." She studied his expression. "Shit, man, don't you know what's going on around here?"

"No. What are you . . ." He roughly pulled his arm out of her grip and moved again in the direction of the house. "If you think you can deceive me with some story you make up as you go along so I won't call the police, you can think again, because I intend to—"

"Roger, you're wanted in connection with the murder of Helen Marval."

His eyes widened and then narrowed in a scowl.

"It's true. The police found evidence at Helen Marval's that was directly traced to you." She assessed the expression rolling over his face and decided to hit him with everything. "They also want you for questioning about Gayle's disappearance. Your car was identified as the one that left Max's parking lot that morning. You're the prime suspect."

Wynn dropped the shotgun and kicked it away as if it were a cobra ready to strike. Folding his hands in prayer, he pressed his thumbs against his forehead and squeezed his eyes shut. "Dear God, forgive me. Forgive me the sin of my pride which has cost another precious life."

He ran, stumbling, the rest of the way to the house. The pain in her back forgotten, Cynthia caught up with him at the door and took hold of his arm. "What the hell is going on?"

Roger shook her hand off. "Get away from me. I've got to call the police right away."

She blocked him. "You can't do that."

He stared at her.

"Not yet," she said in a more reasonable tone. "Talk to me before you go walking into the lion's den, and I'll tell you the rap the police have on you."

He hesitated, distrustful of her motives. "How would *you* know what the police . . ."

"Let's just say that at this point in time, I'm solidly in bed with the police department."

Leaving Jeeves and his floppy disk as she found them, she went into Douglas's office meaning to check out the wall art. The phone on his desk reminded her to call Henry.

Adele chuckled. Considering the fact that she'd taken a major tour of his house without his knowledge, she was sure Douglas wouldn't mind if she used the phone either. The appropriate aphorism for anal-retentives, she decided, should be: "What you don't know can't hurt you."

Sitting at the desk, she dialed Henry's number, which was still busy. Idly she looked around, trying like hell to ignore the computer screen less than a foot from her nose. It proved difficult since the screen saver was a colorful animated display of red strawberries raining down from a blue sky. As soon as the strawberries hit the ground, they turned into red gummie worms inching their way to the edge of the screen, where they automatically recycled back into strawberries.

Why don't you open the top drawer? asked one of her

jet set–type imaginary friends. *I'm sure it will be perfectly all right to do so.*

"Oh. Well, okay," chirped Adele cheerfully. "As long as I have your permission, I think I will."

There was, of course, a picture-perfect array of pens and pencils, scissors, a set of neatly labeled keys, and other desk basics. She started to close the drawer, when her eye was caught by a glint of gold in the paper-clip holder. Adele pried off the clear plastic top and shook out the contents into the palm of her hand.

A gold chain holding an elegant moonstone pendant sat conspicuously in the nest of steel clips. Her stomach tightened. She was used to seeing the unusual pendant on someone . . . someone she knew. She closed her eyes and relaxed her shoulders, trying to picture the neck from which the piece hung. Freckles. Light skin prematurely damaged by too much sun; skin that belonged to a blond woman . . . a woman not usually given to such touches of femininity as jewelry. Had it been in with Chloe's personal effects and he'd brought it home by mistake? No. Whose was it?

Adele opened her eyes and found herself staring at a framed black-and-white photograph on his wall. It was a picture of a naked pregnant woman lying on her back, screaming in pain. The title of the photograph was "Childbirth."

She returned the piece of jewelry to the world of paper clips and put the holder carefully back into its proper place. The answer to the question of who it belonged to would probably wake her out of a sound sleep sometime during the night.

Deliberately, she brought her eyes to the computer

screen and boldly hit the space bar. The whimsical screen saver instantly disappeared, revealing Douglas's desktop menu. Rolling the cursor to "Shortcuts," she clicked the mouse. It would be interesting to see what he'd been working on the last few days.

Clicking on "File Menu" revealed he had been working on four recent documents. The first was titled "HAIR."

It was with the rationalized guilt of a woman who goes through her husband's pockets searching out clues which might point to illicit love that she opened the file and devoured the first three screens of material.

She held her bottom lip between her teeth, holding off a giggle. Douglas had been doing his homework on hair transplants. The file contained data on the various techniques, and lists of doctors and fee schedules.

She was musing over the various donor sites for hair when the sound of a car motor set her fingers in fast motion to return to the main menu. She ran out the back and arranged herself on the patio chaise longue.

The car passed.

Like an addict who'd hit the lottery, she returned to his desk and opened the second file, labeled, "TAX RPTS ST. HILARY'S," which proved to be just what it said—boring tax reports for the church.

The third, titled "FINANCE," was nothing more than downloaded information about the S&P 500. Nothing about how much he made or what he invested his money in.

She clicked on the last file, titled "PULSE." The machine made a bleeping noise and a message appeared: "CANNOT ACCESS THAT FILE."

She returned to the list, studied the document title, and

saw that it was a D drive file. That meant it would be on a floppy disk. Making a beeline for Jeeves, Adele violated him without a care as to which of her imaginary friends saw her do it.

Unmarked floppy in place, she clicked on and received the command "ENTER PASSWORD."

Instead of deterring her, the command was like flashing a slice of moist Jarlsberg cheese at a starving rodent. She tried a variety of words, each time getting the "PASSWORD INCORRECT. DOCUMENT LOCKED" message.

Think, said the imaginary Nancy Drew. *Yeah,* said Mike Hammer. *Some small thing . . . a favorite number or color.*

"Six," she remembered. "His lucky number is six, and his favorite color is salmon."

There you go, doll, said Sam Spade. *Find a six-letter word.*

Salmon. Corpse. Embalm. Baldie. Pulses. Deaths. Secret. Diener. Gummie. Fucked. All earned "PASSWORD INCORRECT" messages.

The grandfather clock in the hall chimed seven times. It reminded her to call Henry again. Adele took several gummie worms from the crystal candy dish and chewed thoughtfully.

She typed "S-T-R-B-R-I," got a "PASSWORD INCORRECT" message, and punched in Henry's number.

"S-T-R-B-E-I"—"INCORRECT."

A man answered the phone. "Yo?"

"Henry?"

"Yeah?"

She typed "S-T-R-B-R-E." "INCORRECT."

"It's Adele. What's up?"

"Hey, sister. I was thinking 'bout how you asked me to remember anything strange 'bout Sony getting herself killed, and I remembered something else that was weird."

"Shoot."

"S-T-R-B-E-R."

"But it ain't 'bout Sony, right?"

"INCORRECT."

"Shit. I mean, yeah, okay. No problem."

"It probably don't mean nothing, so don't be making any big deal out of it."

She typed "S-T-R-B-R-Y."

"Everything means something, Hen. Just spill it and don't—"

The machine made a whirring groan and the screen opened onto a document edged with a thick black line.

Thrilled, Adele began to scroll down.

"Adele?"

"Oh my God."

"What're you doing, girl? Where you at?"

Her eyes were rapidly scanning screen after screen of information on the Women's Clinic—lists of all physicians and nurses who had volunteered at the clinic, and the periods of time during which they had worked.

Below that information were statistics, broken down into columns of how many abortions had been performed each month since it had opened six years before. Below that were lists of the ages, incomes, races, and religious affiliations of the patients.

The following screens held the names of fifteen medical-professional volunteers who had worked specifically in the abortion clinic.

Next to the first six names was a skull-and-crossbones symbol. Sonya Martin, John Ganet, Gina Ducke, Chloe Anne Sedrick, Aaron Milton, Gayle Mueller. After the symbol was a date, a time, a location, and a paragraph or two of notes. Her eyes blurred with the rush of adrenaline.

She forced her eyes back to the woman in the black-and-white photograph. Her respiratory rate was up to the mid-30s.

"Everything means something, Henry," Adele repeated numbly, sounding out of breath. "What did you remember?"

"The morning Uncle Milty got himself killed?"

"Uhn-huh?" Adele tried to swallow. She'd just remembered who wore the moonstone pendant and had bragged that she'd never once taken it off since the day her father fastened the clasp on it forty years before. Automatically her eyes sought out Gayle's name, stumbled over two words—*fought hard*—and stopped.

". . . so I had to do a night shift and there weren't nothing happening so I took myself a snooze down in the engineer's room." Henry laughed. "Now you don't go telling nobody 'bout this, 'cause they'd fire my black ass if they knew I was sleeping on the job.

"I mean, it don't harm nothing. They can beep me if they need me, right?"

"If I worked nights I'd do the same thing, Hen." Adele's eyes drifted back to the screen and sought out Sonya's name. She dared to read the first paragraph beyond the name.

Present in the House of Murder during the killing of The Son. October 12, 6:22 a.m. Ellis utility room, Ward 8.

Defiled the Priestess of Female Filth and Temptation. Main airway, internal and external jugulars severed. Complete cessation of physical activity: 62 seconds. No struggle. Minor seizure at 21st second.

Witness to be dealt with at future date.

"That's all right, sister," Henry said.

Adele was barely listening.

"I got paged about two A.M., so I was coming out of the engineer's office, and I saw the coroner coming out of the incinerator room, right?

"Now, Adele, you don't know this, but don't nobody go in there at night 'cept those housekeeping boys when they're sneaking around for a place to flop. Coroner went whiter than a nigger's teeth in a dark alley when he saw me. That man was burning something—something he didn't want anybody to see. Why else would that man be in the incinerator room? So when I tell one of the housekeeping boys about it, he tells me he's seen him in there before too."

Adele's hands were shaking so badly she could barely hold the phone. She stood up and sat back down immediately, her knees gone to jelly.

She pulled out the pager, frantically trying to remember the code numbers.

"Uh-huh," she mumbled, took a deep breath, and pressed 1-9-6-7. She hit the pager's send button, remembered to breathe, and forced her eyes back to the screen.

Gina Ducke: Direct accomplice to The Son's Murder. Extermination executed: October 1, 12:36 a.m. Partial ether administration. Abducted from underground garage 3441 Elliston St., Sacramento, without complication.

Extermination site: 3.8 mi. east of Northface Rd., Sacra-mento. Hunter's car park.

1:14 a.m.: Defiled orally and rectally before partial disembowelment. Allowed to come to full consciousness. Vomited twice. Death struggle: Total 14 minutes 6 sec-onds. Mental function fully intact: 6 min. 22 seconds.

1:19 a.m.: Holy Uterus removed and consumed in full view of Bitch Filth.

Verbalizations: "Why?" "Please no." "Jesus help me." "Mommy." Wept first two minutes of consciousness. Two seizures during last five minutes before initial extermina-tion complete (Seizure A: Two minutes four seconds. Seizure B: Twenty seconds). 1:43 a.m.: Hands and breasts amputated and preserved. 2:01 a.m.: Rest of remains prepared and packaged for transport and easy disposal. Reported missing 10/4 by mother to Sacramento PD.

Adele retched. *Holy Uterus consumed? Prepared and packaged?*

Unable to stop herself, her eyes went to Gayle's name long enough to read:

Transfer of body from BMW to storage room achieved within garage. Defiled rectally. Death struggle spectacu-larly active despite disembowelment and amputation of hands and breasts. Total record time: 32 min. 14 sec-onds!! Consumed Holy Uterus and one breast. Observed by whore. Unusually large amount of adipose tissue in breasts. Sweet. Similar to pork.

Preparation for disposal delayed while car returned to rectory.

Her finger accidentally clicked the mouse, and another screen replaced what she was having a hard time compre-hending. It was the schedule of abortions performed on October 12 two years prior. Highlighted in red was the 8:15 A.M. appointment: *Dana Collier, 31, primipara, fetal age: 11 weeks, referred by Dr. Aaron Milton. TAB by Dr. John Ganet, assisted by Gina Ducke, R.N.*

She clicked the mouse again, and the next screen exploded in shades of deep purple and red. In the center was a graphic of a devil-like form dressed in a hooded robe, holding out a baby in his taloned fingers as if in offering. The Old English script on the hood of his robe read, "Death to the Murderers of The Lord Satan's Children."

The text below the display began, *Death to all foul whores who steal the sperm from good men and murder their children. Death to all butchers who murder the babes of The Lord Satan in the Holy Wombs.*

He killed them all, Adele thought. He killed them one at a time in order—systematically, the way he ate his food.

Henry's voice, loud and sharp, came from far away.

"Hey, Adele! You hearing me or what?"

"Uhn?"

"What's wrong with you, girl? You hear what I was saying? I said I think the man was—"

The call-waiting beep interrupted his words.

"Gotta hang up now!" Adele said, panicked. "Talk later."

The phone rang almost immediately after she hit the disconnect button on the handset. At the second ring the answering machine picked up. Adele held her breath. If it was Douglas calling to retrieve his messages, he'd notice the phone had rung an extra time or two.

Instead of the rewind of messages, the red room-monitor light flickered on. She froze in place, a thousand reasons to panic parading through her mind. It was Douglas, and of course he'd have noticed the extra ring, and what if the computer suddenly made any one of its numerous computer noises, or what if he could hear her breathing?

She held her breath and instantly had an uncontrollable urge to cough. Breaking into a sweat, she covered her mouth with the bottom of her sweater. Her eyes glued to the red monitor light, she tussled with the cough, as though it were a demon inside her trying to get out in order to destroy the world.

The second the call disconnected and the monitor light went off, the mother of all coughs violently erupted. When the respiratory explosion was over, she returned the computer to the main screen, replaced Jeeves's floppy appendage, and in a daze headed toward the door leading to the garage.

SIXTEEN

". . . THE CAR AT MAX'S, THE HISTORY, THE SHOE tracks, the disappearing act the day Helen was murdered—it all pointed to you." Cynthia warmed her hands on the coffee cup, alternately keeping a watch out the window for Adele and an eye on the man as he paced.

"Thank you for telling me this," he said finally, stopping long enough to give her arm a squeeze. The small gesture engendered a sense of trust in her. She'd begun feeling sorry for him; he was wearing an old, knotty gray sweater that had a hole near the underarm. He looked pitiful.

"The police will find you here," she said quietly. "They'll arrest you and charge you with—"

"I hope they do find me." He smiled sadly. "It'll save the church a toll call."

He was close enough that Cynthia got a good look at his teeth—a little yellowed, but otherwise a normal set; she had half expected something akin to broken fangs. "Why do you want them to find you?"

"I'll tell them to get a search warrant for Douglas Collier's home and office. I'm sure they'll turn up enough to put the man away for a couple of lifetimes."

A surge of panic ripped through her, settling in her stomach. "What are you talking about? What's Doug got to do with this?"

He shook his head, mimicking her. "What's Doug got to do with this?" He laughed derisively and resumed pacing. "Everything. He . . . he's . . . a . . . I can't say. I'm under an obligation of confidentiality."

She slapped the table with the flat of her hand and stretched her neck forward. "Are you kidding me? I took a major risk spilling my guts to you." She glared at him, ignoring the stinging of her palm. "I want to know what the hell Dr. Collier has to do with this. Adele is with him as we speak. If she's in danger, I have to know."

"She's with him? Right now?" He stopped pacing. He was perspiring heavily. "Did she ever volunteer at the Women's Clinic?"

"She's a good nurse, but not much of an altruist. She doesn't volunteer—she guards her time off like a miser guards his money."

He visibly relaxed, rubbing the side of his face where the stubble was thickest. "Okay. She's probably not in danger for the time being—or as long as she stays in the dark about who she's dealing with."

"Who *is* she dealing with, Roger? What are we talking about here?"

He paced the length of the dining room, obviously having a moral battle with himself.

Cynthia sighed irritably.

Shoulders slumping in reluctant concession, he began. "Collier had a wife named—"

"Dana," interjected Cynthia impatiently. "I know her. We went through mortuary college together."

He nodded absently. "She and Douglas were my parishioners. Two years ago, she got pregnant while on birth control pills. For reasons that weren't clear to me at the beginning, she didn't want children—not with Douglas, anyhow—so she decided to have an abortion.

"Douglas was so adamantly opposed to terminating the pregnancy, and she was so determined to have the abortion with or without his consent, that he handcuffed her and locked her in their attic.

"Dana begged him to let her free, finally promising that she would go through with having the child. The day after he let her go, she had the abortion."

Roger found some coins in his sweater pocket and began rubbing them together. "Doug went raving mad when he found out. He came to me, wanting to have some sort of bizarre memorial service for the fetus. He talked crazy about how the Son of the Lord had been ripped from the holy womb of life, and the evil of woman was destined to destroy the world.

"I wanted to take him to the crisis unit, but I realized that would be the end of his career, so I kept him here at the rectory. I sedated him so he'd at least sleep. After that, Mrs. Muten, my housekeeper, looked after him, nursing him until he got himself together.

"It was about two months before he forgave Dana. He even seemed to accept the idea of a childless marriage. But six months later, right around the time the baby would have been born, she confided in me that Douglas's behavior was becoming erratic and violent.

"I wasn't blind—I could see the bruises for myself. She'd try to hide them with makeup and clothing, but

I've seen the bruises men leave on women plenty of times before, believe me."

He poured himself a shot glass of whiskey from a decanter on the sideboard and downed it.

"Over the next couple of months Dana continued to see me in secret, mainly because Doug didn't want her talking to anybody. He kept her like a prisoner in that house. She wasn't allowed to have friends, and the only time she could leave the house was if he was with her. She'd wait until he left for work, and I'd meet her on the trail behind their house.

"She told me things about him that . . ." He hesitated, careful in choosing his words. ". . . weren't right. He forced her to do disgusting, inhuman things. Drinking menstrual blood and . . . and . . . eating parts of . . ." Roger shook his head.

"He was one of those men who had to degrade a woman in the basest of ways in order to function in the marriage bed . . ." He trailed off again and waved his hand in dismissal. He was quiet for a few minutes, as if to marshal difficult thoughts. When he spoke again, his voice was low and dispirited.

"Crumb by crumb Dana fed me pieces of information about Doug's past that seemed too fantastic to believe."

"Like what?"

Roger clasped his hands together and put them to his mouth. "She told me his parents were high-ranking members in a Satanic cult in Chicago," he said carefully, biting his lip. "Dana indicated a couple of times that they'd done something that was . . . something terrible happened and . . ."

Cynthia leaned forward, almost off her chair. "What? What happened?"

He shook his head. "Afterward, Douglas came out here and became the leader of another, larger and more influential Satanic cult. That's why he was so upset over the abortion. Supposedly his firstborn son was to be raised as the next master of the cult.

"Frankly"—he waved his hand in the air—"at first I thought she was making most of it up. You know how women have a knack for blowing things out of proportion when they're upset."

"No, I don't," Cynthia interjected sourly, making a face.

"Sorry," he breathed. "But the behaviors she described were so deviant and perverted it didn't seem possible she could have made it up."

Cynthia nodded, recalling that Dana had been a world-class prude/snob at the beginning of college. The pierced body parts and the shaved head came only after she started dating Collier.

"She decided to leave him and go live with her family in Seattle. I tried to talk her out of it."

He poured another shot and laughed bitterly. "I actually suggested that she and Douglas come in together for marriage counseling. I offered to talk to Douglas about getting some psychiatric help. See, I just thought that if I could bring the Spirit into their lives, they might make it."

Roger looked to her, his eyes pleading for some understanding. Cynthia didn't blink.

He drank off the shot and wiped his mouth. "So, she agreed to stay with him for another month and work on the idea that they see a counselor together."

He went still and clasped his hands over his face. His breath came in jagged sighs. "I never heard from her again.

"Previously I'd been meeting her once a week on the trail. When she didn't come two weeks in a row, I asked Douglas if I could stop by the house and say hello to Dana and maybe pray with her, since I hadn't seen her at church. He told me that she'd left him and gone to live with her family in Seattle.

"I expressed my apologies and offered counseling, but when I prodded him, he quickly became very unpleasant. There was an evil violence brewing in that man beyond anything I'd ever experienced.

"Right then and there, I knew something bad had happened to Dana. Douglas knew Dana and I were close, but he didn't have any idea how close. I'm positive that he never even suspected that she might tell me about what went on between them—he'd threatened to kill her if she ever told anyone. She discovered the details about his past by going into his private files. God knows what he'd have done to her if he'd realized what she'd found. I think I was the best friend she'd ever had. She would never have left without contacting me.

"Not long after that, I noticed Douglas's behavior was becoming more unpredictable. I don't think most people would have picked up on it, but I'd spent quite a bit of time with him, so I knew something was off. It was almost as if he had two or three completely different personalities. One day he'd be the old Douglas, and the next time I'd run into him, he'd be a really nasty SOB. Another time he'd be like an automaton. It was frightening.

"That was around the time John and Sonya were

murdered. I remember asking Douglas for Dana's address, but he wouldn't give it to me. He said she'd moved from her folks' without leaving a forwarding address.

"I lost my temper—called him a liar and told him I thought he knew exactly where Dana was. I said if he didn't tell me where she was, I'd go to the police and report her as a missing person."

Cynthia held up a hand. "Why didn't you do that to begin with?"

"Because he blackmailed me."

"Blackmailed? With *what*? Not the child molestation stuff? I mean, everybody knows about—" A thought hit her and she turned in her chair to regard him with an air of shocked amusement. "Oh my God. You slept with Dana!"

Roger sat down. "Not Dana." He went on with a kind of flustered sincerity: "The night before Sonya was murdered, I went to her apartment to plead with her to quit her volunteer work at the Women's Clinic. While we were talking, she was getting ready to work night shift at the hospital. She had on one of those flimsy . . ." Roger faltered, embarrassed. ". . . robes, and she said she had to get dressed, so I told her to make an appointment to come to the rectory and was getting ready to leave when she began touching me in a way that . . .

"Somehow Douglas found out about it. I don't know how, but he did. I think now that he was probably stalking her . . . or maybe he was actually in the apartment already. I don't know, but he knew what happened.

"When I threatened to report Dana missing, he told me he took sperm samples from Sonya's body and he could prove that she'd been with me that morning in the supply room." The chaplain shrugged, his eyes hollow and sunken.

"So, I said and did nothing until Chloe was murdered. I realized then that all of the killings had to do with the clinic and Collier was involved. I decided to go to the police, but I didn't want to go empty-handed. I wanted to be armed with information.

"First I checked with the authorities in Chicago to verify what Dana had told me, then I tracked down her parents in Seattle. The last they heard from her was a phone call a few days before she disappeared, saying she was leaving Douglas and coming home. Two days later, she called again and said she'd changed her mind and was going to go to Europe instead and that when she felt ready to talk to them, she'd let them know. Her mother said she sounded strained . . . not like herself.

"They sent her letters, addressed to Douglas's house, none of which have ever been returned . . . or answered. After a couple of months, they called. Douglas told them then and has continued to tell them that he doesn't know where Dana is but he thinks it's a phase she's going through and it's probably best if they follow his example and let her go through it and not force themselves on her.

"Of course, he being the respected and successful son-in-law, they believe every word he tells them."

"What a bastard!" Cynthia cried, then, turning quickly, narrowed her eyes at him. "What about your car being seen at Max's?"

"He had keys made, Cynthia. I've lent my car to him on numerous occasions when the Lexus was being worked on or if he had to do some driving for the church. He knows Mrs. Muten doesn't get here until nine, and that I get up at eight. When I got in the car on the day Gayle disappeared, I knew it had already been driven. I didn't really think about it—I just figured that Douglas had borrowed it to run an errand for St. Hilary's."

"And your shoes? How did he get your shoes?"

"I couldn't find them when I packed. Douglas could have easily taken them from my closet. He had to have access to the church files I keep here, so he had a key to the house. Most of the time he pretty much came and went as he pleased.

"And," he added, "we wear the same size shoe."

Her beeper went off with all the noise of a smoke alarm with new batteries gone rabid.

They yelped in unison.

Adele yelped and jumped back from the freezer. It was the same noise and movement she'd made the time she'd seen a human toe poking through the pile of dirt on her Mr. Greenjeans shovel. Outside in the car, Nelson was barking like a wild animal. She focused on the familiar racket to keep from losing her mind.

Her eyes returned to the contents of the freezer, making sure she wasn't hallucinating.

She wasn't.

That's what you get for sniffing around like a dog, she thought. *Digging up all sorts of odds and ends, toes and hands.* She stopped herself from going mad with rational thought. First, she would drive to the police and tell them about the freezer full of hands and breasts . . . packages labeled with the names of humans she'd once known. It was hard, cold evidence, no pun intended.

Her eyes settled on the official "Coroner's Evidence"

tags, doubt at once sprouting in her stomach and winding itself around her guts.

But was it really evidence? This was the county coroner, after all. Finding hands and amputated limbs in his freezer wasn't really *so* suspicious, was it? And the descriptions in his computer could be something as innocent as him writing a mystery/thriller based on a true story. He was going to sell it to Hollywood. After all, if Patricia Cornwell could do it, so could he . . . couldn't he?

She glanced at the breast marked "Victim Mueller" once more and closed the freezer lid. Maybe the police had found the missing people, parts and pieces, and were keeping it a secret from the public until they found the killer.

Hurrying back to his office, she picked the set of keys out of the desk drawer, twirled them around her finger once, then went to the locked room on the second floor. The key marked "Dana's Room" opened the door.

Completely ignoring the fact she was in the presence of a man of the cloth, Cynthia swore like a sailor as she tore through the Blessed Virgin Mary's glove compartment looking for the list of number codes.

"Think about when you had it last," Roger offered, more to stop her swearing than actually advise.

Cynthia sat back in the driver's seat and retraced her movements. She'd untaped it from the back of the pager and put it where she'd be sure to see it if the pager went off. She remembered it being right in front of her eyes . . .

She sighed, stuck her hand into the observation box, and pulled the code sheet off the inside. Going down the list of codes, she punched in the numbers. "Call the police. Stat. Go to Douglas's. Danger, proceed with caution."

Roger and Cynthia looked at each other for half a second before setting off at code-blue speed. "You call the police," Roger shouted. "I'll back the car out."

The room smelled faintly like creosote, Pine-Sol, chalk dust, and grease. It was cluttered, like his office, except there was an aura of femininity to the clutter—a basket of silk flowers, half-finished watercolors of pastoral scenes, a pair of pink-and-black Rollerblades. A baby-blue prom gown and a pearl-encrusted wedding gown hung, curiously, over a cradle filled with baby clothes still in their original wrappers. Flung on top was a woman's straw hat, the band made up entirely of silk roses.

Impulsively, she flipped on the night-light and knelt next to a pile of framed photographs. She picked up the closest frame and studied the vanity photo of the dark-haired woman she now recognized as Dana Collier. The woman was prettier than she remembered. In the dark eyes, Adele read a joyful, almost impish nature.

The pile of photos toppled to the floor and slid like dominoes in a sideways stack. Automatically, she began gathering them back into a pile, when, in the farthest corner of the room, she spied a narrow mound covered with a sheet.

The hairs on the back of her neck sprang upright and her bowels clutched in spasms. She didn't need to pull the sheet down to know what was underneath.

But she did.

She was back in Dr. Ryno's anatomy class with Molly the Mummy—a dried-up female cadaver who'd been pried open and violated by sixty students a day for two years. The cadaver in front of her was fresher and in better shape, though not much. A female in her thirties, Adele estimated, with shoulder-length black hair. The mandible had been removed, along with the hands. The lower abdomen had been cut open, then clamped together with a single surgical clip.

"Ohmygodohmygodohmygodohmygod."

She stood, fell against the wall, unintentionally knocking the night-light out of the wall plug. The dark of the room caused terror to surface as her senses went to full reception.

Outside, Nelson had stopped barking. He would have indulged himself for hours unless he'd been tended to. The thought that Cynthia or the police had arrived sent her flying down the stairs. She hastily threw the keys back into the desk, grabbed her shoes, and ran out the back door. Turning the corner of the house, she collided with someone holding Nelson by the scruff of his neck.

The hands left Nelson and grabbed for her. She screamed, maneuvering herself away, and took a stance of defense.

Douglas stepped back. "Adele? What's wrong?" His eyes moved to the patio door, then back to her.

"You . . ." She thought fast and forced herself to smile. "You scared me. Someone broke into my house tonight, so I came here to wait for you. I fell asleep on your patio chaise longue. Had a bad dream—it spooked me."

He reached out and put his arm around her. "Poor sweetheart, you must be cold, you're shaking."

She nodded, wanting to get away from him—get to the police as soon as she could. "I'm . . . I'm freezing."

He took her hands—hands that were hot and sweaty—
in his. She didn't want to see his expression. Breaking
free of his grasp, she knelt to stroke Nelson. He whined
bitterly at the smell of Her fear and nuzzled Her face.

"Why didn't you call me?" he said sternly. "I would
have come immediately."

"I was so scared I wasn't thinking straight." She
stepped around the other side of him. "I think I'm going
to head over to Cynthia's and sleep there. I've got a
migraine and I want to go to bed."

He slipped his arm around her shoulder and pulled her
back, placing himself between her and the front of the
house. "Come in and have a cup of hot tea first. Get
warmed up. I'll change and drive you to Cynthia's."

He placed a finger under her chin, tipping her face
upward. "Or, you're more than welcome to stay with me.
I have a futon I can put anywhere in the house. You can
even sleep in front of the fireplace if you'd like."

Or in the spare room with your wife, thought Adele.
We can share the same sheet.

He pulled her toward the back of the house. "Come on,
I insist. Besides, the police came up with some information on Helen that I think you'll appreciate. I'll tell you
over tea. If you're hungry I could make quattro stagioni."

She imagined what quattro stagioni might be—some
Italian dish, teeming with tomatoes, basil, garlic, ovaries,
odd fingers, and wrist bones. "What's in it?" she asked
doubtfully, in spite of her fear.

He laughed. "A pizza to die for."

Her eyebrows shot up to her hairline at his choice of
words, allowing herself to be corralled into the house. If
she resisted too much, it would rouse his suspicions.

The second he opened the patio door, Adele panicked. She was sure she'd left the door to Dana's room unlocked. The thought caused her to step back. Glancing at the stars, she felt an immense sadness that she might never see the night sky again.

"This yours?" Douglas held out her hair band, which had fallen next to the chaise longue—probably when she'd run out of the house.

Adele smiled and took it from him. "I have a tendency to thrash around when I sleep," she said, ecstatic over the small stroke of luck.

He fit his key into the lock and frowned, mumbling that he thought he'd locked the door. She paled, waiting for him to accuse her of breaking into his house. When he didn't so much as look in her direction, she relaxed her shoulders, which cracked with the released tension. The moment the door was open, Nelson ran barking into the house, disappearing toward the front hall. A new panic that he would go to the cadaver room and have a barking-scratch fit outside the door caused her to run after him.

She caught hold of his collar in the foyer.

Douglas came up noiselessly behind her. "Would you like a tour of the house?" he said in a low, seductive tone, putting his arms around her waist. "We could start in my room."

He turned her around and, taking her face in both hands, kissed her, his tongue thrusting into her mouth. He pressed himself against her so that she could feel his erection. His body tightened against hers as his intensity grew. Pushing his hand down the front of her sweatpants, he probed her roughly with his fingers. She whimpered out of fear and pain, which seemed to increase his passion. Almost at once, his breathing changed to harsh gasps.

The constant invasion of her mouth with his tongue was making her nauseous, and the thought that he was going to orgasm using her as a sort of masturbatory post infuriated her. At their feet, Nelson whined constantly, pawing at Douglas's leg. He roughly shoved the dog away and pressed himself harder into her pubic bone, hurting her. He pushed her sweatshirt over her breasts and fumbled with the back of her sports bra, searching for the hooks that did not exist.

To her relief, the momentary awkwardness of his search allowed her to break the tension. "Tea and food first." She faked a shiver. "I'm too cold. I can't get in the mood."

"Don't worry, I'll warm you up." He pinched her nipple through the cloth of her bra.

"I'll bet you will," she said seductively, pulling free of him. "But let's put Nelson outside first. He's very protective. He gets upset when people get too close to me."

An expression of disgust passed over his face. "You treat the damned dog like it was a child!"

Adele shrank back. *Here it comes,* she thought. *I've sent him over the edge.* She felt for the Colt and realized with a flood of panic that she'd left it under the front seat of the Beast.

He forced a smile, his anger just under the surface. "Put the dog in the garage. I'll make us some tea."

"I think I'll put him back in the car. He'll be more—"

Without a word he grabbed Nelson's collar and pulled him toward the garage. "I said he can go into the garage.

I don't want him barking in the car, disturbing my neighbors."

He turned back to her, the irritation again replaced with a tight smile. "Besides, he'll be more comfortable out here." Pushing Nelson down the garage steps, to her utter amazement he added, "If he gets hungry, he's got a freezer full of meat."

He steered her toward the kitchen. As they passed his office, Douglas glanced in, stopped two feet beyond the door, and retraced his steps. His hands tightened around her wrists, pulling her with him.

Adele glanced around, rapidly canvassing the desk and surrounds. It took a second before she saw that the handset of the cordless phone was not in the charger base. She closed her eyes and swallowed. In her panic, she'd mindlessly put it in the desk drawer; she remembered doing it. She wanted to slit her own throat—anyone as anal-retentive and obsessive as Douglas would notice the slightest thing out of place.

"Nice office," she said, her temples burning with fear. She pulled him toward the kitchen. "Onward to tea and food. You'll need to fortify yoursel—"

His grip loosened but he looked at her with a puzzled, disbelieving expression. He opened his mouth to ask something, changed his mind, and tightened his grip again. Her wrists were beginning to throb.

She very tentatively tried to pull her hands out of his grasp and found she could not. "After tea, I want that tour . . . starting in the master bedroom."

The disbelief disappeared from his face and was replaced with anger and injury. "Why are you lying, Adele?

More than anything in the world, I hate a woman who lies."

She smiled and cocked her head as if not understanding his mood change. "I'm not lying to you," she said softly. Again she tried to move her hands. "Why do you think I'm—"

"You've already been in the house, haven't you?"

"No," she said quickly. "No, I wasn't. I told you, I fell asleep on the patio chaise lon—"

He let go of her wrists and walked past her into his office, jaw clenched. He paused, pulled open the drawer, found the handset, and put it in its proper place. He briefly fingered the set of keys she'd used to get into Dana's room, then picked up the handset again and hit one button—redial.

The panic had turned to a raging fire in her brain. How could she have been so stupid? How many times had Kitch said that not paying attention to the small details was what got people killed?

"Yeah, who's this?" he said into the mouthpiece. Without a word, he hung up the phone and looked at her.

"I don't normally keep the handset in the desk drawer. And the last call I made on this phone was to you, Adele, not Henry Williams." He walked toward her. "Why'd you lie to me?"

"I wasn't in your house, Douglas," she said, affecting a snotty, defensive tone. "I don't know who Henry Williamson is, and even if I did use your phone, I think I'd remember where the handset went."

He approached her and she stepped back into the hallway. She mentally calculated the distance to the back door, trying to remember what kind of lock it had and if he'd engaged it or not when they came in.

"I don't like people prying into my private things, Adele," he said. The vein running crookedly down the center of his forehead was pulsating. "Did you find anything interesting?"

The thought that she would casually answer, "Yeah, baldy, how's the hair transplant going?" brought up a strong threat of the hysterical, crazy-woman laughter. Instead, she brought a self-confident and deeply offended edge to her tone. "I'm going to go home now, Douglas. I don't like this conversation, and I especially don't like being accused of something as shitty as snooping through your things. All it does is make me wonder what you have to hide. I suggest you put your investigatory powers to use and find someone else to accuse of snooping."

Without waiting for a reply, she turned and headed for the back door. She employed all the willpower she had to keep from breaking into a run.

He, however, did run, coming to stand between her and the door. "I can't let you leave."

"Tough shit, Doug. I don't like you very much right now." She was astonished by her own insane coolness. "Get out of my way." Boldly, she reached for the handle and pulled the door against his back.

He forcibly removed her hand from the doorknob and pulled her tight against him. "I don't want to argue with you," he said, his tone changing abruptly from accusatory to amorous. He pushed his erection into her crotch. "You can't leave me now . . . not like this." He unzipped his pants and guided her hand around his penis.

"I love you, Adele. Please don't ever lie to me. Dana lied. It tore me up."

He guided her hand up and down in a slow rhythm that he obviously liked. "You're not like other women, you're different. You're ready for this. You're ready for me—I can feel it in you."

There was a sudden outburst of Nelson's frenzied barking. She prayed it was Cynthia with the police and not just some wild hair of Nelson's.

"Let me initiate you into my life. You can have any-thing you want if you accept my ways. You won't want to leave once you give us a chance. I want . . ."

The barking grew more hysterical. His hand faltered in its rhythm.

"I want us to have a . . ." His hand stopped, as the rest of his body tightened. "The dog needs to learn manners," he said, hurrying for the garage.

"Don't hurt him!" Adele screamed, running after him. She tackled him as he swung the door open and stepped down. She might have been a fly landing on his shirt for all the difference it made.

Douglas grabbed Nelson's collar and yanked him off his front legs.

"Stop it!" she shouted, trying to push the man off balance.

He jerked the dog again, and the barking turned to a strangled yelp. "You've got to let them know who the master is," he said, shoving her away with his shoulder. "You can't let a dumb animal run your life!"

He yanked on the collar a third time and Adele flipped into self-defense mode, jamming both elbows into his kidney. At once he let go of the collar, arching back in pain.

Nelson cowered and ran to the door, where Cynthia and Roger stood looking confused and somewhat horrified.

There was a beat of silence where everyone stood still.

"What's going on here?" Douglas groaned. He sucked in a breath. "What are you people doing in my house?"

All eyes—including Nelson's—shifted to Adele.

"They're here because I called them," Adele said. "There are some questions you need to answer."

"Questions *I* need to answer?" he said sarcastically. "It appears to me that I'm the only one who isn't trespassing on private property. In California we have laws about breaking into a man's home."

Adele shrugged, shards of doubt resurfacing. He seemed too poised, too self-possessed. "Fine. You don't *have* to answer anything until the police get here."

His smile faded. "What are you talking about? Have you lost your mind?"

"No, but I think you have," she said. "You left your door unlocked, and your computer on. It didn't take a genius to figure out the password to your locked files." She looked at him and mentally took in a deep breath. "I read the Pulse file. I know what you did."

"What . . . ?" Douglas locked eyes with her, staring her down the same way he'd done the first night they met. His gaze pierced through her resolve, making her acutely uneasy.

"First of all, I never leave my house unlocked, nor do I ever leave my computer on. I don't have a 'pulse' file. Basically, I don't know what the hell you're talking about, Adele, but I hope the police find it as absurd as I do."

To hide her discomfort, she steeled herself, not wavering under his stare. "Shall I recite a couple of the descriptions of how you got off on watching your victims die after you raped and then disemboweled them?"

"What?"

"Or how about the fact that you seem to have some interesting meat in the freezer?" She opened the freezer lid and pulled out a plastic bag holding a pair of hands. A tag dangled from the twist tie.

A cry escaped Cynthia as she clasped her hand to her mouth.

Douglas looked from Adele to Cynthia and Roger. "This is ridiculous." He took the bag and glanced at the tag. "I don't know where those came from. Someone's playing a sick joke and I—"

"A sick joke, Douglas?" Adele said. "Really? I suppose the cadaver upstairs—the one with all the identifiable parts missing—is a joke too?"

Douglas clenched his jaw. "You went through Dana's room?" There was a pause in which he fixed her with a look of such hatred that she stepped back, as if his glance could harm her physically.

"How dare you. For your information, that cadaver belonged to the mortuary college. It was a Jane Doe the public administrator was going to have cremated—I thought I might be able to use it in the lab for teaching some of the new trainees. I've had to store it here because there's no space for it at the lab."

Made bold by the presence of Cynthia and Roger,

Adele got up in his face. "Okay, so then how did Gayle's pendant get in your desk drawer?"

"Pendant? I don't know what you're talking about. When I left this house this afternoon—"

Roger stepped close to the man, his face a mix of rage and determination. "Where's Dana? Did you kill her the same way you killed the rest of them, or did you do something really special to her?"

Roger grabbed Douglas's shirt and shoved him against the front of the freezer. "What did you do with her, you son of a bitch?" His voice broke. "Didn't you make her suffer enough while she was alive?"

Douglas pushed the man back, his face flushed. "You bastard. You planted this crap, didn't you?" He looked at Adele. "He was in love with Dana. He destroyed our marriage. I'm telling you that whatever you found or think you found was planted by this psycho asshole."

"Where *is* Dana?" she asked.

"I wish to God I knew. She left me over a year ago." Douglas glared at Roger Wynn. The hatred in his eyes was almost palpable. Leaning against the freezer, he passed a hand over his eyes. "I was selfish and immature. Dana wanted a baby—I didn't think I was ready for a family. The truth was I didn't want to share her with anyone . . . not even a child.

"I talked her into having the abortion. I . . . I never realized she'd fall apart. She started to despise me—with the reverend's help of course.

"I did everything I could to get her forgiveness, but she was blinded by him. She was always talking about how Roger was so good, and Roger wouldn't have made her kill her baby, and Roger was such a loving man and Roger was so sensitive, and on and on until I was sick with it.

"A few months after the abortion I came home one night and found Dana drunk. She'd tormented herself until she was sick. I truly believe she wanted to reach out to me for help, but I'd hurt her too much. So, instead of letting me in, she lashed out, trying to make me feel her pain. She got more and more hysterical until finally she told me the child hadn't been mine."

He looked at the floor and shut his eyes for a moment. "The baby was Roger's. She said he'd wanted her to leave me and marry him, but she'd been too confused to make up her mind. Later, he'd gotten violent when he found out she had the abortion and threatened her. She was convinced he was going to do something awful."

Douglas rubbed his temples, pressing hard into the flesh with his fingers. "Still, she was protective of the bastard. God only knows why. She made me promise on her life that I wouldn't go to the police about him no matter what. I promised because I loved her—I didn't want to hurt her anymore. I thought if I kept my promise, she'd realize how much I loved her.

"We tried for another month or so to make the marriage work, but she couldn't pull herself together. She decided she wanted to get away from Marin for a while and move back in with her parents. A couple of days later, she changed her mind and said she wanted to make a complete break and go to Europe for a few months. I thought it would be best to let her go."

There was a sincerity in Douglas's expression that made Adele's stomach churn with apprehension. She glanced over at Roger, who remained standing next to Cynthia. Silent, eyes downcast, he wore an odd expression, as if lost in a daydream.

"How can you stand not knowing where she is?" Cynthia asked. Adele heard a sympathetic inflection in her tone. "I mean, didn't you try to find her?"

"When I didn't hear from her after two months, I did everything possible to find her without making a federal case out of it. I've gone through hell trying to find her. It was as though she vanished off the face of the earth."

Adele grabbed at a passing straw. "Why did you lie about the psychiatrist's evaluation of Roger?"

Douglas stared at her. "I didn't lie."

"I spoke to Dr. Wilmont," Adele said. "He said Roger wasn't violent at all, and that he didn't fit the profile of a—"

Douglas shook his head. "Dr. Wilmont didn't do a full evaluation. It was Dr. Thomas Muday of Seattle. Dr. Wilmont did the first evaluation—he was the one Roger snowed. When Muday interviewed him two weeks later, he got the real story. That's the evaluation I read."

"Tim said there was supposed to be another psych report," Cynthia said quietly, "but the shrink died and the file was lost."

"They couldn't find it because I have it," Douglas said. "When I realized how involved Dana was with Roger, I did my own investigation on him. In the course of examining the information about the child molestation cases, I found out that he'd seen Muday, so I contacted Muday's office.

"As it turned out, Muday died two weeks after Roger

saw him. His notes on those sessions couldn't be found and as a result, a report was never made.

"I went to Muday's home in Seattle and spoke with his widow. She was very ill and I'm ashamed to say I took advantage of her age and poor health to persuade her to let me go through his files. It took me three days, but I eventually found his notes on Roger. I told Mrs. Muday I couldn't find them and that they had probably been lost or accidentally destroyed.

"After I transcribed the notes, I wanted to go to the police, but I'd already promised Dana."

"You are a liar," Roger said, unruffled. "Muday interviewed me for all of twenty minutes. We talked about his advancing cancer and his concerns about his wife. I counseled *him* about returning to the church before his time came." Roger faced Adele. "Whatever he told you about Muday's evaluation came out of his warped brain. If he really did steal Muday's notes, he also found a way to manufacture a false report."

Adele looked from one man to the other, trying to gauge who was lying. Will the real serial killer please sit down.

"When did you last use your fireplace?" she asked Roger.

"The night Milton was murdered," he answered promptly. "There is a whole storeroom full of old files on the church that needed to be destroyed. Douglas brought over some of the boxes and insisted I burn them, even though he knew the fireplace wasn't supposed to be used. He said he didn't want to take the chance of someone finding them in the garbage. I was up until two that morning burning the stupid things."

"Tell them all of it, why don't you?" Douglas stepped toward him and then stopped himself. "I'd been using the incinerator at the hospital to get rid of the files because you're too damned lazy and cheap to go out and buy a shredder. I've been asking you for months to buy one. I was sick and tired of playing garbageman."

Random phrases from the description of Gina Ducke's death struggle went, uninvited, through Adele's mind. Her eyes settled on Douglas. "Where did those descriptions of the murders come from on your computer?"

"I don't have a clue as to what descriptions you're referring to, but think on this—half of St. Hilary's records are on my computer and Roger knows the password. He's got keys to this house."

Feeling as though they were at a Wimbledon match or a rerun of *To Tell the Truth*, the two women looked at Roger Wynn, who suddenly applauded, shaking his head.

"Great performance, Doug, but then again, you're only being yourself—or should I say one of your many twisted selves." He glanced at Adele. "I don't have the keys to this house, which, I might add, he keeps locked up like Fort Knox, nor do I have access to his computer. I have my own computer. Getting copies of the church's current financial records from him is like trying to get top-secret files from the CIA."

Roger moved to the small steps and sat down. "How long did you think you could fool people, Collier? Or should I call you Kolinger?"

At the name, a flicker of anxiety came into Douglas Collier's eyes. He at once seemed frozen in place, oddly at attention.

"You know, Doug, I flew to Chicago yesterday, before

I went to Seattle to talk to Dana's parents. Interesting place, Chicago. Don't you think so?"

Roger wiped his mouth and went on. "I found out some things there, and since we're into telling horror stories tonight, how about one about a family named Kolinger who lived in a South Chicago suburb?"

Adele watched the changes going on in Douglas's face. He began to resemble a man who'd had his testicles kicked up into his throat but hadn't fully realized it yet.

"Once upon a time," Roger continued, "there was a South Chicago bus driver and his wife, who, to the public eye, looked like very fine, upstanding folk. They gave to charities and volunteered for all sorts of community services. They took in mentally disabled foster kids and runaways, and when they had time left over, they worked at the local halfway house for troubled teens. Once a week they opened their home to their church group, and mostly they raised a nice boy named Stephen—an Eagle Scout kind of kid.

"Except what no one knew about the nice Kolinger family was that the minute the door closed and the shades were pulled, they turned into hooded monsters. Sadistic, sick animals. Satanists.

"The potluck church dinners were actually cult orgies where ritualistic sex was practiced on the victims they pulled in—mostly young females, runaways and retarded women. The vileness of what went on there put them in the highest order of Satanists. Copulation with animals, child pornography, the consumption of human blood, the breaking of all laws of decency, and worse.

"But, as with all filth, they finally went too far with a poor retarded girl named Anna Meckstroff . . ."

Douglas looked to Adele, and although he shook his head and laughed, his face glistened with sweat. "What has this got to do with anything? I was born and raised in Philadelphia. I have documents to prove it. He's trying to cover—"

"The reports were conflicting," Roger went on, shouting over him. "The authorities couldn't decide if nineteen-year-old Anna Meckstroff bled to death from the violent, repeated rape performed by each member of the cult, or from the wounds they inflicted in order to obtain the required amount of blood for their communion service. In the end it didn't really matter to the jury, most of whom were devout Catholics. Five people were convicted and sent to prison. Two were life sentences.

"Mr. Kolinger died by his own hand in a prison cell in Joliet, and Mrs. Kolinger expired of heart failure one month after she was sentenced to life.

"Little Stephen was placed in one foster home after another until he graduated from high school. His last foster mother was a widowed Austrian woman by the name of Helga Baumann. She remembers Stephen Kolinger as troubled, an Eagle Scout who mutilated small animals and then tried to see how long he could keep them alive to suffer. He called it scientific experimentation.

"Mrs. Baumann knew nothing about multiple personalities, but eventually she asked the youth authority to take Stephen out of her house because she was afraid to be alone with him."

Roger stood. "Exactly the same way Dana was afraid of you, Mr. Kolinger.

"When I showed Mrs. Baumann your photograph she said you could change your name and move to the other side of the world, but she could still see the meanness in your face."

Roger was only inches from him. "It's over, Stephen," he said in a quiet voice that was almost kind. "It's time to pay the piper. There'll be no more killing for you."

Outside, several cars pulled into the driveway. Doors opened and closed. Douglas, his face set in a moue of contempt, brushed roughly by them and disappeared into the house, slamming the door behind him. In a flash Adele envisioned him returning to the garage armed with a handgun, and methodically (soup, meat, vegetables, salad) blowing each of them away with a single, neat bullet to the head. They stood immobile and silent for a moment, not knowing what to do next.

From a distance, they heard Tim Ritmann's raised voice. "Sheriff's Department. Open the door, please."

As if waking from a nightmare, Cynthia sucked in a breath and lunged for the door. Adele scrambled after her, pulling her back into the garage. Somewhere in the house a door slammed.

Adele hit a black switch on the wall. Instead of the garage door opening as she had hoped, they were pitched into complete darkness.

"Turn on the light!" cried Roger. "My God . . ."

The door opened. Silhouetted in the doorway was Douglas, dressed in a garment with a large cowl . . . like a priest at High Mass. There was something wrong with his stance, Adele thought; he seemed slouched, less balanced. He stepped into the garage, moving slowly toward her.

Instinctively, Cynthia and Roger flattened themselves against the nearest solid object. Sensing fear, Nelson whined and cowered near Roger, who reached over and laid a comforting hand on his rump.

Adele took a wide-footed crouch, ready to spring and knock Douglas off balance. If she could get him in a hold, she could at least disable him until Tim located them.

"Adele?" Douglas's voice wavered, as though he was crying. "I wanted you. I wanted us to create another son for the Order. We could have raised him as the Master." He took another step toward her. "You were so perfect for the breeding . . ."

Behind them, Cynthia cried out: "Tim! Hurry! In the garage!"

Almost at once a broad-shouldered figure, silhouetted against the light of the house, filled the doorway. A second later Tim Ritmann turned on the light.

"Dear Jesus," Roger whispered, staring at Douglas.

The front of the white robe was entirely stained with blood. Douglas, his eyes glassy bright and fixed on Adele, took another unsteady step toward her. "Adele, come with me. We'll go to the Master together."

She tensed. "Stay where you . . . are."

He took another step. She saw the deep longitudinal slashes down the inner part of both his forearms and the crosscuts at each end and in the middle. From a distance, the wounds took on the look of elongated swastikas.

He held her eyes with his, until she felt mesmerized. "Please, Adele. They murdered my son. They made Dana turn against me and the Order. You were different. You were the one sent to absolve them . . . to make it clean again."

Tim had his gun aimed, ready. He motioned for Cynthia and Roger to get down on the floor.

Adele couldn't take her eyes away from Douglas's, just as she could not make her legs obey the command to move.

He raised his right hand. In it was a number twelve scalpel.

She was dimly aware of someone weeping, Nelson's barking. Her vision blurred, then cleared. A measure of time passed, but she wasn't aware of it. She was in a different world, dealing with other planes of awareness.

He stretched out his other arm, slick with blood, motioning her to come to him. "Will you come with me now?"

She shook her head.

The arm dropped. "I love you, Adele." He said it quietly—barely above a whisper. There was a graceful, slow-motion movement as his hand brought the scalpel up and, with as much care as a surgeon, made an incision over his right jugular, and then his left. The fine incisions closed immediately behind the blade, but not before a tiny spray of warm blood landed on her cheek.

The scalpel fell to the floor less than an inch from her foot. He clutched his throat, not moving his eyes from hers. A thick cascade of blood oozed over his fingers and spilled down the robe.

In the one second that seemed like forever, his eyes rolled back and time returned to normal.

Cynthia's hoarse screams competed with Nelson's bark. Needlessly, Tim lunged against the still-standing Douglas. As the men fell to the floor, Roger grabbed Cynthia and pressed her face into his chest, shielding her from the sight. Detective Cini charged through the door, his gun drawn.

Jarred back into real time, Adele automatically knelt

next to Douglas's body and put her hand over the wound, as if to stanch the flow of blood—the blind instinct of a nurse fully functioning. As soon as she laid her ear to his chest, she realized there would be no breath sounds.

Getting oxygen into him seemed like the thing to do next, until the understanding came to her that both his carotid arteries had been cut. She calculated the amount of time it would take to activate 911, get a surgeon, drive to the scene . . .

No. There would be no purpose.

Nelson pawed at her leg and whined.

Cynthia knelt down and hugged her, pushing back her bangs. "Are you okay? He didn't touch you with the scalpel?"

Adele shook her head, sitting back on her haunches. She reached around for Nelson and buried her face in his fur. She felt cold and suddenly very much alone.

Someone kneaded her shoulder.

Tim.

"Adele? Are you okay?"

"Yes." It was barely audible. There was a beat of silence interrupted only by the approaching sirens. After a moment, Enrico Cini and Roger lifted her off her knees to her feet. Cynthia and Tim slipped their arms around her waist and helped her to the living room.

Out of the presence of the dead man, they all began to talk at once.

SEVENTEEN

ADELE AND CYNTHIA RAN INTO ROOM 806, where the voluminously large Mrs. Flagg, lying halfway between her bed and the bathroom, was busy having a seizure.

"She held it too long!" shouted Mrs. Cornelius, Mrs. Flagg's roommate. "I told her she shouldn't hold it so long! I told her, the toxins from the pee in your kidneys goes to your brain and kills ya. I told her that, but she doesn't listen and she holds it and now look at what happened!" Mrs. Cornelius started to cry. "She shoulda listened. I told her. She shoulda . . ."

Skip cooed at the elderly woman, while leading her away from the possible code-blue scene about to unfold.

Inside of six seconds, Adele verified the presence of a pulse while Cynthia hooked the patient to the crash cart monitor and outfitted her face with a green oxygen mask.

They waited patiently until the seizure activity stopped, before they could accurately evaluate the woman's respiratory, cardiac, and neuro status.

"You want me to call a code or not?" Tina, returned to her usual cantankerous mood, asked the question from the hallway.

"Nope," Adele answered. "She's fine. Put a call in to Dr. Harrison and get the lab up here for the usual post-seizure blood work. Then call Henry and ask him to bring the mechanical lift. He's going to need more than muscles to get this mountain back to bed."

Adele and Cynthia glanced at each other over Mrs. Flagg's enormous abdomen as she lingered in the post-seizure state of semiconscious lethargy. Both knew perfectly well what needed to be done next, but they were bound by archaic rules and policies which forced them to wait for the physician to dictate orders.

"No wonder Nelson was spooked," Adele said, picking up the thread of the same conversation they'd been having on and off for a week. After a hundred or more times of analyzing and discussing the night Douglas Collier cut his own throat—when the details no longer awed them—they'd moved on to the broader aspects of the case.

"Douglas must have broken into my house a number of times and gone through my stuff with a fine-tooth comb. He needed to do research before he settled on me as his chosen breeder. He knew everything about me, from my favorite pie to the fact I didn't own a minirecorder."

"What's really scary is that you fit all his criteria," said Cynthia. "I'd worry about that."

"Actually, it *does* bother me," she said thoughtfully. "I can't figure out what the hell I did to get him going like that."

"It's your devilish ways."

"Telling me to record Helen was an ingenious stall," Adele said. "I'm sure my going out to the Marval house pushed his schedule up, but that extra time was enough for him to get out there, kill her, make it look like a fake suicide, *and* set up Roger."

"She was ready to spill her guts." Cynthia assessed Mrs. Flagg's color and reduced her oxygen flow. "He had to kill her before you or Tim got there."

Mrs. Flagg raised a finger. "I'd like that pie à la mode, please."

Cynthia smiled and patted the patient's shoulder. "Sure, Mrs. Flagg. The pie's coming out of the oven right now."

"I'll bet he wasn't more than ten feet away from me when I found her," Adele went on. "He could have killed me so easily."

"Naw," replied Cynthia. "Not the new breeder for the Satanic cult."

"Yeah. A pure womb for the Chosen Son of Beelzebub and the next Cult Master—*Rosemary's Baby* revisited. And there I was walking into his office and practically offering myself to him. Whichever one of his personalities didn't hate women must have thought I was a godsend . . ." Adele frowned.

"A Satan-send," Cynthia corrected. "You resembled Dana, didn't work at the Women's Clinic, weren't a born-again Holy Roller or some other religious fanatic, never had an abortion, wanted kids, and were just over the edge enough to suit his tastes."

"Antichrist on a bicycle, he must've thought he'd died and gone to hell."

"What I want to know is where the hell did he get all his money?"

"From hell," Adele replied. "It's one of the benefits of

being a Satanist. There are plenty of bored, wealthy folk who like to play around on the dark side. Several people in the cult had him invested in major moneymaking deals. He was making money hand over cloven hoof."

They watched the monitor for a minute, lulled by the sound of the rhythmic bleeping.

"I still don't get why he kept all that evidence in his house." Cynthia cocked her head slightly. "I mean, anybody could have walked in and found that stuff."

Adele shook her head. "Not likely. If Roger and I hadn't screwed up his plans, I think he would have destroyed everything—including the computer files—that night."

"But why did he have it at all? Why would he keep those body parts?"

"My guess is that he was saving everything for some Satanic ritual on a particular full moon or something." She paused. "Probably a feeding frenzy or a bonfire—maybe both.

"The guy must have been majorly stressed out—I mean, here he is living in a house that's protected by a state-of-the-art security system, and he goes off and forgets to set the alarms or even lock the door."

"But he was *so* paranoid," Cynthia said. "Why would he do that? Doesn't make sense."

Adele raised her eyebrows. "Ah yes, my dear Watson, but on *that* day, he came home to a message from Dana's parents saying they'd had a visit from Roger and demanding he call them back. They threatened to contact the police if he didn't tell them where Dana was.

"He panicked. He'd always figured he was above suspicion, and suddenly he's got Dana's parents asking

questions and Roger stirring up shit. Here was this misguided sap who he'd been carefully setting up to take the
rap, and who was now on the run, except—oops!—it
turns out the sap isn't misguided, nor is he on the run.
Instead he's out there digging up info on *him*.

"He probably broke speed records getting to his office
to destroy whatever evidence he had hidden there and in
the lab."

Drawing her knees up, Adele rested her elbows on
them. "I'll never know for sure, but I think part of why
he broke into my house that night was because he
thought I was in contact with Roger, or there'd be information on my answering machine, or I'd leave something lying around."

Adele shrugged. "Who knows? Maybe he flipped into
his killer personality and decided to kill me. Like I said,
he was stressed to the max and probably had less control
over his other personalities than usual."

Skip swung by the door. "Not off the floor yet,
ladies?"

They shook their heads in unison. Mrs. Flagg turned in
his direction and asked what happened to her pie à la
mode. He assured her the waitress would bring it to her
table right away.

"There goes a lucky man," Cynthia said after the
nurse left.

"I'd have to say you were right about that, considering
he was the next in line to be murdered, and that Douglas
already made notes about exactly where and how he was
going to kill him."

"Too bad Gayle and Helen weren't as lucky."

"Psssh." Adele shook her head. "Helen was doomed

from the moment Douglas realized she'd seen him kill Sonya. I'm surprised he let her live as long as he did.

"He had a dossier on every nurse and physician who worked in Marin County. He knew her psych history and he knew how to manipulate her to his advantage. As soon as he saw Chloe's name on the surgery schedule, he called Helen and ordered her to visit Chloe before surgery, then go to recovery and hang the IV that he'd put into Chloe's med box."

Mrs. Flagg stirred and then yelled at the top of her lungs: "Waitress! Did they burn my pie?"

Cynthia and Adele both smiled. Adele turned the oxygen flow back up.

"The whole thing about Douglas making Roger burn those church files in the fireplace seemed pretty weird," Cynthia said.

Adele thought for a minute. "Not really. Douglas may have thought that Roger suddenly having a fire in a condemned fireplace in the midst of another flurry of messy, grisly murders might look suspicious to the police later on.

"The fact is, Douglas was probably telling the truth when he said he'd been burning the church files in the Ellis incinerator. I'm sure he had lots of creative ways to dispose of the remains of his victims, but I'd be willing to bet that the incinerator got most of them, along with the scalpels, syringes, and bloody clothes. Plus, the church files were a plausible, convenient excuse if he was ever questioned about using the incinerator."

Grace Thompson, a fiftyish woman who could be described as "severely handsome" in her starched white uniform and white stockings, stood glaring at them from the doorway. "Are you ladies enjoying your picnic?" It was an English spinster's voice right out of a *Saturday Night Live* routine.

Adele turned a deaf ear to the woman's scolding tone and laughed. "Want to join in, Grace? There's enough ham here to feed the entire British army several times."

The new head nurse of Ward 8 pursed her lips, unamused. "We're too understaffed for this nonsense. This is quite unprofessional. Get up off that filthy floor, both of you. This sort of slacking off isn't fair to the rest of the staff." She arched an eyebrow and added under her breath, "Such as it is."

Neither of them made a move to get up, though both nodded in agreement. The staff hired to replace Helen and Meg were nurse's aides and "med techs"—people barely qualified to change beds, let alone take over the tasks of a registered nurse.

"Whose patient is this?" Grace pointed a pudgy white finger at Mrs. Flagg.

"She belongs to the med tech with the moss-green teeth," Cynthia volunteered. Grace Thompson scowled and cocked her head in an attitude of not understanding.

"Oh, you know who we mean, Grace," Adele said, putting forth all the sarcasm she could muster. "The former stock boy who had all those three days of training."

"No matter. Get up and get on with it." The woman clapped her hands like a schoolmarm and marched off.

Adele and Cynthia groaned.

"And just when we had Gayle almost trained," sighed Adele.

Cynthia's whole body drooped perceptibly and her face

took on a melancholy cast. "Oh, poor Gayle. What a horrible way to die."

"Oh, poor all of them who suffered at the hand of that madman."

"God! To think I actually f—" Cynthia looked down at Mrs. Flagg, who was coming around. ". . . I was intimate with the guy."

"You've got to be extra careful these days about whose horns are lying on the pillow next to yours," Adele said.

"But . . ." Cynthia smiled sadly. ". . . there were some good things that came out of it."

"I suppose. You met Tim."

"And we don't have to walk around being afraid of getting our throats slit anymore."

"Harold Marval resigned."

"There's more locker space in the nurses' lounge."

"And Nelson's back to normal."

Cynthia held up a finger. "Now, I don't know if I'd go so far as to say *that*, Adele. Nelson isn't exactly your run-of-the-mill dog. He's had some pretty dysfunctional parenting." She paused. "Just look at Gavin."

The thought of Gavin living with his mother and placing ads in the personals columns for a cross-dresser support group didn't make Adele feel particularly sad. She knew it would only be a matter of time before he disappeared again, or fell in love with someone his own size who didn't mind sharing her clothes.

"Yeah, well, at least Nelson's not sleep-deprived anymore."

"Speaking of sleep-deprived," Cynthia said, brushing invisible hospital microorganisms from her uniform, "I talked to Roger last night. He's seeing a shrink a couple of times a week about his nightmares. He's still tormenting himself over not going to the police about Douglas when Dana disappeared. He thinks some of those people would still be alive."

Adele repressed an amused smirk. The friendship which had developed between Cynthia and the chaplain seemed odd—even for Cynthia. But, as long as it remained platonic, it would provide Cynthia with some moral grounding, and Roger with some concrete insights into the modern woman.

"Unfortunately, he's probably right. Somebody would have checked with Dana's parents, and maybe gotten curious enough to have started asking Mr. Satan a few probing questions." Adele snapped her fingers. "Oh! I just remembered—I stopped by Meg's yesterday, and the guy who owns the Granary told me she bought an apartment building in Pacific Heights."

"Whoa!" Cynthia raised her eyebrows. "Sounds like she dipped into her trust fund."

"Let's just hope she has some money left over to pay for a shrink. She's a Future Helen Marval of America waiting to come out of the closet."

"Where's my pancakes?" Mrs. Flagg pinched Adele hard.

"What happened to the pie à la mode?" Adele asked.

"It's still in the oven," Mrs. Flagg moaned.

An odd-looking contraption came clanking through the doorway.

"Hey now, looky who we got here," said the smooth, low voice of Henry Williams from behind the Hoyer lift. "Our own Miss Hero Nurse."

"Hey, my man, how're you doing?" Adele got to her feet to give him a hug.

Smiling hugely, he removed his earphones, and spoke to Cynthia over Adele's shoulder. "This girl's something, ain't she? We were talking on the phone, right? And there she be, sitting at the man's house while I'm filling her in on the bad dude himself."

Henry made the African-American men's head-flip motion. "Cool as ice, man. Most girls I know? They'da been screaming and carrying on like wild women.

"This one?" Henry hugged Adele off her feet. "All she said is, 'Hey, I gots to go, bro.' Cool as ice. And the dude is right there, man, getting ready to cut her ass up into a hundred pieces."

"Oh Henry, he wasn't—"

"I want my steak cut into smaller pieces!" demanded Mrs. Flagg, struggling to get up. The sight caused the exact same thought in all three of her observers: *Beached whale.*

"Comin' right up, ma'am." Henry said, pulling the canvas cradle from the hydraulic lift.

After putting a strain on the lift, the three of them managed to get the woman back into bed with only a moderate amount of grunting. They had just begun to clean up the mess on the floor when the PA system crackled to life.

"ATTENTION ALL PERSONNEL. CODE BLUE . . ."

There was an unprecedented pause in the message.

Adele, Henry, and Cynthia, wearing astonished expressions, looked at one another.

The switchboard operator, still hooked into the public address system, could be heard to say, "You're kidding!" in a disbelieving tone. After a few seconds, she cleared her throat and, in poorly disguised bewilderment, finished the broadcast.

"CODE BLUE . . . ah . . . ADMINISTRATION OFFICE?"

Adrenaline surging, Adele and Cynthia were out the door and running for the first floor.

In the sixth-floor stairwell, Adele, two steps ahead of Cynthia, called back, "This ought to be interesting."

"Yeah," Cynthia said dryly. "The chief administrator probably just realized managed care is here to stay."

"Well, if he is the person down, you cover for me while I go through the financial files. I'll bet I can find some really incriminating stuff in there."

"Oh God," moaned Cynthia, pushing open the stairwell door.

"It's Sam Spade with a nursing degree arisen from the ashes."

They spilled out into the first-floor corridor, where they were met by the small crowd of sprinting people who made up the rest of the code-blue team.

Joining in, they raced toward the unknown together.